Praise for earlier Crampt mysterie

"I found myself quickly wrapped up [illegible] put it down until it was done!" ***Me & My Books***

"A fun read with humour throughout…" ***Crime Thriller Hound***

"An excellent novel, full of twists and turns, plenty of action scenes, crackling dialogue - and a great sense of fun." ***Fully Booked***

"A good page-turning murder mystery, with a likeable protagonist and great setting." ***The Bookworm Chronicles***

"A highly enjoyable and well-crafted read, with a host of engaging characters." ***Mrs Peabody Investigates***

"An amiable romp through the shady back streets of 1960s Brighton." ***Simon Brett, Crime Writers' Association Diamond Dagger winner***

"A highly entertaining, involving mystery, narrated in a charming voice, with winning characters. Highly recommended." - ***In Search of the Classic Mystery Novel***

"Part adventure story, part politically incorrect comedy, this is a fast-moving and funny book. I would recommend it as a light and satisfying read." ***Northern Reader***

"A romp of a read! Very funny and very British." ***The Book Trail***

"Superbly crafted and as breezy as a stroll along the pier, this

Brighton-based murder mystery is a delight." ***Peter Lovesey, Crime Writers' Association Diamond Dagger winner***

"It read like a breath of fresh air and I can't wait for the next one." ***Little Bookness Lane***

"By the end of page one, I knew I liked Colin Crampton and author Peter Bartram's breezy writing style." ***Over My Dead Body***

"A little reminiscent of [Raymond] Chandler." ***Bookwitch***

"A rather fun and well-written cozy mystery set in 1960s Brighton." ***Northern Crime***

"The story is a real whodunit in the classic mould." ***crime author M J Trow***

"A fast-paced mystery, superbly plotted, and kept me guessing right until the end." ***Don't Tell Me the Moon Is Shining***

"Very highly recommended." ***Midwest Book Review***

"One night I stayed up until nearly 2am thinking 'I'll just read one more chapter'. This is a huge recommendation from me." ***Life of a Nerdish Mum***

"I highly recommend this book and the author. I will definitely be reading more of this series and his other books." ***The Divine Write***

"Bartram skilfully delivers one of the most complex cozy mystery plots I've read in years." ***Booklover Book Reviews***

The Poker Game Mystery

A Crampton of the Chronicle adventure

The Poker Game Mystery

A Crampton of the Chronicle adventure

Peter Bartram

Deadline Murder Series Book 4

THE BARTRAM PARTNERSHIP

First published by The Bartram Partnership, 2019

ISBN: 9781700011497

For contact details see website:
www.colincrampton.com

All characters and events in this book, other than those clearly in the public domain, are entirely fictitious and any resemblance to any persons living or dead is purely coincidental.

Text and Cover Design: Barney Skinner

Also by Peter Bartram

Crampton of the Chronicle Mystery novels

Headline Murder

Stop Press Murder

Front Page Murder

Deadline Murder Series novels

The Tango School Mystery

The Mother's Day Mystery

The Comedy Club Mystery

The Poker Game Mystery

Novella

Murder in Capital Letters

Morning, Noon & Night Trilogy

Murder in the Morning Edition

Murder in the Afternoon Extra

Murder in the Night Final

The Morning, Noon & Night Omnibus Edition

(All four Morning, Noon & Night books are also in audiobook)

Short stories

Murder from the Newsdesk

Prologue

11th July 1965

The young woman hitched up the hem of her red Lycra mini-skirt another inch and winked at the man standing next to her.

She said: "The word on the street, my lord, is that you're shacked up with a bevy of girlfriends."

The woman's name was Deirdre Telford. She was twenty-one and, in the last few years, she'd jigged around the maypole with an assortment of men. None of them worth tuppence. She'd never had a boyfriend with a title before.

Viscount Rackham looked at her with languid aristocratic eyes that took in everything, gave away nothing.

He noted the long raven hair, the deep hazel eyes, the high cheeks, the pert nose, and the full kissable lips. He tried not to ogle the long legs under the mini skirt and cup-like breasts which mounded Deirdre's Rolling Stones tee-shirt.

Deirdre winked again. "So how many girlfriends hang out their smalls on your washing line, my lord?"

"Girlfriends?" Rackham said in a dark resonant voice. "Oh, five at the moment. But I'd really like six - one for every day of the week."

"You mean seven."

"No six. The girls play cards to be with me on Sunday."

"Not Happy Families, I bet," Deirdre said.

Rackham's thin lips twitched into an indulgent smile.

"No, not Happy Families. Generally, poker. A game at which I fancy myself as something of a hustler."

A hustler? Deirdre wasn't sure what Rackham was talking about. Hadn't she seen a film called *The Hustler* a few years back? That's right. That dreamboat Paul Newman starred in it. But he hustled pool not poker.

"I ain't much good at cards," Deirdre said. "My friend Angie used to beat me at Snap. And she had a stutter."

She paused to take a look around. They were in what looked like a huge greenhouse. What had his lordship called it?

An orangery.

Deirdre couldn't see any oranges. But there were a lot of trees like those ones she'd seen in pictures of hot places such as deserts. And there were fern things and creeper things that climbed up the side of the walls.

"Are your girlfriends good at cards, then?" Deirdre asked.

"Some are, but it's not necessary to live here. And, by the way, I don't call them girlfriends."

Deirdre's eyes flashed with alarm. "You're not one of them gits that goes around mouthing off about 'my slag' are you?"

Rackham laughed. The sound rumbled up from his broad chest and burst out of his mouth. It shook his shaggy beard and the wavy fair hair that touched his shoulders. It made him look like the picture of Jesus Deirdre had seen in the front of her school Bible. Rackham's green kaftan shimmied as he chuckled.

"No," he said. "I call them my Little Darlings."

Deirdre puzzled about that. She wondered what would happen at meal times if he asked, 'Little Darling, please pass the HP sauce'. Everyone would make a grab for it.

Still, perhaps this was the kind of place where you just asked the butler.

She looked through the windows at the lawn beyond. It rolled down to a walled garden. Beyond, the land sloped upwards to a clump of trees. A small cottage nestled close to the trees. The clump straggled along the foot of the hills and thickened into a dense forest. It stretched as far as she could see.

"I dig your pad," Deirdre said.

"Pad?"

"Drum."

"Drum?"

"Gaff. Don't you speak English?"

"You mean the house," Rackham said. "It all belongs to my father, the Marquess of Bognor. He inherited it from his father – as I expect to do from mine."

"It's that eldest son dodge, isn't it? The one where the man gets the lot and the girls get nothing."

Rackham frowned. "Dodge? I think primogeniture is the word you were looking for."

Deirdre certainly wasn't looking for that word as she'd never heard it before. But after living with her father for so many years, she knew a scam when she saw one.

"Hrrrumph!" Rackham cleared his throat. He had something important to ask.

"Deirdre, would you like to be my sixth Little Darling?"

Would she? Why was she here?

Does a mouse squeak?

Does a lumberjack cry 'Timber'?

Does Acker Bilk play the trumpet?

No, she thought, actually he plays the clarinet. And wears a bowler hat. Not that he needs one to play a clarinet. Or even a bass tuba.

My mind's getting into a muddle, Deirdre thought. She'd expected Rackham to pop the question, even if the question wasn't quite the one she'd have liked him to pop.

But it wouldn't do to seem too eager.

So, she pressed her lips together in a thoughtful gesture, looked at the ceiling, and hitched her skirt up another half-an-inch.

She turned back to Rackham. "I wouldn't want to be called Little Darling," she said.

"You don't need to worry about that," Rackham said. "I've named each Little Darling after a day of the week. I got the idea from the American film actress Tuesday Weld. If she could be named after a day of the week, why not others?"

"Oh yeah? I saw Tuesday in that flick *The Cincinnati Kid* at the Regal."

But who cares about her, when there's that Steve McQueen to lust after, Deirdre thought.

"I want to call you Saturday," Rackham said.

"My name's Deirdre." She pouted. Rackham liked that. It brought out the sensuality he suspected lurked only just below Deirdre's rough exterior. He made a mental note to annoy her occasionally when he wanted her to capture that look.

"You'll shorten the name and start calling me Sat," Deirdre said. "Every time you use it, it'll sound as though I'm lounging on my arse with my feet up."

Rackham stroked his beard. This could be a problem.

"What do your friends call you?" he asked.

"My best mates call me Nibbles. On account of I eat my chips with my front teeth when they're really hot. The chips, that is, not my teeth."

Nibbles, Rackham thought. Sounded a bit like nipples. And Deirdre's were rather a fine pair. He could see their provocative outline protruding through her tee-shirt.

He grinned. "Nibbles it is, then. You can stay in the cottage next to the copse."

"Cops? I ain't staying next to no rozzers. We had enough trouble with them at home, what with my dad's work and everything."

Rackham's broad forehead wrinkled with a frown.

"Not cops, but copse – a small collection of trees."

"Oh, so no boys in blue waving their truncheons?"

"Not here. But your father's work brought the police to your door?"

"He's in security."

"And that interests the police?"

"Sometimes he has to thump people."

Rackham's frown deepened. His fair eyebrows beetled

together. Perhaps it would be wiser not to pursue this point.

He said: "I'll show you up to the cottage later. It's just a short walk through the rose garden and past the ha-ha."

"Ha-ha?" Deirdre asked.

"It's like a long trench used as a boundary instead of a fence."

"You won't be laughing if you fall into it in the dark."

"Perhaps not," Rackham said. "Later you can meet the other Little Darlings. They all get on awfully well with one another. Well, perhaps Thursday is a little standoffish. I put it down to her having been head girl at Roedean a couple of years back. But she fits in very well and, of course, her public-school background means she can get credit with the dealers."

"Which dealers?"

Rackham shot Deirdre a wary glance. This wasn't going to be a problem, was it? Didn't Deirdre realise that this was a commune where the love was free but the drugs were paid for?

He flashed one of his sunburst smiles – all eyes and teeth. "Just dealers who supply things we need," he said.

"Yeah, we've got a bloke comes round the door once a month selling clothes pegs. My mum used to buy some from time to time. Of course, that was before…"

"She passed on," Rackham said gently.

"Yeah, croaked it. The bloke still comes with the pegs but my dad never buys any on account of he never does any washing, so hasn't got anything to hang out. Just another thing about him I can't stand. Anyway, I'm twenty-one now, so I've just left him to it."

Rackham pursed his lips irritably. He hoped he was making the right decision.

But then the sun peeped out from behind a cloud. It shone into the orangery. Deirdre looked like she'd been lit by a spotlight. Her raven hair shone like ebony.

And, anyway, Saturday nights had been lonely these past few weeks, Rackham reflected.

"Let's walk up to the cottage," he said.

"Yeah! Best foot forward."

"You'll enjoy the copse. There are rabbits and blackberries as big as your nipples in September."

"They get stuck between your teeth, my lord."

"Your nipples?"

"No, blackberries. The pips in blackberries."

Deirdre glanced down at her tee-shirt to hide a secret smile. This one might be a lord but, in the most important way, he was like all the rest.

Rackham said: "It's good to walk in the copse. But you mustn't go into the woods beyond."

"That forest on the other side of the cottage?" Deirdre asked.

"The Dark Wood, we call it. It's dense with thick undergrowth, not like the copse. And there are old traps that gamekeepers set in times past – and worse. Yes, best not to go into the Dark Wood. Bad things have happened there – and not so long ago."

"What kind of bad things?" Deirdre asked in a whisper.

"Things we don't want to remember," Rackham said.

He turned to Deirdre and took her hands. "But there's no need to worry about the Dark Wood when you've got the cottage by the copse."

He threw his arms around Deirdre and hugged her tight. She felt soft and warm. He gently rubbed her back and he felt her relax into his arms.

"Remember that we'll always have just the two of us," he said.

"Only on Saturdays," Deirdre said.

Chapter 1

Three months later...

The news that shattered our world at the Brighton *Evening Chronicle* came late one Thursday afternoon in October.

It was one of those hot autumn days which seem like a bonus after a dreary summer. I sat at my desk in the newsroom - jacket off, tie loosened – and mused on some half-forgotten line from Keats. Something about having "o'er brimmed their clammy cells". I vaguely recalled he'd been talking about bees. Not like the clammy cells I see down the nick as a crime reporter. On a bad night, you'll find a couple of drunks who've puked up eight pints of Harvey's bitter and a vindaloo supper.

Yes, very clammy cells.

Anyway, it was a day when a breeze as light as fairy dust barely stirred the flags on the Royal Pavilion. The air carried the warm scent of the sea. Through my open window I could hear a street busker round off his number – *Summertime Blues.*

So it wasn't the kind of day you'd expect bad news to barge in uninvited like a four-letter word at a vicar's tea-party.

I'd just typed a nib – news in brief, in case you were wondering – about a bank manager who'd shoplifted a packet of frozen fish fingers. The subs – that's sub-editors - would use it as a filler at the bottom of a column if a story under-ran. Especially if they could think of a pun as the headline. I could just imagine one of the subs scratch his head as he weighed up the comedic merits of "Light fingered" over "Fishy business". Neither of them raised much of a smile for me.

The phone on my desk rang.

I lifted the receiver and said: "Colin Crampton."

A soft burr of a voice that reminded me of country lanes overhung with leafy trees said: "You're not going to like this."

The harbinger of gloom was Detective Inspector Ted Wilson. He had mournful eyes and a shaggy beard. He walked around in a crumpled suit with a couple of Biros in the breast pocket. But Ted was probably the only straight 'tec on the Brighton force. Which meant he would price the tip-off I suspected he was about to give me at a strong whisky rather than real folding money.

I said: "If I couldn't handle bad news, I wouldn't have gone into crime reporting. I'd have become a circus clown."

"You wouldn't have enjoyed a custard pie smashed in your face. But this news is worse."

"Just get to the point," I said testily.

"Your employer has died."

I laughed. "Is this some kind of leg pull? I've just seen Frank Figgis walk through the newsroom."

Figgis was my news editor and occasional tormentor. He was a wrinkled relic of the paper. He smoked seventy Woodbines a day and smelt like a Craster kipper. He walked with a high-stepping gait like a trick pony on account of the settings on his braces were adjusted too tight.

At the other end of the line, Ted tut-tutted in his quiet kind of way. "Listen up, I shouldn't be telling you this. Lord Bognor has died."

Now that was bad news.

Did I say bad? I meant terrible.

Make that catastrophic.

Then multiply it by ten.

Every muscle in my body tightened. Like I was a marionette and the puppet-master had just tugged viciously on the strings. I felt sick. Not "clammy cells" sick. But sick enough to reach for my handkerchief and dab my lips.

I couldn't believe it. "You mean the Marquess of Bognor, who owns the *Chronicle*?" I blurted.

"Is there any other?"

"How did he die?" I asked.

"We don't know yet."

"Is it suspicious?"

"Can't be sure. But it looks like a heart attack. We'll need to wait for the post-mortem."

"How do you know this?"

"I'm actually at Bognor's house now."

"Ethelbert House? Out near Washington on the London Road?"

"That's the place. Not your average two-up, two-down is it?"

I ignored Ted's factitious comment. Bognor lived in a stately pile at the centre of a big estate surrounded by high stone walls. The house was a vast place built out of grey limestone. It had diamond-paned mullion windows. Outside there was a terrace and a walled garden. There was an ice house, from the days before you shoved the milk in the fridge. Inside, there was a library and a billiards room and a gun room with, for all I knew, a Chieftain tank parked outside. There were enough bedrooms to put up Brighton and Hove Albion's first team and the reserves as well. But it was the kind of house where the bathwater gurgled and ran cold. Where there'd be a roaring fire in the drawing room grate but the place still felt like an igloo. Where, if you walked into a room unexpectedly, you'd hear the scurry of little feet as the mice dived for cover. Or so I'd heard.

These thoughts jumbled through my mind as I tried to absorb the news.

"When did Lord Bognor die?" I asked.

"We think late last night. The butler found his lordship in the orangery. He was slumped in a basket chair as dead as Hector. He had a look on his face like he'd just seen a tiger about to pounce. But heart attacks do that to you."

"Does anyone know about this?"

Ted lowered his voice. "Not yet. I'm calling on a phone in the butler's pantry. Or it may be the housekeeper's parlour. This place has more rooms than a Sultan's harem. Tomkins is lording it around the place – pardon my pun – like he's Fabian of the Yard. That's why I've got to be quick, before he sees me making this call."

"I understand."

Detective Chief Superintendent Alec Tomkins was a man who proved that cops' big feet weren't just a cliché. Over the years, we'd had the occasional difference of opinion. We didn't get along.

Or, to put it another way, he hated me.

Ted said: "I've just heard Tomkins coming down the corridor. Got to go."

The line went dead.

I replaced the receiver with added care, like I was balancing it on eggshells. Then wondered why I'd done it that way.

I stared around the newsroom. It was winding down at the end of the day. The last edition had gone to press. I could feel the vibrations from the rotary presses. Their rumble came up through the floor from the print room below. The last of the run – the papers that were sold at Brighton station to commuters on their way home.

That rumble was part of everyday life in the newsroom. None of us took any notice of it. Especially when the day's work was done and it was time to head to the pub.

Susan Wheatcroft put the cover on her typewriter. Phil Bailey made a couple of jottings in his notebook, then shoved it in his desk drawer. Sally Martin reached for her handbag and headed for the door.

They all thought tomorrow would be just another working day.

But it wouldn't.

Suddenly, the rumble from the presses stopped. The last papers of the day had been printed.

An ominous silence descended on the newsroom.

I stood up and put on my jacket. Straightened my tie. Fussed with my hair.

I don't know why. This was bad news whatever I looked like.

I walked slowly across the newsroom.

I was about to spoil Frank Figgis' evening.

Chapter 2

Frank Figgis drew a long slim Sobranie Black from its elegant packet.

He shoved it between his lips like he was thrusting a plunger down a blocked drain.

He flicked his lighter, sucked hard, and the tip of the posh fag glowed red.

I said: "What happened to the Woodbines?"

Figgis lifted the Sobranie from his lips and blew out a stream of pure white smoke.

He said: "I decided to smoke these black fags until Lord Bognor's funeral. I have to show some respect and Mrs Figgis threw out my black tie after what happened at her Uncle Whitrow's wake."

I decided to ignore what happened to Uncle Whitrow.

Instead, I said: "Bognor's funeral was yesterday."

"I know. I've got only one of these black beauties left. Don't worry, it'll be back to a packet of coffin nails tomorrow."

We were in Figgis' office. It was two weeks after I'd told him Bognor was dead.

I said: "I heard today that the police have closed the book on the investigation. The post-mortem clearly showed a myocardial infarction."

"Heart attack."

"His heart had been showing signs of disease for years. After all, he was eighty-three."

"I thought he'd go on for ever."

"You mean, you hoped he'd go on for ever."

Figgis took a last gasp of his Sobranie and stubbed out the dog-end on the edge of his desk.

"I liked him because he never interfered in the paper. Not like those megalomaniac press barons. The first Viscount

Rothermere used the *Daily Mail* to promote fascism - and he supported Hitler."

"Bognor wasn't perfect," I reminded Figgis. "He appointed His Holiness as editor."

Gerald Pope was an upper-crust dimwit who thought news gathering was a dirty game. He spent his time complaining about difficult clues in the crossword puzzle or demanding to know why the astrologer's predictions hadn't come true.

"Bognor knew I wouldn't like a hands-on editor in the news department," Figgis said.

"How come?"

"I told him."

"You met him?"

"He came to the office to interview the candidates for editor."

Of course, I should have worked that one out long ago. Figgis had applied for the job. It would've been natural. He'd been the paper's news editor since the crack of doom – long before I joined. He'd be the natural choice to step up to the editor's chair.

I said: "Did Bognor turn you down as editor?"

"He told me I was too valuable to spare from the newsroom. Said he'd make sure he appointed an editor who would leave me to get on with my job."

"So that was why we ended up with a useless article like His Holiness."

I glanced out of the window. The Indian summer we'd enjoyed a couple of weeks ago had gone. Now grey clouds hung in the sky. It was late afternoon and the light was fading over the Royal Pavilion gardens.

I said: "What happens now that Bognor's dead? Now the paper has a new owner."

Figgis reached for his Sobranie packet. Shook the last black fag out of it. Lit up and savoured the flavour for the final time.

"A change of ownership is always a dangerous moment for a paper," Figgis said. "Especially for a successful paper like the *Chronicle*. Why a new proprietor who's never owned a newspaper before thinks he can run it better than someone who's done it for years is a mystery to me."

"And you think the new owner will shake things up?"

"It's what new owners do."

Figgis flicked the ash off the end of his Sobranie. It fell on his waistcoat and he brushed it away.

"This new owner is more unpredictable than most," Figgis added.

"The new Marquess of Bognor," I added. "The late Lord Bognor's only son. I guess he relinquishes his courtesy title of Viscount Rackham now."

"Sure, he inherits the paper as well as the house and estate – even though Bognor allowed him to use it for his own private pleasure for years. All those girlfriends! Little Darlings he calls them. How many at the last count?"

"Six, I believe."

Figgis shook his head. "I shudder to think what Mrs Figgis would say if I decided to keep five other women in our place."

"It would make for a queue outside the bathroom in the morning."

Figgis shook his head. "How does he do it?"

"It's the hippie culture," I said. "It's all to do with free love."

"There was nothing like free love when I was a young lad. There was Dirty Dora who used to stand under the lamppost outside the Duck and Trombone on a Saturday night. But there was nothing free about her love. She charged five pounds a time. Extra if you wanted to lie down."

"Do you think Rackham will want to appoint a new editor?" I asked.

"How should I know? I don't even know whether he's realised he owns the paper. Unless one of his Little Darlings has told him."

"I heard that the lawyers are still looking at the documents to see exactly what Rackham inherits. I gather Bognor tied a lot of the estate up in a trust so Rackham can't fritter it away on girls and grass."

Figgis said: "When you say 'grass', I take it you don't mean the kind you cut with a lawnmower."

He took a final drag on his last Sobranie and said: "What I do know is that we'll keep the new owner happy if we boost circulation – and that means we could do with a good running story. Perhaps something with a dead body and a killer on the loose."

The door opened and Cedric, the copy boy, stuck his head into the room.

He flashed his toothy grin and said: "Phone call in the newsroom for Mr Crampton."

"Did he say who it was?" I asked.

"It's a woman. Sounds like Miss Goldsmith."

"Shirley?" I said, surprised.

I stood up and headed towards the door.

Figgis smirked. "Your own little darling. How many do you think you'll finally end up with? Six, like Rackham?"

I turned at the door. "One's quite enough when it's Shirley."

Back at my desk, I picked up the phone.

Shirley said: "Strewth, Colin, what kept you?"

Shirl's accent always became stronger Australian when she was stressed. And I could tell she was now.

I said: "I was chewing the cud with Figgis, but what's up?"

"I've just had a call from Stella Armstrong."

"The name means nothing to me."

"Stella is the photographer's assistant on the shoot I'm doing up at Devil's Dyke."

Shirl worked as a fashion model. She'd mentioned the night before she was modelling next spring's collection for a department store chain.

"Stella called me ten minutes ago," Shirley said. "She's worried sick. She lives in a top-floor flat and she heard raised voices and commotion earlier from the flat downstairs – sounded like something had been knocked over - and now the owner's dog is whining down there. Won't stop."

"Has she knocked the door?"

"Sure. No answer. But the dog snarled and barked, then went back to whining."

"She should call the cops."

"She's no Dumbo. They told her whining dogs were a matter for the Royal Society for the Prevention of Cruelty to Animals."

"That figures. Brighton cops' first reaction is how they can get out of a job."

"Does Stella know who lives there?"

"Single man, apparently. Said his name was Steve. Late forties, beefy type. Looks like he could handle trouble. So does the dog. It's a Staffordshire bull terrier."

"A Staffie? Aren't they supposed to be ferocious fighters?"

"Apparently, this one's a real softie. I said we'd go round and take a look."

"Take a look?" I asked.

I knew what Shirl meant. She wanted us to break into the flat. She knew I'd done it before – strictly in the line of duty as one of Her Majesty's Journalists, you understand.

"Sure, just take a look," Shirl said. "I'll meet you there in ten minutes."

Shirley gave me the address and rang off.

I leaned back in my captain's chair and thought about what Shirley had told me. I knew little about dogs, but I thought they whined when something was wrong. Stella had heard a commotion. But that could mean anything. Perhaps the beefy type Steve had tripped over a rug. Perhaps he'd tripped over the dog. An angry Staffie would create enough commotion for anyone. Perhaps Steve had fallen on something. Hit his head, maybe. Was now lying unconscious.

Or perhaps he'd simply gone to bed and the dog didn't like it because he wanted to play throw-the-ball.

I shrugged. Shirl was on a mission and there'd be no stopping her.

I opened my desk drawer and reached in for the printers' rule I kept there. It was marked in ems, the unit printers use to measure typefaces. I liked it because printers' rules were made out of metal. And mine had a whippy spring action in it when you bent it back.

I put the rule in my pocket and headed for the *Chronicle's* tearoom. When you're breaking into a flat with a dangerous dog you need to think ahead.

Ten minutes later I was standing outside the door to Steve's flat with Shirley and Stella.

Stella was a small girl, late twenties, with close-cropped auburn hair and big brown eyes. She was wearing worn blue jeans, a tee-shirt with a Carnaby Street logo, and a worried frown.

She gave me a lop-sided grin and said: "Shirley told me you're always up for this kind of thing."

"What kind of thing would that be?"

Stella blushed. "Getting into places."

"That's me, the Raffles of the newsroom."

Shirley said: "There may be an injured man in there. We know there's a distressed dog."

"He's called Ruff," Stella said. "I heard Steve call him one day."

"You sure he wasn't asking him to bark?"

Shirley said: "Are you going to stand there making bad jokes or get the door open."

I took the printer's rule out of my pocket.

I said: "You two may want to turn away so you can honestly

say you didn't see me open the door. If we have to call the police, we'll tell them we gave the door a heavy shove and it just opened."

"They'll believe that?" Stella asked.

"No, but they won't be able to disprove it. In any event, if we have to call them, they'll be more concerned about what they find inside – and not getting eaten by Ruff. Which reminds me."

I reached into my other pocket and pulled out a handful of digestive biscuits, courtesy the *Chronicle's* tearoom. I handed them to Shirley.

"Be ready with those if Ruff rushes us," I said.

"Doesn't scare me, cobber. I once faced a charging croc in the Northern Territory."

"How much was he charging? Or did he offer a discount?" I said.

"Ha, bloody ha," Shirl said. "Are you going to open that door?"

I moved towards the door and, with the delicacy of a brain surgeon performing a lobotomy, slipped the end of the metal rule between the lock's strike plate and the cylinder. It's the cylinder which holds the latch when the door is unlocked.

The door was locked and I could feel the end of the ruler move around the curve of the latch. I pushed it until I felt it engage in the angle between the latch and the cylinder.

I manoeuvred the ruler to get as much purchase on the latch as I could. Then in one soft but sharp movement I flicked the end of the ruler so it put heavy pressure on the latch. The ruler bent as the pressure applied to the latch held. The sharp edge of the metal rule cut into my hand as I pressed more. This was tough. It wasn't going to happen.

CRACK!

The pistons in the lock gave way and the latch slipped back. The door swung open.

And Ruff began to bark. Loud and angry. Full of rage.

The flat was dark. Shirl handed me the digestives and I crept into the hall. The light switch was just inside the door. I flicked it on.

There was a short corridor with two doors leading off to the left and one to the right. I took a couple of steps down the corridor and stood still.

I felt the girls crowd in behind me.

Ruff had heard footsteps. He let out a low growl. Full of menace.

He'd been shut in one of the rooms on the left. He threw himself at the door and it shuddered in its frame. He had another go. Then launched another deep growl.

I said: "If we don't quieten Ruff, we'll have the neighbours round."

Shirley said: "Give me the biscuits."

She took them and opened the door. She tossed a couple of the biscuits on the floor. Ruff charged out but skidded to a halt when he saw the bickies. He sniffed them suspiciously. Decided they met with his approval. His huge jaws locked around one and crumbs dripped from the side of his mouth.

I said: "Remember he won't understand when all the biscuits have gone."

"No worries," Shirley said. "By then he'll have rolled over and have me tickling his tummy."

I turned my attention away from Ruff.

There was a sharp acrid smell of something. Not cooking. I couldn't place it.

It was coming from the room on the right.

The door was open but the light was off. I switched it on as I stepped in. Stella pushed in behind me.

We were in Steve's sitting room. There was a beaten-up sofa in front of an electric fire. The fire was giving off the smell.

There was a table and couple of chairs and a small desk on the other side of the room. There was a television set in the corner.

I didn't notice anything else.

Because Steve was lying in the centre of the room. A chair had been knocked over beside him. Magazines were scattered across the floor. The remains of a clock lay near the fireplace.

Steve was dead.

There was a heavy thump on the floor behind me.

I spun round. Stella had fainted.

Chapter 3

I must have been away the day my journalism course covered what to do when you're stuck in a house with a dead body, a fainted woman, and a fierce dog.

But it turned out to be just common sense.

Shirley and I lured Ruff into the kitchen. We ransacked the cupboards and found his Kennomeat. We piled a large portion of it into a bowl and left him to tuck in. Then we shut the kitchen door on him.

We went back into the sitting room and gently lifted Stella off the floor. We carried her upstairs to her flat. Shirl rummaged in Stella's pockets and found her door key. We let ourselves in and laid her on a bed.

I asked Shirl to call the cops from Stella's phone, then play nursemaid and comforter to the girl.

Then I scooted back down stairs. I reckoned I'd have about five minutes to snoop around before the cops arrived.

I took a good look at the front door as I went back inside. It hadn't been damaged in any way. Whoever killed Steve hadn't forced their way in. Steve must have known the caller who became his killer.

I went back into the sitting room. I forced myself to look at Steve. It wasn't a pleasant experience. He hadn't died easy. His eyes stared at the ceiling from beneath drooping eyelids. Snot had run down his nose. His mouth was open in a silent scream. A stream of drool had run over his chin onto the floor. His lips were blue. His legs had contorted in what must have been a terrible spasm. One ankle looked as though it could have broken. His hands and fingers had crabbed into claws which spoke of agony in his final moments.

I wondered whether it could have been a natural death. Perhaps a massive heart attack or stroke. Could that account for the knocked over chair and the magazines scattered around the place? But, no, that didn't explain the commotion and raised voices Stella had heard.

It looked as though Steve had been playing with a pack of cards. Loose cards were scattered among the magazines. But five cards were laid in a line next to Steve's right hand. I didn't think they could have fallen like that. They were in too straight a line. Steve must have arranged them. But why do that in his dying agony?

I leant over to look more closely at the cards. In order, the Jack of spades, the king of diamonds, the two of clubs, the five of hearts, and the ace of spades. It was like a hand in stud poker. But not a good hand. Ace high. I wouldn't have staked my shirt on this hand. But had Steve staked his life?

If he'd been murdered, it was not easy to see how the killer had finished him. Blue lips suggested Steve had struggled to breathe in his final minutes. But there were no strangle marks around his neck. No wounds from a knife or a bullet.

Perhaps the killer had slipped Steve some deadly poison in a drink. But there was no sign of a glass in the room. No remnants of food either.

Steve would be posing a puzzle for the pathologist.

The minutes were ticking by before the cops arrived.

I had a quick shufti around the room. There was a desk in one corner, loaded with papers. There was a thin film of dust over much of the stuff. That suggested Steve hadn't touched it for some time. Perhaps he didn't like paperwork. There were three drawers in the desk's right-hand pedestal. The two lower ones were half open but the top one had been pushed completely shut.

I wrapped my handkerchief around my hand – you won't find me leaving fingerprints around – and pulled the drawer open. There was a pile of folding money inside. Ten-pound notes, too. The tenners had only been reintroduced by the Bank of England two years earlier. And Steve had a stack of them. Perhaps as many as two hundred. That would be two thousand pounds, a huge sum to keep around the house.

On the top of the pile was a train ticket. Brighton to London Victoria return. It had been dated a couple of days earlier and clearly used as it had been clipped. Why was Steve hanging on to an old railway ticket?

I picked it up in my handkerchiefed hand and turned it over. Steve had scrawled a telephone number down the edge. I pulled out my notebook and jotted down the number CRO 7362. Three letters, four numbers – a London telephone number. I replaced the ticket in the drawer, face down, just as I'd found it.

I stood there thinking for a moment. Could the killer have come to steal the money? Perhaps Steve refused to tell him where it was. Even for two thousand pounds, he'd sold his life cheaply.

In the distance, I heard the bells of a cop car approaching. I had to be quick.

I hurried out of the sitting room, along the corridor and into the next room. It was Steve's bedroom. Three pairs of trousers lay in a pile on the floor. There was a tangle of dirty shirts and underwear in a basket. Evidently, Jeeves didn't work here.

I moved over to his bedside table. There was a lamp, and a paperback of the James Bond novel *You Only Live Twice*. In French. There was also a glass with the remnants of a whisky in it. I picked up the glass using the handkerchief and sniffed the contents. It smelt like whisky should. Couldn't detect any poison. But no doubt the cops would analyse it.

And speaking of the cops…

Outside the flat, a car screeched to a halt. The bells sounded shrill in the flat. Ruff started to growl like he wanted to eat anyone who came near him.

I hurried back into the corridor.

Seconds later Tomkins came through the door. His hair had

flopped over his forehead and there was sweat around his jowls. A couple of uniformed coppers barged in behind him. Ted Wilson reluctantly brought up the rear.

Tomkins glared at me. "How did you get in here?"

I smiled pleasantly. "Same as you," I said. "Through the door. I came to aid a concerned neighbour. What's your excuse?"

A couple of minutes later, I was upstairs in Stella's flat.

I couldn't get out of Steve's flat fast enough. I didn't want Tomkins asking any more awkward questions about how I'd entered the place. For the time being, he had enough to do rather than worry about me.

I found Stella sitting up in bed. She was sipping a cup of tea Shirley had made for her.

Stella's face was pale, and her eyes watery. Her shoulders gave a little involuntary spasm from time to time. That would be shock and it would pass.

Shirley and I perched on the edge of Stella's bed. It had a quilt with a teddy bear motif on it.

Stella put down her tea and said: "I don't think I could live here anymore after what's happened tonight."

I said: "When you look for new lodgings steer well clear of the place run by Beatrice 'the Widow' Gribble in Regency Square. I don't know why I stick it."

Stella managed a thin smile. "Will I have to speak to the police?" she asked.

I said: "Yes. They'll want you to make a statement. But not just yet. They've got plenty to do downstairs before they can be bothered about us."

"I don't think I can sleep yet."

"Sometimes it helps to talk about it," Shirley said.

Stella nodded. "I don't want to talk about the body. That was horrible."

"Perhaps you could tell us a bit about how long you've lived here – and whether you knew Steve," I said.

Stella reached for the tea and had a gulp.

"I suppose it will help to pass the time. I moved in here three years ago. Steve already lived downstairs with that dog – what a brute."

"Ruff by name and rough by nature," Shirley said.

"True, but knowing there was a vicious animal in the building somehow made me feel safer."

"Pity it didn't work for Steve," Shirley said.

"It's more evidence that Steve knew his killer," I said. "If Steve was relaxed in his presence, the dog would be, too. Maybe the killer acted scared and got Steve to lock the dog in a room like we did."

Stella shuddered. "Are killers really as cold-blooded as that?"

I nodded. "But, tell me, did you ever get to know Steve's family name?"

"It was Telford," Stella said. "The mail for his flat and mine just came through the front door letterbox. He also had a daughter, Deirdre, about twenty-one, I think. She was living with Steve when I came here but moved out about three months ago."

"Do you know where she's gone?"

Stella shook her head. "I'll miss her. Steve never said much if we passed in the hallway, but Deirdre would always have a comment about the latest fashion or what was top of the pops. Pretty girl, too, the kind men go for."

"They go for anything in a skirt as long as she's not on life support," Shirley said.

I harrumphed. Then realised I sounded a bit like Figgis. I'd have to watch that.

I said: "Do you know where Deirdre is? She'll have to be told."

Stella said: "Could be anywhere. I remember the day before she left, I ran into her going out. She said she was off tomorrow. I asked her where. And she said: 'Somewhere I can have an easy life.' I asked her what she meant, but she just giggled and rushed out. Never saw her again."

"Presumably Steve knew," I said.

Stella shrugged. "If he did, he never mentioned it to me. But, as I've said, we rarely spoke."

I said: "Do you know what work Steve did?"

"I asked him a few weeks after I'd moved in and he mumbled something about being in security. It was obvious he didn't want to talk about it. But then I saw him a month ago. I was out on the town with a couple of girlfriends and we decided to end up at Sherry's. He was on the door."

"You mean he was a doorman?"

"I mean he was a bouncer. And not afraid to bounce people either. When we were coming out, a young lad was getting a bit lippy and Steve thumped him. Knocked him down right into the gutter. The lad scrambled up with his lip bleeding and scarpered."

So Steve was no stranger to a touch of freelance violence. But could Steve have upset some local hoodlum enough to have had a death threat hanging over him? And – I remembered the London train ticket – perhaps Steve's killer wasn't so local. Wherever he did his work, a bouncer could make enemies.

Some colour had returned to Stella's cheeks but her eyelids drooped and she looked tired.

Shirley said: "If you like, you can come back to my place tonight. Get away from the blue meanies downstairs. They'll be crashing about all night."

"I'd rather stay here tonight," Stella said. "But I'll take you up on that offer if I definitely decide to move."

As Shirley and I made our way downstairs, a piercing scream came from Steve's flat.

"That bloody dog has just bitten me," Tomkins yelled.

I reached for Shirley's hand. "At least one good thing has come out of a terrible evening," I said.

Chapter 4

I couldn't resist a smirk when Tomkins limped into the police press briefing the following morning.

Ruff's teeth had left a lasting mark.

Tomkins sat down behind the top table and began to study the statement he planned to read. There were black circles under his eyes. His slicked-back hair flopped over his ears. He looked like a man who'd had a hard night.

Mind you, I didn't exactly feel a bundle of energy myself. By the time I'd called the story of Steve Telford's killing into the night copytaker at the *Chronicle,* it was past three before I hit the sack.

My one consolation was that Jim Houghton, my rival crime reporter on the *Evening Argus,* the other paper in town, would have had a tougher time. He'd have had to pick up the details of the story direct from the cops.

Not that Tomkins wouldn't have been helpful. He'd have done anything to take the shine off what would otherwise be a scoop for me.

Jim didn't look like a man who'd lost a race when he sat down beside me.

He nudged me in the side. "I hear this could be difficult for you," he said.

"I've never found it difficult to land an exclusive news story, Jim. I believe it's the reporters who play catch-up who have the trickiest time."

"Cocky bastard. It's the reporters who stick around who find out what's really happening."

"Or think they do," I said.

"Could be Tomkins will have some questions for you to answer, sources tell me."

Jim's "sources" would be Tomkins. I'd been around long

enough to know exactly what Jim had done. Because Tomkins knew I had the story, he'd have tipped off Jim personally. That's why Tomkins hadn't tried to stop Shirley and me leaving Stella's flat before giving statements. He'd rather put off basic police work until later so he could cast a shadow over my triumph. But he wouldn't know how much I'd seen inside Steve's flat until I wrote about it in the *Chronicle*. And Tomkins wouldn't see that until the midday edition was on the street.

I said: "I'm always pleased to answer Tomkins' questions, Jim. But usually he has more trouble answering mine."

"Apparently, the cops will want to know how you came to be inside a flat with a murdered man," Jim said.

"I've already told Tomkins. I was called by a concerned neighbour."

"And managed to enter without a key."

"The front door hadn't been closed properly."

Jim was about to say something. But Tomkins decided he'd studied his statement enough and called the meeting to order. A dozen journos around the room pulled out their notebooks and licked the tips of their pencils.

I didn't bother. The only interest for me was in what Tomkins would reveal and what he'd keep to himself.

Five minutes later, Tomkins sat down after setting out a cock-eyed theory about the killing. In Tomkins' view, Steve had blabbed about the two thousand pounds he had in his flat. The killer had come to steal the money while he thought the flat was empty. He'd unexpectedly run into Steve and killed him. The police would be questioning anyone who knew Steve had a large sum of money in his flat.

Even the opening premise of Tomkins' theory – that Steve had blabbed about the money – was nonsense. There wasn't a shred of evidence to support it. And the theory didn't explain how the killer had entered a supposedly empty flat when, in fact, Steve was at home. It didn't explain why the killer hadn't taken the money, when it was easy to find, after he'd croaked Steve.

Before Tomkins called for questions, I stood up and asked: "Have you any leads?"

Tomkins glared at me. But he answered: "Yes."

The lead would be the train ticket with the telephone number. I'd called the number last night and received no answer. I'd called again early this morning. The number turned out to be a greengrocer in Croydon, a suburb of south London.

"Have you followed up the lead?" I asked.

Tomkins snarled a bit – or maybe his leg was hurting. He said: "We're doing that at present."

I didn't think it would lead anywhere. I'd spoken to the greengrocer. It had been clear he'd never heard of Steve Telford. He was more concerned about an imminent delivery of tomatoes. But there must've been some reason why Steve scrawled the number on the ticket.

A reporter from one of the nationals asked whether the search of the flat had yielded any other clues.

Tomkins said the police were still evaluating the evidence.

I wondered whether that included the cards next to Steve's body I'd thought might be a poker hand. Well, I thought, good luck with evaluating that. At the moment, I had no idea of what it meant – or even whether it was relevant.

But Tomkins didn't mention the cards. So I couldn't tell whether he considered them a clue or whether he'd not even noticed them.

As there were no further questions, Tomkins stood up and limped towards the door. I passed him on my way out.

"Trouble with your leg?" I asked.

"You know perfectly well I was bitten by that bloody dog."

"Ruff luck."

I arrived back at the *Chronicle* ten minutes later.

I sat at my desk and batted out half a dozen paragraphs about the police press briefing. Not that it added much to the copy I'd already written. But the fact other papers now knew what only I'd known last night, meant that my lead on the story had gone. When you're under pressure for scoops, you need to keep ahead of the pack.

Figgis wouldn't be happy about that. And neither was I.

I sat back in my captain's chair and thought about what to do next. I badly needed a lead into the story. There were three possibilities.

The first was to find Steve Telford's daughter Deirdre. She'd taken off into the wide blue yonder three months ago. Nobody seemed to know where she was. Stella Armstrong didn't know and I didn't think any of the other neighbours would have a lead on her whereabouts.

There could be something at Steve's flat – such as an address book or letter from Deirdre – that would provide the answer. I hadn't seen anything last night – not even a photo - but then I hadn't had time to conduct a proper search.

I didn't think Tomkins had the information, either. He was asked at the press briefing whether there were any other clues but he hadn't mentioned Deirdre. He could have discovered where she was and be keeping the information close to his chest. But that wasn't Tomkins' style. If he had a scintilla of advantage over me, he'd boast about it.

I thought about asking Figgis whether we could run an appeal for Deirdre's whereabouts in the paper. Have you seen this woman? But that would only alert other papers to what we were doing.

The second possible lead was the pack of cards and the poker hand. If it was a poker hand. I flipped open my notebook and looked at the list of cards I'd written down – Jack of spades, king of diamonds, two of clubs, five of hearts, ace of spades. Why would Steve lay out a poker hand in his dying agony? Was it some way to distract his attention from the pain his twisted body must have suffered? Or was he trying to convey some message – perhaps about his killer? If so, it made no sense to me.

So that left me with just the third lead - the train ticket with the phone number. I flipped a page of my notebook and looked at the number again.

CRO 7362.

I didn't think a Croydon greengrocer could be involved in this mystery. But why did Steve need the number? A greengrocer would hardly need Steve's services as a doorman to keep the cauliflowers safe.

I'd scribbled the number down quickly as I was searching Steve's flat. I wondered whether I'd made a mistake when I'd copied it. Perhaps Steve was also in a hurry when he'd written it down. And why had he written it on a train ticket? Perhaps he had nothing else on him. Or perhaps he'd been on a train when he'd written the number. That would account for the scrawl – as well as the fact it's not easy to write anything on the side of a train ticket.

I closed my eyes and tried to picture the original ticket. The writing was untidy and now I remembered that the letters had been run together. The lower tail of the C had run into the R. What if the first letter wasn't a C? What if it were a G? The cross-stroke on the bottom of the tail of the letter would have been hidden by the fact that it ran into the R.

If I was right, the number wouldn't be CRO 7362.

It would be GRO 7362.

GRO stood for Grosvenor Square, a swanky part of Mayfair in central London.

There was only one way to find out if I was right. I lifted the telephone receiver and dialled the number.

The number rang three times before the phone was answered.

A woman's voice said: "Clansfield Club, Ethel Fotheringay,

manager's secretary, speaking."

I sat up straighter, like the headmaster had just walked into the room.

I knew about the Clansfield Club. Even though it was one of those places that preferred to lurk beneath the public's eyeline – a members-only gaming club for high-rollers. Not a place for your ordinary Joe. Members were captains of industry. Celebrity gangsters. Members of Parliament. Bankers and money men with their fingers in the pie. The word was the two things you needed to get in were money and discretion. So why did Steve have the club's number on the train ticket?

There could be only one answer. Stella had told me she'd seen him work as a bouncer outside a Brighton dance hall. So he must have been employed by the Clansfield as a doorman. Perhaps it had been a one-off hiring and he'd noted the number in case there was a chance of a further booking.

"How can I help you, caller?" Miss Fotheringay said.

I breathed deeply and played my hunch. "I'm calling on behalf of Steve Telford."

"Is he a member?"

"No, he worked as your doorman a few days ago."

"Ah, yes, I remember. One of our regular doormen was away sick. Mr Telford fills in occasionally when one of our regular staff is off."

"I've got some bad news, I'm afraid. Steve Telford won't be able to work again. He's dead."

"Oh, dear, that's very sad," Miss Fotheringay said in the least sad voice I've ever heard. "Thank you for informing us, Mr, er..."

"Burtenshaw," I said. "Eric Burtenshaw."

"I will inform Mr Hector Clansfield of the news, Mr Burtenshaw. I'm sure all of us here at the club would like you to convey our sincere condolences to the Telford family," Miss Fotheringay said. "Good day to you."

The line went dead.

I sat back in my chair with a grin on my face that wouldn't have shamed the Cheshire Cat.

I now had a lead which meant that I'd be ahead of the pack again.

"What's so special about Welsh rabbits?" Shirley Goldsmith said.

"They're not rabbits," I said. "The dish is called Welsh Rarebit."

"So we won't be eating the bunnies?"

"No. They make the dish by grating Cheddar cheese then mixing it with beer, mustard and Worcestershire sauce. They spread it on toast and brown it under a grill. It'll be delicious. Just wait and see."

It was evening and we were on the Brighton Belle whirling towards London.

As we were visiting a plush club, I'd decided the *Chronicle* could pay for us to take a plush train.

We were sitting at a table for two in a first-class compartment. It was dressed with fine white linen and laid with silver-plated cutlery. An ornate lamp threw a mellow light across the table.

Shirl and I had decided to have an early supper on the train. I'd told her the rarebit was a Brighton Belle special.

"And, Jeez, where did you get that monkey suit from?" Shirl asked.

She had never seen me in the black dinner suit with shiny lapels and bow-tie before.

"I bought this three years ago when I was invited to the annual press awards dinner. I haven't worn it since."

"Smells like it," Shirl said.

"The moth balls' odour should clear before we reach London. But you look – and smell – great."

Shirley was wearing a low-cut sleeveless dress with a crazy

psychedelic pattern of blue and red zig-zag lines and yellow dots.

"Yeah! This was kinda left over from one of my modelling assignments. And the fragrance is Rafale by Molinard."

"Send him my compliments. It more than passes the sniff test."

The steward brought our Welsh rarebits. We hoisted our knives and forks and tucked in.

Shirl's lips smacked in appreciation. "Hey, this is ace tucker. I guess the Welsh bunnies make a tasty snack after all."

I said: "Let's enjoy it while we can. We won't have time to eat when we're at the Clansfield Club. And we'll need to be discreet. The place is super-exclusive. If they suspect I'm a crime reporter we'll both be shown the door."

"But I don't get it," Shirl said. "What connection has this posh club got with Steve Telford?"

I cut off a piece of the rarebit. "He worked at least one shift as a doorman. Someone must have murdered Steve and the fact he had two thousand pounds in his flat suggests that big money is at the bottom of this. So far, the Clansfield Club is the only link between Steve and big-time cash."

"You think someone from the club killed him?"

"I don't know, but I hope we can learn more tonight. We'll just watch what's going on and see whether anything looks suspicious."

"How are we gonna get into this swanky joint?" Shirley asked. "Neither of us is a member."

"We've had a bit of luck there. Dickie Waterford, the *Chronicle's* parliamentary reporter, is a member. The place is thick with Members of Parliament – just the types Dickie schmoozes. Personally, I'd rather spend my time pursuing honest criminals. Perhaps we'll find some of those in the Clansfield as well. Anyway, Dickie has promised to get us into the club as his guests. Then we're on our own. In the meantime, let's sit back and enjoy the grub."

"Yeah," Shirley said. "This sure is a bonzer choo-choo. Guess I'll take it again tomorrow. I've got a London job for a magazine shoot."

"I didn't know. Which magazine?"

"Only got the call this morning. Apparently, it's a new mag that's launching in six weeks. Called *Switched On*! Crazy name if you ask me."

"That's a new one on me."

"The guy who called me said it's going to be a bit like that *Reveille* paper."

"The conscripts' comforter."

"What?"

"*Reveille* is a paper with lots of sports and showbiz articles topped up with pictures of pretty girls in swimsuits or bikinis. When service in the army, navy or air force was compulsory for young men, *Reveille* was called the conscripts' comforter, because the cheesecake pictures of the girls were all the young lads had in their lonely bunks at night."

"Sounds a bit freaky to me," Shirl said.

I was about to say something, but the steward came in to ask whether we'd like coffee.

"With two large brandies," I said.

"Yikes!" Shirl said. "Is it gonna be that kind of night?"

I grinned. "Worse, I expect."

Chapter 5

We met Dickie Waterford in the bar of the Goring hotel, just around the corner from Victoria Station.

Dickie was wearing a dinner suit so sleek it made mine look like the beggar's rags. He had the comfortable padded body of a man who spends his days lunching contacts in the best restaurants. The way his double chins wobbled suggested he was happy with his lot in life. His cynical brown eyes peered at the world from between folds of flesh. But Dickie knew his business as a journalist.

Dickie ordered gins and tonics all round. After the brandies on the Brighton Belle, Shirley and I were getting fired up for the task ahead.

He said: "I hope I'm not putting my Clansfield membership in any peril if I introduce you as guests."

"We'll be the very soul of discretion," I said.

"And we won't spill our drinks on the carpet," Shirley added.

Dickie didn't look convinced. He took a good pull at his gin. He looked like a man who needed to steady his nerves.

He said: "I'll take you in – I'll have to be with you when you arrive to sign you in as guests – but I'll slip quietly away afterwards. I have a dinner with the Secretary of State tonight."

I said: "When you sign us in remember that I'm Eric Burtenshaw."

"And I'm Estelle Clapworthy," Shirley said.

Dickie's chins shimmied as he shook his head.

"Anything we should know before we arrive?" I asked.

"The Clansfield is very discreet. There's no sign outside, no plaque on the door. If you don't know where it is, you're not welcome anyway. We'll enter through the foyer. There are usually a couple of doormen there. Don't get the wrong idea about them. Most of the doormen at the Clansfield are former army. Some of them special forces. I've heard it said they like nothing better than practising their old tricks."

"I know how to handle tough guys," Shirley said.

Dickie gave Shirl the once over. Took in the low-cut dress, the psychedelic colours.

"I don't doubt it," he said. "Anyway, inside you'll find the main bar and beyond it the gaming rooms. One is for roulette, the other for cards, usually poker. There's also a restaurant, but you won't be going in there. You'd never get the expenses claim past Frank Figgis. Watch out for Hector Clansfield, the owner. He normally spends his evenings in a private sitting room with a couple of favoured clients. But sometimes he mixes with the *hoi polloi* in the rest of the club. He's shrewd and he's tough – and I've heard tell he can be nasty. So if he comes your way, don't get on the wrong side of him."

"Sounds like a charmer," I said.

"He can be, but it's the charm of the king cobra," Dickie said. "Are you sure you still want to do this?"

I lifted my gin and drained the glass.

"Let's go," I said.

We took a taxi to the Clansfield Club which turned out to occupy a Georgian house near North Audley Street.

Dickie had been right. If you'd not known the place, there was no way to tell it wasn't a stately private residence. The house had three main floors and a row of attics, which would have been home sweet home for the servants when the place was built two hundred years ago. A pair of pillars in one of those Greek styles like Ionic or Doric - Ironic for all I knew – flanked marble steps. These led up to the kind of front door – darkened oak and a hefty brass knocker - that would discourage casual callers.

As I paid off the cabbie, Dickie said to Shirley: "If you get into trouble, leg it around the corner to Grosvenor Square and claim sanctuary in the American Embassy."

"I'm an Oz," Shirl said. "Our place is in The Strand. If you believe I can run that far in these heels, think again."

She pointed at her four-inch stilettos.

Dickie raised his eyebrows to Heaven. But I had a feeling we wouldn't be getting any help from that direction tonight.

Dickie led the way up the steps. The front door opened before he'd even reached it. A muscleman straight out of those Charles Atlas adverts opened the door. He'd been shoe-horned into a blue uniform with gold braiding and brass buttons. He looked like a cross between a railway porter and member of the chorus in an Italian comic operetta.

A neck the size of an ox's gave a deferential nod. He said: "Good evening, Mr Waterford."

Dickie said: "I have two guests this evening, Hilary."

Shirl couldn't resist a little snigger at that.

Hilary gave me the kind of look like he wanted to eat me.

He pointed at a tasteful walnut desk with red inlaid leather top on the other side of the entrance hall. Another gold-braided gorilla was standing behind the desk. He had a petulant pose with one hand on his hip. Like he'd just sung his song in the operetta but hadn't got as much applause as he'd expected.

"Evelyn will help you to sign in your guests, Mr Waterford, sir." Hilary said.

We crossed the hall.

There was a slight hitch during the signing when I couldn't remember whether I should write Burtenshaw with an S H A W, or an S H O R E at the end. But Evelyn was too busy eyeing up Shirley to notice.

We pushed through a couple of those green padded doors which look like they belong in lunatic asylums and entered the bar.

Once again, Dickie pushed the boat out. We hoisted our G and Ts – this time served in cut crystal tumblers – and took a good pull at them.

I had a quick look around the place. We were in a long room with rosewood panelled walls lit by three large crystal chandeliers. Red leather armchairs were grouped around small tables. The place was full of well-fed men in dinner suits and slender women in dresses that didn't look like they'd come from the bargain rail in Dorothy Perkins. The women had bouffant hairstyles like beehives and lots of diamonds. There was a hum of subdued conversation. This didn't look like the kind of place you'd come for a lively night out.

The bar itself was a long arrangement in some kind of hard black wood. It was lined with red velvet stools. We perched on them and viewed the place.

Dickie said: "Those two doors on the other side of the bar lead to the gaming rooms. The one on the right is for roulette, left is for cards."

He glanced to the far end of the bar. "Don't go through that door marked 'Private'. I know you. Stick a sign like that on a door and you treat it as an invitation."

"Not tonight, Dickie. We're on our best behaviour. Anyway, what's in there?"

"That's where Hector Clansfield has his private sitting room and office."

Dickie pointed to the other end of the room. "The loos and cloakrooms are through there. But don't think you can get up to mischief. There are attendants permanently in the gents' and ladies' toilets."

Dickie downed the last of his gin and tonic. "Well, I must go or the Secretary of State will think I've stood him up. You're on your own. I'll slip out of the fire exit beyond the toilets so the doormen don't realise I've left."

Dickie slid elegantly off his stool. "Good luck," he said.

We watched him glide across the room and disappear through the door.

Shirl looked at me. "What now, big brain?"

I said: "We're here to see whether anyone knew anything about Steve Telford. Especially people he knew or was friendly with."

Shirley grinned. "Didn't Dickie say there was an attendant in the ladies'? A woman who spends her evening washing down the dunny will enjoy a good gossip. I'll start there."

I nodded. "That sounds a good idea, but be careful. I'll begin by taking a look in the card room."

I watched Shirl flounce across the room towards the ladies'. Clever. A girl who'd made that much show of wiggling through the place couldn't be up to no good. At least, not the kind of no good she was actually up to.

I took my drink and headed for the card room.

It turned out to be smaller than the bar. There were four elegant green baize-topped tables, each surrounded by four Chippendale chairs. Each table was lit by a single bulb framed by a green conical shade. It hung a few feet above the table by a long flex from the ceiling.

A few armchairs were grouped around the edge of the room. Only one was taken by a thin man in a double-breasted dinner suit. He wore half-moon glasses with tortoise-shell frames. He was pretending to read an old copy of *Country Life*.

I nodded to him in the way I imagined old members of the club would do and took a seat a few feet away. I swirled the ice in my drink and pretended to be fascinated about whether or not it would melt.

Just two of the card tables had games in progress.

On the far side of the room, three men stared morosely at their cards and pushed betting chips around the table. They seemed to communicate with one another by nods and shakes. They confirmed a truth I'd always believed. Losing your money is not a lot of fun.

There were four men in the game on the table nearest to me.

They looked like a serious poker school, but an odd assortment to be old friends. The man who dominated the table I put at around forty-five. He had the broad shoulders of someone who'd done manual work in his life. He had a head of thinning hair but a full beard that covered the lower half of his face. His thin lips were just visible through it. He had cold eyes below thick brown eyebrows. But it was his nose that grabbed attention. It dominated his face, like it had just landed there and decided to colonise the place. It was completely out of proportion to his other features. A Cyrano de Bergerac homage of a schnoz to nasal architecture. The man was wearing a blue velvet dinner suit and a cerise show handkerchief in the breast pocket.

The man to his left was younger, probably late twenties. He had the thin worn face of a guy who has a lot of late nights. He had thick black-rimmed glasses and held his cards close to his face.

To the left of the younger guy, a worried looking man fidgeted in his seat. He was older than Big Nose. He had a round fleshy face and a tonsure of brown hair around a bald head. His forehead looked damp from sweat. He licked his fleshy lips nervously.

The fourth man at the table had his back to me. I couldn't see his face, but he had the lithe body of a young man. And an energetic one, too.

I fiddled with my drink and tried not to look conspicuous. But the four were absorbed in the game. The guy with his back to me was acting as dealer. He flicked a final card to each of the players and a fresh round of betting began. Big Nose chipped in two hundred pounds. The betting moved to the younger guy. He saw that and raised three hundred pounds.

The worried guy looked at his cards. He stared anxiously at the cards of the other players. He glanced at his small pile of chips.

"I'll fold," he said in a soft voice.

The betting moved back to Big Nose. "I'll fold, too," he said. But he made it sound like a triumph.

The younger guy scooped a pile of chips towards him and the dealer collected the cards and shuffled for the next game.

I looked hurriedly at my gin and tonic as the players around the table relaxed. It would be embarrassing if they thought I was watching them.

Big Nose glanced in my direction. He watched me for a moment longer than I felt comfortable.

I stood up and ambled back to the bar. Like a guy who's bored with his surroundings. Like a guy who couldn't care less that four guys were playing poker.

Out of the corner of my eye, I caught a glance from the man sitting in the chair a few feet away. The man with the tortoise-shell glasses and the *Country Life*. He also seemed a damned sight too interested in me.

There were fewer people in the bar than before. There was no sign of Shirley. But she'd be learning all the secrets of the ladies' lavatory attendant.

I sauntered up to the bar and ordered another gin and tonic. I hadn't made any progress in my investigation but I was beginning to feel happy.

The barman served up my drink and I hoisted the glass.

Someone sat down beside me. I turned and looked into the face of the man who'd been reading *Country Life*. He'd removed his tortoise-shell glasses.

He said: "I'll have a whisky and soda if you're buying."

"Why would I be buying?" I said.

"A fellow in a strange place on a mission needs a friend."

I nodded to the barman to bring the drink.

"And what mission would that be?" I asked.

"I'm not sure yet, but I'm right, aren't I?"

"You weren't reading *Country Life* in there because you're thinking of buying a place in Berkshire."

"You're quite right. Because I'm on a mission, too."

The barman put the whisky and a soda siphon in front of my new best friend.

He picked up the glass, gave the whisky a squirt of soda, and sampled the result. He nodded contentedly.

He said: "If I tell you my mission, will you tell me yours?"

"Why should I want to do that?"

"Because if I'm right about you, we'll be able to help each other."

"And why do you think I'd be able to help you?"

"Because I think you're a private eye. Or perhaps a reporter – an investigative reporter."

"And how do you think you'd be able to help me?"

"Because I understand stud poker better than most. How to play it – and how to cheat."

I took a pull at my gin and tonic while I thought about that.

I said: "Suppose I were a reporter, would there be a story in it for me?"

My new best friend grinned. "Think of a headline in big black type on the front page."

"Who are you?" I asked.

"Archie Stamford. And I'm assuming you're not Eric Burtenshaw."

"How did you know I'd signed in under that name?"

"Because I checked the visitors' book. I'm a member here – I have certain rights."

I shrugged. "Colin Crampton, *Evening Chronicle*." I handed him my business card.

"Excellent." Stamford fished in his pocket and handed me his card.

I said: "So what's this story that'll make me big black headlines?"

Stamford drained the last of his scotch.

He glanced around the room. Hilary had just barged in

through the padded doors. He was giving Stamford the evil eye.

Stamford's hands began to shake.

"Not here. We need to speak where we're not going to be noticed. I'll be in touch."

He glanced at his watch, like he'd just remembered an urgent appointment.

And with that, he levered himself off the stool and hurried out.

I lifted my glass and took a pull at my gin and tonic as I tried to work out what that was all about.

Stamford had been watching the four guys playing poker. He'd mentioned cheating. There had to be some connection there. But I didn't know who the poker guys were. I wasn't sure who was cheating whom. And I didn't know why it mattered to Stamford.

This visit had turned out to pose more questions than answers.

I wondered how Shirley had fared in the ladies' loo. But it didn't look as though we were going to find out anything useful about Steve Telford. It had been a mistake coming.

As I put the glass down on the bar, a large hand landed on my shoulder.

I turned around. Hilary, the doorman crowded me.

"We wouldn't want to break any of the glasses, would we?" he said.

"Or anything else, I hope," I said.

Evelyn had been standing behind Hilary. Now he moved around and loomed up in front of me.

I said: "Shouldn't you be watching the door to keep the peasants out?"

Evelyn said: "Our colleagues Beverley and Meredith are doing that."

"Are they as big as you?" I asked.

"Bigger," Evelyn said.

Hilary said: "Mr Hector Clansfield would love to meet you."

"I get a lot of that," I said. "I put it down to my magnetic personality. Perhaps another time."

Evelyn said: "Mr Clansfield wasn't offering an invitation."

Hilary said: "He was issuing an instruction."

"That's the trouble with bosses," I said. "They think they can do what they like."

Evelyn grabbed my right arm and twisted it behind me. He marched me across the room.

I said: "Be careful with that arm."

"Why?"

"Because it's the one I'm going to use to give you a bloody nose."

Evelyn laughed, a deep uproarious rumble from deep in his chest.

He was still laughing as we pushed through the door into Hector Clansfield's office.

Chapter 6

Evelyn shoved me into Clansfield's office and I stumbled forward.

I came to a halt in front of a large oak desk. It was furnished with a fancy brass inkstand with two crystal bottles. Black ink in one, red in the other. There was a leather blotter and a white telephone.

A man with a large round face sat behind the desk. He had a thick thatch of brown hair parted down the middle. He had a broad fleshy body and a stomach that hung over his waistband. He smelt of *Eau de Cologne*. He was wearing a dinner suit with a red bow-tie. He lounged in a high-backed leather chair which moved on casters.

He pushed back the chair and stood up as I stumbled up to the desk.

I said: "Don't get up on my account, Mr Clansfield. You look like the kind of man who needs a sit down."

He said: "And you look like the kind of man who needs to be taught a lesson."

Clansfield turned to Hilary. "Where's the other one?"

"Where's the other what?" Hilary asked.

"The other snake-in-the-grass."

"There ain't no snakes here, Mr Clansfield."

"I mean the bird."

"No birds, either. We could try London Zoo."

Clansfield thumped his fist on the desk. The crystal in the inkstand tinkled against the brass.

"I'm talking about the woman who came with this interloper, you moron," Clansfield thundered.

Hilary's face creased into a smile. "You mean the blonde, boss. She's real tasty."

"Yeah, the blonde. I don't care how tasty she is. Where is she, cretin?" he screamed. His eyes were bloodshot and a red vein pulsed in his nose.

"She's talking to Chloe."

"Who the hell is Chloe?"

"You must have seen her around the place, boss. She's the girl who wears that scarf on her head knotted at the front and that blue overall thing. She's the attendant in the ladies' lavvies. Dab hand with a bog brush. Best this side of Sloane Square."

Clansfield shrugged, calmed down a bit. "The blonde bit can't do any harm there. We'll pick her up when we've dealt with this unwelcome visitor."

"Signed in all nice and proper by one of your members, Dickie Waterford," I said. They already knew that and it looked as though Dickie wouldn't be coming here anymore. Not after this.

Clansfield walked round the desk. Stood legs akimbo in front of me. He smirked like a big man who gets his thrills by making everyone else feel small.

He curled his lip to show he intended to enjoy every minute of what he wanted to say. "Journalists are like rats who gnaw at the very foundations of your home."

"Too right," Hilary, the creep, said.

"They're like weevils who infest your cupboards and your storerooms and eat away at everything," Clansfield said.

"Couldn't have put it better myself," Evelyn, the sycophant, added.

"And let's not forget the moles who dig away and scupper the foundations." I decided I might as well join in.

Clansfield snarled. "You think you're clever, don't you?"

"Someone has to. And at least I can rely on my own opinion. I don't need a pair of arse-lickers to boost my morale."

"Here, boss, he just called Hilary and me arse-lickers," Evelyn protested.

"Just because I'm twenty-one stone don't mean I ain't got

feelings," Hilary said.

Clansfield held up his hands. "Don't worry, boys. You're going to feel really good in a minute."

"You're going to give us a bonus?" Evelyn said.

"In a manner of speaking," Clansfield replied.

"In money?" Hilary asked.

"In blood."

"I trust you're not looking to me as a source of supply," I said.

Clansfield turned to his two goons. Stood up straighter. Stuck out his chest. His belly still sagged over his trousers. Threw back his head like he was General Montgomery addressing the troops before the battle of El Alamein.

He pointed at a fancy Persian carpet in front of his desk.

"In a moment, our unwelcome visitor is going to trip on the rug, stumble forward, and break his nose on the edge of my desk," he said. "There will be a lot blood but no long-term damage."

"No damage, boss? Guess he'll have a crick in his nose 'til the day he dies," Hilary said.

"I was referring to the desk," Clansfield said. "We can wipe the blood off the polished wood."

Evelyn and Hilary exchanged glances and grinned.

"That's funny," Evelyn said.

"There's more," Clansfield said. "As this clumsy reporter stumbles, you, Evelyn, will grab his arm and try to save him. But you won't try too hard. Instead, you'll break his arm."

Evelyn chuckled like an asylum inmate who's just found the key to open his padded cell.

"What about me, boss?" Hilary said. "Don't I get no fun?"

"You will raise your leg to try to prevent this jumped-up journalist from falling forward. But, instead, you will kick his kneecap."

Evelyn and Hilary shook with laughter. Their rumbling guffaws filled the room. The place sounded like the palace of varieties.

"That's a cute idea, boss," Hilary said. "I'd have never thought of that."

"That's why I'm the boss and you're an ape in a uniform," Clansfield said generously.

"That leaves me with only one course of action," I said. "I reached into my jacket pocket and pulled my notebook. I flourished it in my left hand.

"I'm going to write down every word you've all uttered and use it in evidence against you when this comes to court," I said.

Evelyn and Hilary exchanged worried glances.

"Can he do that, boss?" Hilary said.

"It's what any one of Her Majesty's Journalists would do," I said.

I waved the book tauntingly in Clansfield's face. The vein in his nose pulsed. He moved closer. His breath smelt like a dead hedgehog. His eyes were on the book.

Clansfield's hand reached out to grab it. But he was just too slow. My right-arm curved in like a deadly arrow on his blind side and my fist connected with his nose.

There was squelch followed by a crunch. It felt like punching a blancmange and finding someone had hidden a horseshoe inside it.

Blood spurted from his nose and the pulsing vein ruptured. Blood ran over his lips and down his chin.

Clansfield staggered back. He waved his arms like he was sending semaphore.

His goons looked at one another like they thought they'd stumbled in on a stunt.

Clansfield mumbled something through the blood. It had formed a satisfying crimson patch on his dress shirt.

Evelyn and Hilary lunged towards me and grabbed at my arms. I stepped back but there was nowhere to run. Not unless I could get out of the room.

Evelyn got his giant grip around my left arm. Hilary hung onto my right.

Clansfield was looking at his black shoes which had red spots, like a clown's.

He burbled something like a death threat. The idea of breaking a few of my bones wasn't going to satisfy him now. He wanted the hot pokers and thumbscrews.

There wasn't anything I could do. I'd taken my chance. Played my cards. And I'd lost.

And then the door opened.

A high-pitched Cockney voice shrieked: "Can I do you now, sir?"

We all turned in astonishment. A young woman stepped into the room. She had her hair tied up in a scarf with a front-knot. She wore a blue uniform. She carried an enamel bucket full of soapy water and a large mop.

It was Chloe, the bog washer.

No, it wasn't, I realised. It was Shirley, dressed as Chloe, the bog washer.

Shirl moved towards Clansfield, who staggered around in a daze.

"Strewth, sir, would you Adam and Eve it? You've got blood all over yer ones and twos. Let me give them a going over with my mop."

Shirl moved forward and looped the mop head between Clansfield's legs. She yanked the mop to one side and he tumbled over. He hit the ground and lay floundering like one of those walruses you sometimes see on a beach.

Evelyn and Hilary still clung to my arms but their grip had loosened.

Shirl swung round in a circle to give herself some traction and the bucket swung wide. The water sloshed over the room as the bucket crashed into Evelyn's hip.

He yelled in pain, and gripped at his side. He let go of my

arm and staggered across the room.

Shirl changed direction and used the reverse end of her mop as a spear. She charged at Hilary and the mop connected with his crotch. Hilary's hand flew to his crown jewels and he doubled over in agony.

"Right in the orchestra stalls," Shirl yelled in delight. "Looks like your trouble and strife will be on rations when it comes to naughties for a few nights."

"Come on, let's go," I shouted.

Clansfield staggered to his feet as we rushed for the door.

We charged out of Clansfield's office and raced down the corridor towards a sign that read FIRE EXIT.

Behind us, we could hear Clansfield yelling for Beverley and Meredith.

We reached the door. It was one of those fire exits which opens when a bar is pushed. I shoved it hard. The door creaked but didn't open.

Shirley was breathing hard as she looked over my shoulder.

"Jeez, Colin, is the door locked?"

"It can't be."

"Let me try."

Shirl barged past me and pushed down on the bar. It didn't shift.

Way back down the corridor I could hear Clansfield shouting. There was the sound of running feet.

I looked back. Two beefy hoodlums appeared at the far end of the corridor.

Beverley and Meredith.

They wore the same blue uniforms with gold braid and brass buttons as Evelyn and Hilary.

They stopped when they saw us. Glanced at one another. Grinned, like they were hungry lions who'd just spotted a gazelle stuck in a trap.

I shoved the open-bar down again.

"How are we gonna fight these goons?" Shirley yelled.

"We've got to get out of here," I shouted.

Beverley and Meredith started to stroll towards us. Nice and easy. No need to rush. We weren't going anywhere. They wanted to save their energy for the rumble. It would be good. They'd look like champs by the time they'd beaten us to pulp.

"They've got us trapped," Shirley hissed in my ear.

"Look confident. It'll slow them down. They won't want to suffer the same fate as Evelyn and Hilary."

"Look confident? That's all right for you. I'm dressed like a lavvy attendant."

"Just relax," I said.

I leant nonchalantly on the fire door's open-bar. It clicked down. The door swung open.

Shirl snapped: "Why didn't you try that earlier?"

There wasn't time to answer.

We hustled through and slammed the door behind us.

We were in a mews. There were cobblestones like we'd stepped back into the eighteenth century. There were wooden doors that once opened into stables but were now garages. The place was lit by a single lamp at the entrance, where the mews joined the road.

I scanned the courtyard for a quick way out.

There was a Hillman Minx parked in front of one of the garages. There was a BSA Thunderbolt motorcycle propped up behind the Minx. We hustled over and looked at both in case the keys had been left in the ignition.

But that only happens in Hollywood films.

Further down the mews a bicycle had been propped up against the lamppost.

The fire door shuddered as Clansfield's goons rattled the open-bar.

"Let's take the bike," I said.

"What about me?" Shirley said as we hurried across the yard.

"You can sit on the crossbar – just like my friend Barry did when I was a boy. His dad never gave him a bike."

We reached the bike and I grabbed the handlebars. It was a sleek model. Perhaps not fast enough to make it in the *Tour de France*. But quick enough to outrun a couple of overweight goons on foot.

I slung my leg over and sat on the saddle.

"Jump up and sit on the crossbar," I said.

Shirley pulled a "hate you" face at me. But she jumped up like she performed the trick every day.

I took my foot off the ground and pushed off, just as the goons burst through the fire exit.

I pushed my legs hard on the pedals and we rattled over the cobbles.

As we turned the corner into the road, I saw Beverley racing for the Minx and Meredith for the motorcycle.

We were in North Audley Street, heading south. Evening traffic was heavy. A taxi blasted its horn as I swerved to avoid it.

A red bus in front stopped suddenly. I yanked on the brakes and the back wheel fishtailed as we skidded to a halt. An old woman got off and looked at us like we'd tried to murder her.

I glanced back. The Minx had roared out of the mews and was heading towards us.

The bus moved again and I cycled along in its slipstream.

Shirley said: "That Minx is gaining on us."

"If we can reach Green Park, we can lose it in the paths or among the trees."

We swung round Grosvenor Square, past the Roosevelt Memorial, and headed south.

The traffic grew thicker and we put more distance between us and the Minx. But the roads cleared as we raced into Carlos Place and headed towards Mount Street. Behind us, the Minx picked up speed.

"He's only twenty yards back," Shirley yelled in my ear.

But he was closer than that. Seconds later, he came alongside. Beverley steered inwards and I braked hard to avoid running into the Minx's rear wing.

Beverley signalled out of the window for us to stop.

"He's caught us," Shirley yelled.

I mounted the pavement and put a breeze up a courting couple out for a stroll.

Twenty yards ahead, an alley turned off to the left between tall buildings. I didn't know whether I could make it before Beverley caught us. My legs felt like elastic bands about to snap. I gasped for each breath. I'd have given a week's salary for an oxygen mask.

The courting couple had started to yell at us. The cars stuck behind the Minx honked their horns. Somewhere near, I heard the *whoop-whoop* of a police car siren.

It was like Shirley and I were performing in a circus ring. People stared and pointed at us. I summoned up a last reserve of energy to reach the alley.

I cycled into it just as Beverley pulled the Minx to a halt and sprang out of the car. He ran towards us.

But we were thirty yards down the alley and cycling hard by the time he reached the entrance.

I gave him a cheery wave as we disappeared into the darkness.

We shot out of the other end of the alley into Hill Street.

I turned and grinned at Shirley.

"Safe at last," I said.

"That's what you think, buster."

She pointed up the street. Meredith on the Thunderbolt weaved between two taxis and headed towards us.

My feet hit the pedals and we raced towards Berkeley Square.

"I'll throw him off by cycling the wrong way around the square - against the traffic," I shouted above the roar of taxis and buses. "We can get away with that on a bike. He daren't try it on a motorcycle."

We raced into the square.

I twisted left and right as I avoided cars and vans heading towards me. Their headlights blinded me. The cycle wobbled dangerously as I raised a hand to shield my eyes from the glare. Berkeley Square filled with a cacophony of blaring horns.

The nightingale didn't stand a chance.

I was sweating like a mountaineer when I cut into Berkeley Street. But at least we were now moving with the direction of the traffic. And, for the time being, we'd lost Meredith.

Ahead, cars and buses were gridlocked in Piccadilly. I manoeuvred the bike into the flow of the traffic. And stared in shock.

Immediately ahead of us, Beverley was driving the Minx. He hadn't seen us yet, but he only had to look into his rear-view mirror.

"This couldn't be worse if we tried," I said.

"Oh yes, it could," Shirley said.

She pointed behind us at Meredith. He'd just roared out of Berkeley Street. He slid the motorcycle along the side of a bus until he was only feet away.

He tooted his horn and I saw Beverley glance into his rear-view mirror. His mouth dropped open in shock.

He opened his door and climbed out.

Behind Meredith dismounted and walked towards me.

They weren't in a hurry. The traffic was locked solid. We couldn't move forward or back. We were stuck opposite the Ritz hotel.

The cars' headlamps on Beverley's face made him look sinister, like he was Bela Lugosi in a black-and-white horror movie. He grinned and his teeth glinted like daggers in the light.

He was feet away as Meredith closed in from the rear.

I jammed the handlebars of the bike to the right and pushed down on the pedals.

The wheels skidded in a ninety-degree angle and we shot

across the oncoming traffic. Brakes squealed and horns blasted.

Beverley and Meredith shouted as they pounded after us.

I mounted the pavement and shouted at Shirley: "Brace your bum for a rocky ride."

I jumped on the saddle as I bounced the cycle up the steps into the Ritz hotel lobby.

I turned the cycle left and pushed it hard across the green carpet.

A black-jacketed waiter stumbled and dropped his tray of drinks as we flashed by.

The bike's tyres hummed on the thick carpet.

At the far end of the corridor, I could see the doors that led into Arlington Street.

Behind us I could hear Beverley and Meredith shouting the odds. They'd been grabbed by a group of waiters.

We closed on the doors. A uniformed doorman stood in front of us. He wore a frock-coat and a top hat.

His face was an imperturbable mask. He'd seen most things in his time at the Ritz. And what was this?

A *Tour de France* competitor who'd lost his way?

The butcher's boy and his assistant delivering the breakfast sausages?

Or an eccentric millionaire and his wife who liked to cycle everywhere?

One eyebrow twitched. He'd made his decision.

Must be the eccentric millionaire.

He stepped aside and opened the door.

We bounced down the steps into Arlington Street and disappeared into the night.

Chapter 7

Shirley flashed me one of her impish grins and said: "After sitting on that crossbar, I'll have a groove in my bum for weeks."

"I'll check on its improvement every day," I said.

"You and whose army, buster?"

We were sitting at a table in the last Brighton Belle of the day to Brighton. We'd ordered a pot of coffee and ham sandwiches.

We'd bumped down the steps of the Ritz Hotel's Arlington Street entrance like a pair of clowns on a bike with square wheels. But it had marked the end of the chase. Beverley and Meredith had left their Minx and Thunderbird in a traffic jam. They had to move them before the cops showed up.

Shirley and I had leant the bike against the railings outside the Ritz and walked off towards Victoria Station like we'd just come from an evening at the opera.

"I was sure pleased to see you come through the door of Clansfield's office," I said. "I was about to take a serious beating. But I can't figure out how you knew I was there."

Shirl sipped her coffee. "After I'd chin-wagged with Chloe, I slunk back to the bar to find you. The barman admitted you'd been frogmarched off by Evelyn and Hilary to be bollocked by Clansfield. It was obvious you'd talked yourself into trouble again. I'd clocked a staff cupboard while I'd been jawing to Chloe. There were uniforms and cleaning stuff in there. So I made up like a dunny cleaner and armed myself with a mop and bucket. Thought it might buy me those vital first seconds you're always talking about when I barged into the room."

"It was great," I said. "Even fooled me for a second or two."

Lights flashed at the train's windows as we sped through East Croydon station.

I told Shirley what I'd seen at the club and how I'd met Archie Stamford who'd said he had something important to tell me.

"But he left in a hurry and said he'd get in touch. I'm pretty certain that something criminal is going on at the club. But I don't know what it is – and I've not picked up any information about Steve Telford."

Shirley had been munching her ham sandwich while I was talking. She put the crusts back on her plate.

"Looks like I've pulled your nuts out of the fire again," she said.

"You found out something?"

"Turns out Steve only worked at the club a few times, but he got to know Chloe well. She reckons he fancied her."

"A lavatory cleaner in overalls?"

"Some men go for a girl in uniform. And don't knock the bog brush brigade. Their work is a damned sight more useful than the girls who spin the roulette wheels in the gambling room."

I nodded in agreement. "You're right."

"Anyway, Chloe said Steve was always trying to impress her. One night he spun her a yarn that he'd done secret work during the war. Double-O-Seven stuff. She asked him to spill the beans, but he wouldn't tell her. He asked her out on her night off, but she gave him the old 'washing her hair' excuse. He pushed for a date. But she said she only went out with men who were going up in the world. That's when he played his ace. Told Chloe his daughter Deirdre was shacked up with a member of the aristocracy."

"And which of the noble lords had the girl on a string?"

Shirl gave a sly grin. "Viscount Rackham."

My eyes popped at that news.

"He's the hippie peer who has all those Little Darlings living with him on his country estate," Shirl added. "He's always being mentioned in the gossip columns."

I flopped back in my chair. "He also happens to be the new proprietor of the *Evening Chronicle*. His father died a couple of weeks back. Rackham should now be called the Marquess of

Bognor, but I expect the gossip columnists will continue to call him Rackham. This has given me something serious to think about."

Shirley leaned across the table. She had an intense look on her face.

"Chloe told me something strange happened a few days ago. Steve was on duty on the door. When he had his break, he came to see her. His face was white and his eyes looked scared. It wasn't like him, Chloe said. He was usually full of himself."

"Did she ask him what the problem was?"

"Sure. Chloe is a great girl. She won't spend much of her life washing the dunny. She told me that Steve would only say he'd seen a figure from the past."

"At the club?"

"I guess so. He hadn't been all shook up when he'd arrived for his shift, Chloe said. But, later that evening, shortly before he knocked off for the night, he saw Chloe again. He told her he was going to ask her out for dinner. He said she wouldn't refuse him this time, because he was going up in the world. He'd take her somewhere fancy like the Caprice. He reckoned he was coming into money. Big money."

I thought about that. There'd been two thousand pounds in Steve's flat. That was big money in anybody's language. Could it have come from the person he'd seen at the club that night?

Shirley said: "That was the last time she saw Steve."

"He never worked at the club again?"

"No. A few days later he was dead."

The train slowed as it passed through Preston Park. We were only a mile from Brighton station.

I said: "I wonder whether Archie Stamford knows anything about this. Perhaps that was what he was going to tell me before he was spooked and left the club like he was being chased by a nest of vipers."

"What are you going to do?" Shirley asked.

I moved my legs. After the madcap cycle ride, my muscles felt like they'd been set in concrete. Little pains shot up my thighs, and my knees creaked.

I said: "I don't know. I'll just have to hope that Archie gets in touch. And that he can throw some light on the mystery. Otherwise I'll have nothing to show for our meeting but aching legs."

"And don't forget the groove in my bum," Shirley said.

"Mention that once more, and I'll spend the night dreaming about it."

"Kinky," Shirley said.

Frank Figgis' face turned a dark shade of crimson and his eyes boggled like they were bouncing on tiny springs.

"Absolutely not," he said. "That's a definite no. It's out of the question. I totally forbid it."

"So you wouldn't mind if I did it on the quiet without telling you?" I asked.

Figgis' head seemed to pulse like a red warning light.

"It's a 'no' whether you tell me or not," he said. "And if I find you have, I'll kick you out so fast, your bum will have hit the pavement before your mind has even realised you're on the move."

We were in Figgis' office. It was the morning after my visit to London with Shirley.

The morning after I'd discovered Deirdre Telford was now shacked up as one of Viscount Rackham's Little Darlings.

The news had given me a sleepless night. I'd tossed and turned while I thought about what to do.

The obvious action was to head for Ethelbert House, Rackham's ancestral pile, and see what I could learn from Deirdre about her father. Perhaps I'd find Deirdre on her own. But perhaps she'd be enjoying a lovey-dovey moment with the new owner of the *Evening Chronicle*. That could be embarrassing all round.

Especially for me when I signed on at the Labour Exchange.

But now my suggestion had set Figgis on fire.

He was so riled up he'd forgotten he hadn't had a Woodbine for fully two minutes.

I said: "Let's look at this rationally. We've got the chance of breaking open the most sensational murder story any paper has had for months. The daughter of a dead man is linked to a peer of the realm who collects girlfriends like other people collect stamps."

"And who just happens to own our paper," Figgis said. "Have you never heard the old proverb about not dropping a big one on your front doorstep?"

"If we don't chase this story and another rag beats us to it, it'll look like we're hiding something. We'll get tagged with censoring the news when it doesn't suit us."

Figgis reached for his Woodbines, shook one out of the packet and lit up. Evidently, he'd started to think rationally again.

"Who's going to discover the Deirdre connection to Telford? You only found out by chance. From what you tell me, you're lucky not to be in hospital with more bandages than the Invisible Man. We might be having this conversation at your bedside over a bunch of grapes."

"For future reference, I prefer apricots when they're in season. But I can be discreet when I make enquiries."

"And what would the headline be? Murdered Man's Daughter in Lord's Harem. So far, it looks as though Rackham will play a low-key role in the paper. He'll keep our generous editorial budget and let us get on with the job. The last thing we want is him down here giving orders."

"Agreed," I said. "Keeping His Holiness under control is tough enough."

"So you'll keep away from Rackham?" Figgis said.

"I'll do everything in my power to avoid direct contact with him," I said.

I meant it, too. It was Deirdre I wanted to interview.

I stood up to leave the room. Looked back at Figgis when I reached the door. His face had returned to its normal complexion. Battleship grey. He was lighting another Woodbine.

He was content. Normal service had been resumed.

But not as far as I was concerned.

I stomped back into the newsroom in a rebellious spirit.

I felt a bit like Wat Tyler who led all those peasants in revolt. Or those chaps who'd stormed the *Bastille*. But they all got it wrong. Wat Tyler and his chums still went home as peasants. And the mob found little to amuse them in the *Bastille*. They'd have had more fun from a night out at the *Moulin Rouge*.

What they lacked was subtlety and cunning. Crampton specialties.

So I strolled into the *Chronicle's* morgue, where the press cuttings were filed, with a smile on my face and a song in my heart. The song was Chuck Berry's *Don't You Lie to Me*. I wasn't going to lie to anyone. Unless I had to.

Henrietta Houndstooth, who ran the morgue, was sitting at her desk. She was wearing a tweed jacket over a cream blouse with a fancy bow at the neck. Her horn-rimmed glasses were perched on the end of her nose. There was a thick file balanced on her in-tray. She was reading a cutting from the previous day's *Chronicle*. It was my story about Steve Telford's murder.

She looked up as I approached her desk. She took off her glasses.

She said: "I hear you had a lively evening last night."

"All in a day's work for a crime reporter."

"But you haven't come in here to tell me about it."

"I've come in because you're the *Chronicle's* Queen of the Goss."

Henrietta's eyebrows shot up. "Goss? What kind of word is that?"

"An abbreviation. For gossip."

"You can't make up words like that."

"Why not? Horace Walpole invented the word 'serendipity'. I'm not sure why. Hardly anyone uses it. Anyway, I haven't invented a new word. I've shortened an existing one."

"Even worse. If we all go around shortening words, we'll end up like chimpanzees gibbering grunts and squeaks at one another."

"I'll pass on your complaint to the editor of the *Oxford English Dictionary*."

"Unfortunately, Charles Onions died last year."

"Who's the new guy. Bertie Broccoli?"

Henrietta frowned. "You haven't come in here to get into an argument about words."

I nodded. "Sorry. I've got a favour to ask."

"Does it concern this file?" Henrietta asked.

She pointed at the thick monster sitting on her in-tray.

I took a closer look. The tab on the top read: Rackham, Viscount.

Henrietta looked at me with worried eyes.

"Our new owner. What do you know about him?" I asked.

Henrietta pointed at the file. "It's all in there."

"What's in there is the stuff the gossip columnists have written about. I want to know the stuff they haven't written about. You know everything. I didn't crown you Queen of the Goss, sorry, I mean Gossip, for nothing."

Henrietta looked like she wanted to smile but had stopped herself. "In view of my work, I'll take that as a compliment."

She leaned back in her chair and I took that as sign I could perch on the edge of her desk.

"You already know that Rackham was Lord Bognor's only legitimate son. Bognor's wife died when Rackham was only three years old. Bognor was left to bring up the boy, but he passed him on to a succession of nannies and governesses. I heard that few of them stayed long. Young Rackham was a wild boy, just wouldn't submit to discipline."

"Why didn't his father take the lad in hand?"

"Didn't seem interested. The rumour I heard was that Bognor had had an affair with a farm girl. I heard her name was Susan. There was a son. Born on the wrong side of the blanket, as they used to say in those days. But, apparently, Bognor loved the boy more than Rackham. Maybe that was one reason why Rackham was so unruly. Of course, Susan's boy was Bognor's secret, but perhaps the young Rackham sensed there was a rival for his father's affections."

"I thought aristocrats sent their kids off to prep schools and Eton in those days."

"Bognor paid for the best. Rackham was enrolled at Eton but lasted only two terms. Expelled for running a book on Royal Ascot. Then there was Harrow. Three terms. Expelled for procuring girls for sixth form boys. Charterhouse just over a year. Kicked out for running an all-night poker school. At that point, Bognor gave up. Had him educated at Ethelbert House by a private tutor. The strange thing was that Rackham was uncommonly bright."

"Could he have gone to university?"

"That's what I've heard. But he just couldn't be bothered with the conventions of the kind of life he'd been born to. And as he grew into his teens, he became more and more estranged from this father. Did things to annoy him. He knew his father hated insects, especially spiders, so he set up a little menagerie of them in one of the estate's greenhouses. He knew his father was a lover of classical music – patron of the Brighton Philharmonic Orchestra. So Rackham took up *musique concrète*."

"With a cement mixer?"

"Ha-ha, I don't think. No, it's a movement that uses recorded sounds as the raw material for performance pieces. There was a school of *musique concrète* devotees in Paris and Rackham joined them for a while. That's where he also seemed to pick up his liking for girls."

"Lots of them, I hear."

"He knew his father wanted him to find a suitable wife. You know the kind of girl, horsey type you see photographed in *Tatler*. Old Bognor wanted to see the line go on. What old families fear more than anything is dying out. So Bognor would have loved it if Rackham had married and had a son of his own, or perhaps two."

"An heir and a spare." I said.

Henrietta nodded. "I think that's why Rackham defied his father's wishes and set about collecting his so-called Little Darlings – in the way other aristos have a string of racehorses."

"But Bognor allowed Rackham to house the girls in cottages on the estate."

"Bognor indulged him, perhaps through the guilt of neglecting him in favour of his love-child. And maybe Bognor hoped Rackham would eventually make one of the Little Darlings his wife. But it never happened."

"Bognor should have taken a strong hand," I said.

"Easy to say. More difficult to do, especially when you have your own skeletons that could suddenly fall out of a cupboard. But in one way, Bognor did take a tough line with Rackham. He'd had the gambling bug since his days at Eton but it gradually became worse. The word was that Bognor wrote off some big gambling debts. Rackham fancied himself as a poker champion, but usually lost. In the end, Bognor confronted Rackham and told him that if the losses continued, he'd evict the Little Darlings from their cottages. That seemed to focus Rackham's mind. The gambling stopped."

"But I wonder what will happen now that Bognor is dead?"

"That's what fills me with dread for the future of the *Chronicle*," Henrietta said.

"Me too," I said.

Chapter 8

An hour later, I pulled my MGB to a halt outside the gates to Ethelbert House.

The gates were a fine example of fancy ironwork, all twirls and whirls. They had a Latin motto woven into the design. *Ligonem ligonem vocat*. Call a spade a spade. An odd motto for an ancient family, but perhaps the marquesses of Bognor were known for their plain speaking. Nothing wrong with that.

I only hoped I wasn't going to run into Rackham, who was the new marquess.

But it didn't look as though I was going to run into anyone if I couldn't get into the estate. The gates were locked and secured with a stout chain.

The estate was surrounded by a six-feet high wall. The wall looked as though it could have been built a century ago out of limestone blocks. The limestone was weathered and encrusted with lichens. In some places, blocks had fallen out of the wall. I guessed there could be places where it had crumbled completely.

I pulled the car back onto the road and drove a couple of hundred yards. I pulled into a lay-by, parked the car and climbed out.

About fifty yards to my right, there was a spot where the top two courses of stones had fallen out of the wall. It wasn't more than four-feet high. I could practically vault it.

As it turned out, it was tougher clambering over the wall than I'd imagined. I landed on the other side with scuff marks on my shoes.

I was in a wood with oak and beech trees. There was an undergrowth of brambles and nettles. Ahead of me, through the trees, there was sunlight. I made way towards it and stepped out on to a knoll which overlooked the estate. To the south, the hills of the South Downs stretched across the horizon. Old Rudyard

Kipling, who'd lived in Sussex, called them "whale-backed Downs... where chasing shadows skim". I didn't have time today for chasing shadows. I wanted to find Deirdre Telford, ask her some questions, and leave before Rackham realised I'd been there.

I stepped discreetly behind a tree to take a closer look at the lie of the land. About a mile off to the south-east, I could see the main house with its formal gardens. The estate's parkland rolled towards the slopes of the Downs. There was a track which wound its way towards the higher ground. There was a cluster of three cottages at the foot of the track, two more further on, and one near to a copse of trees. Beyond the copse, a thick forest stretched into the distance. I'd heard that locals called it the Dark Wood. It was a source of old wives' tales about goblins with evil spells, of men who vanished in the night, and of tunnels which led to Australia.

Now that I was on the estate, I realised that finding Deirdre without attracting attention from the wrong people wouldn't be so easy. But I decided I wouldn't sneak about. Not a good idea. A gamekeeper might mistake me for a poacher and fire a pot-shot at me.

Instead, I marched boldly towards the house along a path that led down from the knoll.

The path brought me out on a courtyard in front of the house. As I reached it, a country type in riding breeches and rat-catcher's cap, led a horse – a grey – around the side of the house.

He looked at me uncertainly and said: "Are you the vet?"

I said: "I'm looking for Deirdre Telford."

"What do you want with Deirdre?"

"I'm from the undertakers. It's about her father's funeral. Confidential matter, you understand."

The country type looked a bit embarrassed and the horse whinnied in sympathy.

He pointed towards the woods. "You'll find her in the cottage up by the copse," he said.

I loped up the path with a weary tread. Like a bloke who spends a lot of time carrying a coffin on his shoulder.

The cottage by the copse was a small place built out of Sussex flints.

There were a couple of small leaded windows at the front and a thatched roof. The thatch was grey and moss grew in little mounds on it.

I rapped gently three times on the door. A respectful Uriah Heep of a knock. Like a knock from the vicar collecting for the organ fund.

The door creaked as it was opened.

The young woman standing in front of me had a face that might not have launched a thousand ships but would certainly have floated a pleasure steamer.

She had a clear complexion, dark mocking eyes, and enough lustrous black hair to make the ravens at the Tower of London wonder where they'd gone wrong. The shiny hair spilled over her shoulder and down her back to her waist.

She was wearing a kaftan with a green and orange oriental pattern. Could have been Indian. She had sandals on her feet and a long string of beads around her neck.

She said: "Who the hell are you?"

I said: "I've come about your father."

I handed her one of my cards. She looked briefly at it and said: "If you've come to tell me he's dead, I already know, so you can knock off out of it."

"I was hoping you could give me some information about him."

"He did bugger all for me in my life and has just become a great big pain in the bum now that he's dead. So why should I want to do that?"

"Because I've found you."

"So now you can unfind me, smart-arse."

"Sure, but then other people might find you who would be less discreet than me."

"Other people? Like who?"

"Like the police."

Deirdre scowled. "You better frigging come in. But don't expect a cup of tea."

I ducked under the door's low architrave, wiped my feet carefully on the mat, and entered a small parlour. It was a strange room to be home to a young woman. It was furnished with a long couch and a bucket-shaped basket chair which hung from a hook in an old oak beam that held up the ceiling. There was a raffia rug on the floor which looked like an over-sized table-mat. There was a brick fireplace with ashes of an old fire still in the grate.

Deirdre threw herself into the basket chair. The oak beam creaked. The chair swung from side to side. It bounced up and down a bit and the cord fixing it to the ceiling made a deep twang sound. Like someone has just plucked the low E string on a double bass.

She waved her hand around. "Home, sweet frigging home," she said.

I sat down on the couch.

Deirdre seemed to be taking the arrival of one of Her Majesty's Journalists a little too casually. It was time to bring her down to earth.

I said: "Someone killed your father. Do you know who?"

Deirdre laughed. "Who killed the old bastard? Could have been dozens of people. Perhaps hundreds. At some time, he'd screwed every sucker in Brighton."

"I've been told your father was in security."

"If he was in security, then Ronnie Biggs heads the Yeoman of the Guard."

"He'd been working as doorman at a club in London."

"Probably a way to skin the punters."

"If your father wasn't in security, what was he?"

"He was a spiv. A wide-boy. A con man. He made his money by cheating people. Seriously bad karma. And I hate him for ruining my life. There were always people coming round to our house. Rozzers sometimes but other types making threats about what would happen if Steve Telford didn't deliver. How did Lucy - that's my mum - and I know what he was supposed to deliver? He dodged in and out. Sometimes we didn't see him for days. No wonder my poor mum worried herself to death. Yeah! I blame the old bastard for that. He didn't care that his life wore her down to a waif. That she dreaded every knock on the door. Or where the housekeeping money was coming from each week. And then she caught the flu and she was so weak she couldn't recover. So she died. He wasn't even there. I had to close her eyes and pull a sheet over her head."

The tears were streaming down Deirdre's face. She gulped back a sob. She jumped out of the chair, ran across the room, and pushed through a door into a bedroom. She sobbed and wailed for five minutes and then the bedroom went quiet. I waited. She needed to face this herself. To come to terms with her father's death – whatever those terms might be.

It was twenty minutes before Deirdre came back into the room. Her eyes were red. Her nose was moist and her complexion was pale. But she was composed.

She sat down beside me on the couch.

She said: "He was an old bastard."

"At least you had the measure of him," I said.

"He could have been a good old bastard, if he'd wanted to be. Even a brave one."

"In what way?"

"He was in the Home Guard during the war. Used to boast about it on Saturday nights. He'd come home, tanked up after a few bevvies, with a pint of winkles. He'd sit there with a pin, eat the frigging things, and regale Mum and me with tales about how he'd won the war."

I said: "Most of the recruits in the Home Guard were old men. Dad's Army, they called it. Your father must have been young to be a member."

Deirdre shrugged. "Yeah! He told the Ministry of Labour or whatever that he was a farm hand. Thought it was a reserved occupation – meant he wouldn't be called up to the army. That's a laugh. The old bastard only landed himself with what could have been one of the most dangerous jobs of the lot."

"I thought the biggest danger in the Home Guard was that they might run out of biscuits to have with their tea."

"Not the bit the old bastard was in. It was supposed to be secret at the time. They had a special name for it. I can't remember... Axe something or other," I think.

"You don't mean the Auxiliary Units?" I asked.

"Yeah! That's them. You've heard of them?"

I'd heard of them, but only the rumours. In 1940 Winston Churchill feared the Germans would invade Britain from the south coast. He knew the country was ill-prepared for invasion and that the Nazis might make early gains. What was left of the British army – that which had been rescued from Dunkirk – would have had to fall back to defensive positions in the midlands and north of the country. But Churchill wanted to make it as difficult as possible for the Germans to reinforce and supply their invading army. So he ordered the creation of the Auxiliary Units. Independent cells of men would hide in underground bunkers in woods and remote country places and harry German supply lines. It was a desperate plan and the men recruited weren't expected to live for long.

I turned to Deirdre: "So your father was recruited into the Auxiliary Units."

"Yeah! Much to his disgust. They called themselves the scallywags because they were trained to get up to no good when the Nazis arrived. In the old bastard's case, he couldn't bear to wait."

"What do you mean?"

"He couldn't resist screwing his mates – even while they were waiting to do or die."

"He told you that?"

"No. He always saw himself as a hero. But Mum told me the truth. She knew of other blokes who'd been scallywags and didn't have a good word to say about the old bastard."

I thought about that. The scallywags would have been trained in the dark arts of hand-to-hand combat and killing. They'd know how to kill a man in a dozen ways or more. Could one of them have done for Steve Telford? And why would they want to kill him after twenty years?

I said: "Do you know any of the scallywags who were posted with your father?"

"He never mentioned any names, but my mum knew one. Harry Deakin."

"How come?"

"She was engaged to him. That was until the old bastard came along and swept her off her feet."

My eyebrows jumped a bit at that. "Steve Telford stole Harry Deakin's fiancée?" I said.

"You never knew the old bastard. He could be quite a charmer. And during the war years he was into the black market in a big way. I don't know how he managed to fit everything in, but he always found time for making a quick buck. There was boring old Harry Deakin, with barely two pennies to bless himself with. And along comes the old bastard with everything a girl wants but couldn't get in the war. Perfume, nylon stockings, lipstick, and even an occasional orange. Well, which one would you choose?"

"I never wear nylon stockings."

"I didn't think you looked the type."

I thought of Deirdre's mum tempted by perfume and oranges. Then I thought about Deirdre with the opportunity to live on a grand estate as a viscount's girlfriend. Perhaps it was like mother, like daughter.

Deirdre looked away. Wrinkled her brow. Perhaps she was thinking the same thoughts.

She said: "Perhaps if mum was still alive, she'd have got back together with Harry. Now that the old bastard is out of the way."

"Harry is still around?"

"He builds those flint walls you see all over Sussex. He's working on one at Washington church at the moment. I was down in the village one day and saw this geezer at work. I liked it – taking those stones and making them into a wall. It's kind of peaceful, if you know what I mean. He was friendly. He asked me my name. He wasn't so friendly when he knew it was Telford. He didn't want to know when he realised I was the old bastard's daughter. I told him to go screw himself. I was a viscount's girl now."

"And what happens next?" I asked.

Deirdre flashed me a worried a look.

"What do you mean?"

"I mean Rackham has a reputation for leading a rackety lifestyle."

"You're just jealous because you ain't got six girlfriends."

"I've got the equivalent of six in one, but that's another story. What I want to know is whether you're staying on here - or will you go back and live in Steve's flat? I guess it's yours now."

"Haven't thought about that yet. I suppose it depends what happens here. His lordship gives me a free rein to roam around the place. Except I'm not allowed into the Dark Wood."

"That forest around the estate?"

"Yeah! These lord types have a lot of land – pastures and forests and stuff - but they're not always so flush with the readies," Deirdre said.

"Rackham is short of cash?"

"Yeah! His old man always kept him on a tight leash when it came to the moolah. Didn't mind us living here, but didn't want him splashing the folding stuff about in his poker games."

"You've played poker with him?"

"For him. We girls play every Saturday to decide who gets to sleep with him on Sunday night. I've never won. To tell you the truth, I've never tried. As I'm Saturday anyway, I've usually had enough by Sunday morning. It's quite nice to know you've got the rest of the week off."

I stood up. I didn't think I'd learn much more from Deirdre.

I moved towards the door turned to say goodbye. But I'd thought of one more question.

"What do you do here all the time?"

A puzzled frown wrinkled Deirdre's brow. "We live," she said.

Chapter 9

I left Deirdre seeking some much-needed consolation.

She was rolling herself a reefer. Life as Viscount Rackham's Saturday girl had to go on.

I stomped back through the woods, jumped the wall, and sat in my car wondering what the hell to do next.

It was clear that Steve Telford was a man who'd made enemies wherever he went. But if I were to make any progress in finding his killer, I needed to know a lot more about the Auxiliary Units and the scallywags.

Earlier, I'd noticed a telephone box a couple of hundred yards from the gates to Ethelbert House. I climbed out of the MGB, tramped down the road to the box, and put a reverse charge call through to the *Chronicle*. I asked Muriel on the switchboard to connect me to Henrietta Houndstooth.

She came on the line and said: "I might have known I'd hear from you again before the day was done."

"And, of course, I'd hate to disappoint you. Tell me, what would come into your mind if I mentioned the word 'scallywag'?"

"That you were just about to tell me about one of your so-called triumphs. Or that you were about to enlist me in one of your scams," Henrietta said.

"Let's leave me out of it."

"Sometimes, I wish we could."

"If I mentioned Auxiliary Units, would that jog your memory?"

There was a brief silence. Then Henrietta said: "You're thinking of the top-secret wartime organisation that was part of the Home Guard."

"Its members called themselves scallywags."

"I remember now. It was before I came to work in the morgue. Old Miss Esmerelda Fox, who ran the place during the war, told me about it. Of course, because it was secret there won't be any cuttings. Even if reporters had known about the Auxiliary Units, they wouldn't have written about them. It would have endangered the country in a time of war. But there may be some unpublished notes. I'll see if I can find any."

"Soon as you can, please, Henrietta."

"Are you coming straight back to the *Chronicle*?"

"First I've got to see a man about a wall."

I rang off.

Deirdre had mentioned that Harry Deakin worked nearby building flint walls. I thought about that while I walked back to the car.

It was an ancient craft that went back to Roman times. The Normans were also dab hands at flint knapping. William the Conqueror's Normans built castles and churches entirely from flint. They quarried the flints from chalk pits, then used a crude mortar to hold them in place as they erected the walls. Or rather they sat back and stuffed themselves with a surfeit of lampreys while they forced the peasants to do the heavy lifting. Nothing much changes down the years. The bosses loll about while the workers perform the hard graft. It's the same on newspapers.

I thought about what kind of man would dedicate his life to building flint walls as I climbed into the car. It could be a solitary occupation. It would leave plenty of time for reflection. Plenty of time for grudges to fester into hatred. Plenty of time for plans to form in minds.

I wondered whether that's what had happened with Harry Deakin. I sat in the car and turned the theory over in my mind. Someone had killed Telford and it was likely that someone came from his past life.

The only way to test my theory was to question those who had known Telford.

And the first on my list was Harry Deakin.

I fired up the MGB, pulled into the road, and went in search of him.

The tiny village of Washington was deserted when I pulled the MGB into a layby outside St Mary's church.

I climbed out of the car and admired it from the road. I was pleased to see it was flint built – some of it as early as the thirteenth century, a noticeboard by the churchyard gate informed me. There was a slate-roofed nave, a porch faced with red bricks, and a castellated tower. The building was surrounded by a churchyard. Ancient gravestones, encrusted with mildew, leant at impossible angles from the turf. Here and there withered bunches of flowers showed that the dear departed had not yet been forgotten. Long grasses grew at the fringes of the graveyard and ancient yews shaded the path to the church door. It was just the kind of place that would have inspired Thomas Gray's *Elegy in a Country Churchyard*.

Some of the churchyard wall looked as though it had been recently repaired with new flints and mortar. But there was no sign of the workman.

I stood still and listened to the wind rustle the overgrown grasses. I thought about a line from the *Elegy*: "The paths of glory lead but to the grave." No doubt the scallywags thought they were on their way to glory as they waited for the Nazis to invade in 1940. Well, they never had the chance of the glory they expected. And now one had discovered that you don't need glory to end up in a grave.

I pulled my thoughts back to the here and now. There was no sign of Harry Deakin. And then…

CLUNK.

The sound came from the far side of the church.

CLUNK.

The sound of metal on stone. Perhaps I was in luck after all.

A flint wall circled the churchyard. I followed the line of the wall round to the back of the church along a path overgrown with nettles.

Beyond the nettles, there was a stretch of wall which had fallen down. Flints and broken mortar lay strewn on the ground.

A well-built man with a thick thatch of dark hair was bent over the flints. He was wearing a one-piece blue overall.

There was a toolbox to the side of the flints. Several tools – hammers and chisels of different kinds – were piled in the box. A woollen balaclava helmet looked out of place among them.

The man gathered the fallen flints together. He put them in a pile, then selected one of the largest. He took a geologist's hammer from his toolbox and gave the flint a sharp rap. It split neatly into two. The man looked at the flat surface on each of the two halves and smiled. He was absorbed in his work.

I strolled up and said: "As fine an example of flint knapping as you'll see anywhere."

The man glanced up with a scowl on his face. He looked annoyed to be interrupted in his work. Or perhaps he was one of those people who look permanently annoyed. He had bushy eyebrows, a prominent nose and thin lips.

The scowl relaxed to a frown. "Aye. And a better example than any who've worked on this wall afore."

I said: "Harry Deakin?"

"Who wants to know?" The scowl was back.

"Colin Crampton, *Evening Chronicle*."

"Not here to talk flint knapping, I'll bargain."

"Knew I couldn't fool you. I want to talk about murder."

"Whose murder?"

"Steve Telford's."

Harry's bushy eyebrows beetled together. He tested the weight of the hammer in his hands. Looked at it like he wondered how hard he'd have to swing it to smash something. I hoped that something wasn't my head.

"Split a large flint with this," he said. "Daresay, it would split a skull, too."

"Enough to kill a fellow scallywag?"

"No, not that. I read about Telford's killing. It didn't say how he died, but it wasn't with a hammer. Can't say I shed a tear about his death. But then I don't shed many tears these days."

"Since the days when Telford stole Lucy from you?"

Harry gawped like I'd just landed a straight right to his chin. He slumped down on a broken section of the wall.

"Might have expected that from a newspaperman. Can't keep a decent bit a privacy when there's a newspaperman around."

I shrugged. "Someone has to ask the questions."

"And some of us do an honest day's graft and go home with a clear conscience," he said.

"There's no shame in crying for a lost love," I said.

Harry took a deep breath, then let his shoulders slump. "Yeah! I don't mind admitting I shed some tears then. Enough tears to fill the font at this church it seemed like at the time. But you can't hate when you cry. And I determined I'd hate Steve Telford until the day his last breath left his body."

"Did you help that breath leave his body?"

"That's one dream that never came true. And that's not a lie."

"What were you doing two evenings ago?"

Harry shot me a suspicious look. But he knew what I was up to. He knew he'd have to answer before I left him alone with his flints and his hammers. And his memories.

"Thursday nights I helps the vicar with the scout meeting. I was at the village hall."

"Dyb, dyb, dyb and all that," I said.

Harry sighed. "Yeah! And all that."

I moved closer and perched on the wall near Harry.

I said: "Why did you hate Steve Telford so much?"

"What's it to you?"

"I've spoken to his daughter Deirdre. And she hated Steve, too. She blamed the stress and strain Steve's scams put on Lucy for her mother's early death. In fact, Deirdre told me she'd had enough and left home three months ago."

"Yeah! I'd heard. If that girl is mixed up with Viscount Rackham, there must be some of her father in her. But she knew enough to leave him in the end. And that will be the good in Lucy coming out."

"And, like Deirdre, you hated Steve because he'd driven Lucy into an early grave?"

"I hated him because he took away the only girl I ever loved. And not because he loved her, either. Just to show he could do it. Just so he could score one over on me. Because he knew, deep down, that I was twice the man he was. Twice as willing to do my duty and look death in the face if I had to. And I'd do it again if the cause were right."

"And is there a cause?" I asked.

"There's always causes. Ain't you noticed? As the old song goes, 'It's the rich what gets the pleasure, it's the poor what gets the blame.' And sometimes it's worse than the blame."

"What do you mean by that?"

"Nothing. Just me mouthing off."

I thought about that for a moment. Harry had spoken with passion. He clearly hated Telford. But there was something else on his mind.

I said: "Are you saying that Steve Telford was a coward?"

Harry threw back his head in a mirthless laugh.

"Telford was a spiv, a con-man, a chancer. He had bravado – and that's the way cowards cover up the fact that they've not got the balls for true bravery."

"But Telford was a scallywag, just like you?"

Harry turned towards me. Hefted the hammer a couple of times in his hands.

"No, not like me," he said in a quiet voice.

I said: "What was life like as a scallywag?"

"Most of the time it was boring. We sat in our bunkers waiting for the Germans to invade. They never did, of course. We spent the time playing cards. Poker mainly. We became quite good at it. Telford especially. There were six of us in our team."

"You and Telford being two of them?"

"Yeah. Then there was Alec Perkins. He was a fisherman working out of Shoreham harbour before the war started. Went back there after it finished."

"Where would I find him?" I asked.

"Out on his boat – the Jolly Dolphin - when he's not in the pub. He troubles the landlords more than the fish. Try around the Shoreham pubs – you'll find him before long."

"Who else was in your team?"

"There was Fred Youngman, a grave digger from Steyning. He'll dig his own one of these days. He moved to Brighton after the war. Got a job at the municipal cemetery in Bear Road. Still digging graves, when he can't find any other way to turn a quick shilling."

"He looks for the quick buck?"

"Yeah! A bit like Telford in that respect. But not so successful. I think the pair used to see one another from time to time."

"To swap war stories?"

"More likely tales about how to make easy money. But I heard Fred fell out with Telford a few months ago. Everyone does in time."

"I make that four scallywags out of six. Who were the other two?"

"For a few months the team was completed by Patrick Harrison and John King – he was the sharpest poker ace of us all. But neither of them lasted for long."

"Why was that?"

Harry's scowl was back. "It's a long story. I might tell it to you one day. But, then, I might have better things to do. Like building this wall."

Harry picked up another flint and gave it a sharp crack with his hammer.

This time it didn't break cleanly. A chip flew off into the grass.
"Things don't always turn out as you'd like," I said.
"Isn't that just the truth?" Harry said.
He turned his back on me and went back to work.
I heard his hammer strike another flint as I walked away.

Chapter 10

Harry Deakin had told me that Alec Perkins troubled the landlords more than the fish.

I ran Alec to ground in the Duke of Wellington, the third Shoreham pub I visited.

He was propping up the bar.

His brown weather-beaten face had been wrinkled by the sun and wind, but his eyes were sharp. He was raising a glass of beer to his lips.

He was dressed in a one-piece waterproof overall and calf-high boots turned over at the top to reveal the fleecy lining. He had a jaunty sailor's cap on his head and a green duffel bag looped over his shoulder.

The landlord pointed him out to me as he poured my gin and tonic.

I edged along the bar, pointed at Alec's half-empty glass, and said: "Fancy a top-up?"

The sharp eyes squinted at me suspiciously.

"Who's asking?" he said.

"Someone who knows a thirsty scallywag when he sees one."

Alec turned to face me.

"And what would you know about scallywags?"

"Mostly what I've heard from your old comrade-in-arms Harry Deakin."

"Harry never had a blabbermouth in the old days."

"And he hasn't now. But it was loosened when I told him about the murder of Steve Telford."

Alec thumped his glass down on the bar.

"Yeah! I cheered when I read about that in the *Chronicle*."

"I wrote what you read."

"Did you now?"

The wary eyes became a tad less suspicious. Alec nodded at

the landlord who refilled his glass.

I said: "Harry didn't seem too distraught at Telford's passing, either."

"You won't find many who are. Not me."

He hoisted the refilled glass to his lips and lowered the tide line.

"What was your beef with Telford?" I asked.

"Apart from the fact the bloke was an all-round shite?"

"Apart from that."

"Telford was into anything that would turn a dishonest penny. The war was a bad time for most people. There was the bombing, the shortages – but not for Telford. He was into the black market. Made himself a tidy sum. But he didn't care how he did it. There were black-market traders about who treated it a bit like a social service. They knew people needed stuff that wasn't in the shops. They provided it - at a cost. They made some cash for themselves, but they gave a service of sorts. Telford was never that kind of spiv. He was just out to shift anything he could – no matter what it was and the damage it might cause."

"And he damaged you?"

"My sainted old mum, Peggy. It was just before Christmas in 'forty-one. Well, you'd go to the shops or the market of a morning and see the empty shelves. It wasn't going to be a merry Christmas. I was away, but come Christmas Eve all Peggy had for my two younger sisters, Hilda and Winnie, was a tin of bully beef and a pound of potatoes. Not much of a Christmas dinner.. Then Telford appeared on the doorstep. He had a chicken. Scrawny thing it was, or so I heard afterwards, but it was a chicken. Better than the bully beef. Mum paid Telford seven shillings and sixpence for it. Had to dip into her savings. What she didn't know was that the chicken was a reject from a local NAAFI canteen. All three of them went down with food poisoning. Peggy and Winnie got over it, although Peggy was never the same again, but Hilda died."

I took a pull at my gin and tonic.

"What happened to Telford?"

"He slithered his way out of trouble like a slimy lizard, as he usually did. Claimed Peggy had told him to get a chicken at any cost. Even claimed she should have called a doctor to Hilda sooner. I was so angry."

"Angry enough to kill him?" I asked.

"Angry enough at the time. But, then, we were expecting to have other people to kill. Nazis."

"But now?"

"What would the point be? I wouldn't lower myself to do the job."

"Where were you on Monday evening?"

"So now it's the third-degree."

I grinned. "Just a casual enquiry."

"Like hell. But if you must know, I was doing what a fisherman usually does."

"Catch anything?"

"Yes, a bad case of nosey reporter."

"Anyone with you on the boat?"

"No."

"Is that usual?"

"Could you afford a crew's wages on the cash you'd get from a small catch of mackerel?"

"So nobody knew where you were?"

"As it happens, you're wrong about that. I checked in with the harbour-master's office when I sailed out on the high tide. And I made a point on checking in when I returned with hardly enough fish to pay for the diesel I'd used."

"How long were you at sea?"

"About five hours."

"Is that normal?"

"There's a lot you don't know about fishing. When you're at sea nothing is normal."

Alec picked up his glass and drained the beer. He slammed the glass back on the bar and signalled to the landlord for a refill.

He said: "I need a leak."

He lifted the duffel bag off his shoulder, dropped it on the ground, and stomped off to the gents'.

I had a quick look round the bar to make sure no-one was watching me, then stooped down and pulled open the drawstring that tightened the top of the bag.

I looked inside. A cable-knit jersey had been bundled into the bag. On top of it were a briar pipe, a packet of shag tobacco, and a box of Swan Vesta matches.

And a teddy bear.

A cute little brown one with a red scarf tied around his neck. There was a gift label hooked over his arm. It read: "For Pansy Flowers. Happy sixth birthday."

I pulled the drawstring tight again and stood up. I grabbed my gin and tonic and lounged on the bar like I was bored, just as Alec came through the door.

The landlord thumped down another pint of beer on the bar. Alec lifted the glass and had a thirsty gulp.

I said: "When I was talking to Harry, he mentioned two of your scallywag colleagues, John King and Patrick Harrison. He wouldn't talk about them. I got the impression that, like Telford, they might also be black sheep."

"Dead sheep," Alec said.

"How did they die?" I asked.

"They died because they tried to be too clever by half."

"What do you mean?"

"You've probably heard that old chestnut about war."

"You mean the one about it being ninety-nine per cent boredom and one per cent terror."

"Yeah! Well for the scallywags, it was one hundred per cent boredom because the Nazis never came. We spent our time in the bunkers playing poker for pennies. It's surprising how much cash you can lose when you're up against players like Telford and John King."

"They used to cheat?" I asked.

"Telford did. He was a cardsharp as well as a con-man. King, I'm not so sure. He played well, but perhaps he was just a good player. Perhaps not. But it didn't matter in the end. He was blown up in one of the bunkers. We used to keep a ton of explosives in those bunkers. It was going to be used to blow up German supply lines. Anyway, King and Harrison shared a bunker in the woods between Steyning and Washington. And one night there was an almighty blast. When we got to the bunker, there were fallen trees, building debris, and a bloody great hole in the ground. The locals were told it was a controlled explosion of a new weapon. But it was some God-almighty accident."

"And King and Harrison both died?"

"That's where there's a mystery. King died because remnants were identified from his uniform insignia. Big loss to the group, too. He was the radio operator. Used to keep in touch with the French underground. He could speak the language 'coz he'd had a French mother, English father. We used to get news of German invasion plans from the underground. That stopped when King was killed."

"What about Harrison?" I asked.

"It looked like he'd escaped the explosion."

"What do you think happened?"

"I think Harrison caused the blast. He was a cocky bloke. Thought he was better than the rest of us. He'd worked as a schoolmaster before the war – all a bit snooty, while the rest of us got our hands dirty through honest toil. Anyway, Harrison was always yammering on about how to use explosives. I reckon he'd been trying something and it backfired. A few days earlier, he'd said he was experimenting with a new timer device. I think it blew early. I reckon he got clear himself, realised he was for the chop, and scarpered. It wasn't too difficult to lose yourself in those days. Ten of Hearts was never heard of again."

"Ten of Hearts?" I queried.

"Harrison's codename. We all had them – named after playing cards. Harry Deakin was Eight of Diamonds. Fred Youngman was Nine of Spades and John King was Ace of Spades. Telford was Six of Diamonds. Because of our card codenames, we were known as the Joker platoon."

"And what about you?" I asked.

"I was King of Hearts."

"Is there a Queen of Hearts?"

Alec frowned. "No." he snapped. "Now, if you'll excuse me, I've got some fish to catch."

He downed the last of his beer, picked up the duffle bag from the floor, and stomped out of the pub.

I stared after him and wondered how the teddy bear for Pansy Flowers would fit into the picture.

But at the moment I didn't have a picture to fit it into.

Fred Youngman was leaning on a shovel and staring into an empty grave when I found him at Bear Road cemetery.

Even though he bent over the shovel, I could see he was a tall man with a muscular build. He had a large head, topped by greasy brown hair, and a thick neck. He had broad shoulders and bulging biceps. He was wearing a sleeveless pullover and a grubby grey shirt. He had green corduroy trousers, baggy at the knee, and brown boots which laced up around his ankles.

It was late afternoon by the time I'd reached the cemetery. The place was perched high on the hills above Brighton, not far from the racecourse. On a day when the wind was in the right direction, you could hear the punters cheering their horse home.

Not that there would be any cheers for the bods carried into the cemetery's small chapel. They'd already run life's race - and lost.

A few mourners straggled out of the chapel as I drove up and parked the MGB. They sniffed into hankies and hugged one another for comfort, the way of mourners everywhere. Then they brightened up as they realised it was all over. Now they'd be off to the wake – and there'd be sausage rolls and beer.

I picked my way towards Fred between the headstones with their sad epitaphs and withered bunches of flowers.

He looked round as I walked up.

I peered into the grave and said: "Looks like a good job."

"Yours, is it?" he asked.

"I hope not."

"I didn't think so. You look as though you've got a year or two in you yet."

"I was hoping for rather more than that."

"Most of them who end up here do. But you look like the type who looks for trouble."

"Stands out like a corpse at a carnival, does it?" I said.

"Why else would you come to a cemetery to look at an empty grave?"

I moved around to the other side of the grave and looked him in the face.

"I've heard that you've been a bit of a scallywag in your time."

Fred hoisted the haft of the shovel over his shoulder, like a rifle.

He said: "There was a time when I was paid to kill someone who knew about that."

"Happy days?" I said.

"Some were."

"And now?"

"I rub along."

Fred put down his shovel and picked up a long board that was lying on the ground. He laid it along the edge of the grave.

He said: "Don't step too near the edge until I've put a board along your side. The earth at the edge of the grave gives way."

"And I don't want to end up six feet under before my time."

"Five feet is enough in the graves I dig. Seven feet if there are two. Nine feet for three."

I stepped back from the edge. "I think I'll fly solo when my time comes," I said.

Fred grabbed another board, walked round the grave, and laid it along the other side.

He said: "When I heard that shark Telford had been croaked, I didn't think it was long before someone would come calling. Anyway, what's your interest?"

"Colin Crampton, *Evening Chronicle*." I handed Fred a card.

He glanced at it and thrust it into his pocket. "I didn't think you looked like a cop. Could have been secret service. They usually wear better shoes – but they polish them."

I looked down at my Oxford brogues. They were scuffed and dusty.

"I'll fire my valet as soon as I get back to the mansion," I said.

Fred moved back to the other side of the grave and picked up a large hessian sack.

He said: "If you're looking for a lead on the killer, you could start with the entire population of Brighton."

He opened the sack and shook sawdust into the grave.

"The cops are still trying to work out how Telford was killed. The short odds are on poison," I said. "But something's puzzling me."

"If you're wondering why the sawdust, it's because the grieving relatives don't like seeing the dear departed laid on the cold earth. With the sawdust, it makes it look like they're resting on a sandy beach."

"That's not the puzzle I had in mind," I said. "I've heard that you were very matey with Telford until recently. But then you fell out a few months ago. What was that about?"

"What's it to you?"

"Possibly nothing. But it might be enough for the cops to arrest and interview you at the station under caution."

Fred closed the sack and threw it on the ground.

"If I tell you, it stays out of the *Chronicle*," he said.

"At the moment I want to find the person who killed Telford. If what you tell me helps that, but doesn't harm anyone else, I'll see what I can do."

Fred shrugged. "I suppose that will have to do. Well, about six months ago, a rich bloke was buried up here. I dug the grave and there was a whole load of toffs standing round it. The vicar said the words, they all chucked a handful of earth into the grave, and headed off to the wake. You could tell that most of them couldn't get away fast enough. Especially his widow. As cold as a penguin's arse. The mourners only wanted to stick their noses in the trough and knock back the port and brandy. I watched them go and was just thinking about filling in the grave when a younger woman appeared from the side of the cemetery. I don't think she'd been at the service and I certainly hadn't seen her standing around the grave. She produced a photo of herself and the dead guy and wanted me to place it on top of the coffin in the grave. I told her that wasn't what I was paid to do. Well, she turned on the old waterworks and gave me five quid. What could I do?"

"Done it for nothing," I said.

"Easy for you to say. You're not trying to scrape by on seven quid a week. Anyway, after she'd sloped off, I had a look at the picture. It was mounted in a gold frame – hallmarked and everything. Must have been worth a few quid. I thought what can it matter if I put the photo in the grave and sell the frame? She'd be none the wiser. The trouble was, afterwards, I realised it might be a bit difficult to sell the frame, what with it being solid gold and everything."

"So you called in your old mate Telford. Spiv and part-time fencer of stolen goods."

"How do you know that?"

"It wouldn't take old Sherlock to work that out."

Fred scowled. "That bastard Telford screwed me over. Not only sold the frame and kept the money but wanted thirty bob a month from my wages to keep quiet about it."

"And you paid him?"

"Yeah!"

"You should have faced him down. After all, he'd also committed a crime."

"I should have killed him."

I thought about that for a moment.

Then I asked: "Did you?"

"No."

"Where were you on Thursday evening?"

"At the flicks. Astoria."

"With anyone?"

"Yeah! Sophia Loren."

"What did you see?"

"*The Return of the Magnificent Seven.*"

"Anyone good in it?"

"Steve McQueen was great."

"That's what I'd heard."

He turned away. "And now I've got to finish my work. I need to hang green baize cloth over the sides of this grave and cover it with a tarpaulin. If it rains during the night, we can't have the old stiff making a final splash."

Fred stomped across the graveyard to where he'd parked a wheelbarrow loaded with the cloth and the tarp.

I looked after him and wondered whether being a grave digger had given him a taste for drumming up business.

Shirley and I had seen *The Return of the Magnificent Seven* a week ago. Steve McQueen had been in the original film, *The Magnificent Seven*. But his role of Vin was taken by Robert Fuller in *The Return*.

I walked away from the graveyard wondering why Youngman had lied.

Chapter 11

Shirley Goldsmith took a thirst-quenching gulp of her *Côtes du Rhône*.

She said: "And then the slimy bastard asked me to stick out my bum. And me only wearing a pair of French knickers trimmed with eyelash lace."

I grinned. "It must be tough being a photographer's model."

We were sitting at an alcove table in Prompt Corner. It was dinner time. We were waiting for our first course – brown Windsor soup for me, ***pâté maison*** for Shirley.

Shirl was describing the day she'd had posing for cheesecake pictures in a new newspaper called *Switched On!*

She leaned over the table. "You need to take this seriously, whacker."

"I do. But you've been modelling for nearly two years. You must be used to this kind of thing."

"What kind of thing?"

"Sticking-your-bum-out kind of thing."

"Listen up, bozo. I've only ever stuck out my bum for one man."

I nodded and smiled. "I know."

"Not you, you dingbat. I mean Doctor Mackenzie who gave me those injections before I came to Blighty."

"Oh, I see." I'd had a pleasing image in my mind. French knickers with eyelash lace turned to cotton wool and sticking plaster. With the added tang of surgical spirit to dull the ardour.

"I think you'd better start at the beginning."

Shirley had another gulp of the burgundy, reached for the bottle, and refilled her glass.

"Well, as you know, I was a bit leery about this assignment. I normally do fashion not cheesecake, but I thought what the hell? What is cheesecake but fashion with a bit more skin on show? And the money they pay looked good."

"As good as you in the French knickers. *Ouch!*"

Shirley had kicked my leg under the table.

"Peg back your ears, cobber. So, I turned up at the studio in the East End of London. Whitechapel Road, I think it was. Real Jack the Ripper territory. The photographer turned out to be a bloke called Justin de Courtney. I thought with a name like that he should've been lensman at a society wedding. The kind where a bride with ten bridesmaids marries a chinless wonder from the aristocracy. But, no, he turns out to be a sleazy whacker and as slippery as a wombat in weasel grease."

"And probably known to his mum as Fred Splott."

"Yeah! If he'd been to Eton, I'm the games mistress at Roedean. Anyway, he seemed to know his way around the camera and focal lengths and lenses and all that stuff. We started off with me wearing a baby-doll négligée and French knickers."

"*Hmmm!*"

"Keep your mind on the story, buster."

"I was just looking forward to my soup. Honest!"

The waiter came alongside the table and served our first course.

I savoured the soup while Shirley smeared some of the *pâté* on toast.

Shirl munched some of the toast and said: "Anyway, I put Justin right about what I stick out and what I keep in. We broke for coffee and chatted for a bit. He said the new paper was being produced by an Aussie newspaperman who was hoping to break into Britain."

"Anyone I've heard of?" I asked. I supped some of the soup. It was delicious.

"Guy called Quentin Pell, Justin told me. Name meant nothing to me. Justin said he'd met Pell and he was the kind of guy who wanted to shake up British newspapers. Thought they were too old fashioned and fuddy-duddy. Wanted bolder pictures, bigger headlines."

"How about newsier stories?"

Shirl shrugged. "Justin didn't mention that. Anyway, we finished our coffee and Justin wanted to take a second set of pictures with me wearing a bikini. He gave me the kit and I marched off to the changing room. Well, I took a look at the bra and thought I've seen bigger egg cosies. But I put on the kit and checked myself out in the mirror. I thought I looked pretty good."

"Hmmm!"

"Yeah! You just love that soup, don't you? So, Justin rigged up a scene with a blue backcloth and a yellow mat with a deckchair and sun umbrella so it looked like I was on a beach. Although no-one was gonna mistake it for Bondi. He took a few shots. Then he came out from behind the camera. He flashed me a weaselly grin and said, 'Take off your top'. I said, 'There's hardly enough of it to put on.' And Justin said, 'Yeah, but the readers of *Switched On!* will want the full Cinemascope experience.' I said: 'Yeah, they can get it at their local Regal'."

I put down my soup spoon. "He wanted you to pose topless for a newspaper?" I said.

"Yeah! He said this Quentin Pell guy wanted Bristol cities on every page three. Pell told him in Oz there was nothing like a parade of hooters to wake up readers when they opened the paper."

"If John Delane heard that, he would rise from his grave."

"Who is this Delane guy?"

"Editor of *The Times* during the Crimean War. Exposed the bungling and horrors of the war. Praised Florence Nightingale for cleaning up the hospitals."

"We need him around to clean up *Switched On!*" Shirley said. "Anyway, I told Justin that if he wanted to photograph tits, he could find someone else's. Or if he wanted to picture one big tit, he could take shot of himself. Then I left."

"In the bikini?"

"Ha, ha. No, I also put on my socks."

There didn't seem much of an answer to that. And, fortunately, the waiter appeared to take away our empty plates.

Shirley had a slurp of her *Côtes du Rhône*.

I toyed with a breadstick.

Shirl said: "You're thinking."

"Yes, it's become a habit."

"Was it about the Telford murder?"

"I've seen three suspects today – and all had strong motives to kill Telford."

The waiter came with our chicken casseroles. I told Shirley about my meetings with Harry Deakin, Alec Perkins and Fred Youngman while we ate.

"All three claim they have alibis for the time of the murder. Deakin says he was helping to run a boy scout meeting with the local vicar. I can't speak to the vicar until tomorrow to confirm that. Perkins says he was out at sea alone fishing. Says that his boat was checked out of port by Shoreham harbour-master's office – and checked back in again. I've confirmed that with the harbour-master. Perkins was gone for five hours."

"So he's in the clear."

"Only if we can be sure he was at sea all that time. Five hours would have given him time to sail to Newhaven, just up the coast and moor his boat on a quiet quay where no-one would notice. He could have caught the train from Newhaven Harbour station into Brighton, murdered Telford, returned by train to Newhaven, and sailed back to Shoreham. He'd make sure he'd check in with the harbour-master. The perfect alibi."

"What about Youngman?" Shirley asked.

"He told me he was at the cinema – alone."

I explained how Youngman had named the wrong actor who'd played Vin.

"Could have got the two films mixed up," Shirl said.

"It's possible – but I think he lied."

"If you ask me, it doesn't add up. All three scallywags had motives to kill Telford in the past. Why didn't they croak Telford at the time? Why leave it until now?"

I shook my head. "That bothers me, too. But we have to remember they were trained for undercover activities. Perhaps they realised killing Telford so soon after the event would throw suspicion on them. Perhaps they had the patience to wait. Perhaps they believe in that old Sicilian proverb – revenge is a dish best served cold."

Shirl grinned. "But not chicken casserole. Eat more and talk less."

I tucked into the tender chicken and vegetables.

We were drinking our coffee before I brought the matter up again.

I picked up my spoon and stirred it slowly around the cup.

"You've already done that," Shirley said.

"It helps me think."

"What's on your mind?"

"It's the three scallywags. I can't help thinking they're up to something."

"Not that nose for news working overtime again," Shirley said. "You should give it a rest."

"It might be on to something this time around. I just wonder whether men trained to work undercover ever lose those skills. Perhaps they yearn for the excitement of the old days again."

"Sounds a shaky theory to me. If you think they're planning a scam, you'd need some hard evidence."

"I noticed there was a balaclava in Deakin's toolbox. It seemed out of place among the tools. And then there was the teddy bear for Pansy Flowers in Perkins' duffel bag. He'd told me he wasn't married and he didn't admit to having any children of his own. Then there's Youngman's insistence he was at the pictures, when he was obviously somewhere else. Perhaps the three things are all unrelated, but I've just got this twitch at the back of my neck."

"Too much wine," Shirley said.

I grinned. "No. Too much mystery."

I started to unravel the knot of mysteries first thing the following morning in the *Chronicle's* newsroom.

My first job was to check out Harry Deakin's alibi. Had he really spent the evening helping the vicar at the boy scouts' meeting?

Crockford's Clerical Directory informed me that the vicar of St Mary's was the Reverend Simon Tinniswood. The telephone directory provided his number.

Crampton, master of desk research.

I lifted the receiver and dialled. The phone was answered by Tinniswood's housekeeper. There was a bit of confusion while we sorted out that I wasn't the rural dean. And I definitely wasn't the archdeacon the vicar had invited to preach on Solomon chapter seven, verse 11 - "Come, my beloved, let us go forth into the field..." - this coming Sunday.

Tinniswood sounded just as dotty when he came on the line.

"Harry Deakin, you say? Do I know a Harry Deakin?"

"He's mending your wall."

"Which wall is that?"

"The one that's fallen down."

"Like the walls of Jericho?"

"No, like the walls around your churchyard."

"And you say his name is Joshua?"

"No Harry."

"Harry fought the battle of Jericho. That doesn't sound right."

"The builder who's mending your churchyard wall. Harry Deakin.

"Ah, yes, Harry. He helps with the scouts."

"Was he helping you three nights ago?"

"Yes, I think so. That would be Wednesday."

"No, it's Thursday I need to know about."

"Ah, yes, Thursday. No, Harry wasn't helping on Thursday evening. I can be quite certain about that, Mr Joshua."

"Crampton."

"Are you? Well, I hope it gets better. Good day to you."

The line went dead.

So Harry had no alibi for the evening Telford was killed. But had Harry made an honest mistake about the day he was dyb-dobbing with the scouts? Or had he lied?

I was thinking about that when Cedric, the copy boy hurried up to my desk.

"What's up, Cedric? Is the place on fire?"

"Worse than that, Mr Crampton. Miss Houndstooth is having one of her palpitations. She wants to see you right away."

I grinned. "I'd better get in there before she starts to enjoy it."

When I walked into the morgue, Henrietta was sitting behind her desk. Her cheeks glowed pink. Beads of sweat glistened on her forehead.

She was fanning herself with *The Lady*. I refer, of course, to the weekly magazine rather than a passing female. The pages, filled with "situations vacant" for Norland nannies and pleas for companions wanted by elderly "ladies of means" living in Tunbridge Wells, flapped in the breeze.

I hurried up to her desk.

"Is it the usual that's brought this on?" I asked.

Henrietta nodded.

You wouldn't think there was a lot of excitement in running a press cutting archive. You cut up the papers, filed the cuttings, and thumbed through dusty drawers when you wanted to look up something. Routine work with perhaps an ersatz thrill when you found something filed in the wrong order.

But not to Henrietta. If she became really excited her palpitations started.

I said: "Has this something to do with the scallywags."

Henrietta nodded. "When I had your call, I looked up Auxiliary Units in the cuttings files. There was nothing. I checked under scallywags – one or two entries, but nothing relevant to the war. I tried each of the names you mentioned. Nothing under Deakin, Perkins or Youngman."

"But there was something on Telford," I said.

Henrietta's eyes opened in surprise. "How did you know?"

"Because most people who get themselves murdered have had a colourful life. They'll have been in the papers – even though they'd have preferred not to be."

Henrietta reached across her desk for a thin manila file. She handed it to me.

I opened it. Inside were two small cuttings and one larger one. The first small cutting was dated December 1963. It told how Telford had been fined fifty pounds for selling turkeys from an unlicensed market stall in the London Road. The court noted that Telford had one previous conviction.

That previous con was described in the other small cutting. Back in 1955, Telford had been accused of receiving stolen goods. The goods in question were two television sets said, in the formal language of the magistrates' court indictment, to be the property of the Seaford Television and Radio Emporium. Telford had told the court he had bought the televisions from a man in a pub. He couldn't remember the name of the man or the pub. He was fined thirty pounds and warned as to his future conduct.

Henrietta said: "It's the large cutting that matters."

I grabbed the yellowing paper from the file.

The cutting was dated to 1947. It was headlined: WAR HERO ON ASSAULT CHARGE.

It was a typical Saturday-night-in-the-pub story. Telford had fallen into an argument with two other men. One of them had pulled a knife on him. Telford had grabbed his knife attacker's arm, twisted it behind his back, and broken it. He'd thumped the second man on the nose so hard, the bloke had complained of double vision for a week afterwards. The "actual bodily harm" charge was enough to earn Telford prison time – even for a first offence.

And would have done had it not been for a character witness. A senior army officer – the court allowed him to be referred to only as Colonel D – spoke up for Telford. He described how Telford had been enlisted in a wartime special forces operation which was so secret it still couldn't be described today. Colonel D said he was sure Telford would not have launched such an attack unless he felt he was seriously threatened.

The magistrates put their heads together and decided it would be unseemly to send a war hero to the choky so soon after hostilities had ceased. Telford walked free with a slap on the wrist and a modest fine.

I put the cutting back in the file and looked at Henrietta.

I said: "You know who Colonel D is, don't you?"

Henrietta blushed. "I thought he must've been a senior officer in the Auxiliary Units. So I searched the annual index volumes of *The Times*. I started with 1945. I looked through all the entries beginning with the letter D. It didn't take as long as you might think, because I was only looking for the name of an army officer. I found a couple and then checked the full reference on *The Times* microfilm to see whether they had any connection with special forces or secret operations. I found him in 1948. His name is Colonel Carisbrooke Dubbins and he commanded the Sussex Auxiliary Units."

I said: "Henrietta, you're a genius. Now tell me you're a double genius and you've discovered where he lives."

Henrietta frowned. Looked a bit offended that I'd even asked.

"He lives near Heathfield. He's listed in the telephone directory."

Henrietta picked up a sheet of paper from her desk. "Here's

his address and telephone number."

Two minutes later, I was back at my desk staring at the paper.

I was wondering whether to call Colonel Dubbins or turn up on his doorstep unannounced. When you're chasing a reluctant interviewee, it's sometimes best not to give them any notice. If the good colonel knew I was on the way, he'd have plenty of time to call up reinforcements.

So I decided to head out to Heathfield without delay.

There was only one problem. Pansy Flowers. The six-year-old who was getting the teddy bear from Alec Perkins. I needed to know what connection she had to Perkins. But I didn't have time to do that and interview the colonel.

Cedric was over by the telephone booths talking to Sally Martin.

I waved him over.

He flashed his toothy grin as he hurried up. "Got copy for the subs, Mr Crampton?"

"No Cedric, I've got a little job I want you to do for me on the QT."

Cedric moved in closer. I explained how I wanted him to find an address for Pansy Flowers.

"She's just about to have her sixth birthday," I said. "Start by calling all the Flowers in the telephone directory and asking if they know of a Pansy."

Cedric looked worried. "What if they ask why I'm calling?"

"Tell them you've found a children's book lying in the street. It had Pansy Flowers' name written inside the front cover. You want to return the book because she might not have finished reading it. And if they're still not convinced, tell them you work in the children's section at Brighton library and might be able to recommend some more good books for Pansy to read."

Cedric grinned: "You mean you want me to pull a flanker?"

I frowned: "I want you to do some deep research. And make

sure you do it somewhere Figgis won't hear you."

Cedric nodded. "Leave it to me, Mr Crampton."

He bounced off across the newsroom and pushed through the swing doors.

I checked I had everything I needed to interview the colonel.

Notebook.

Pen.

Spare pencil.

Perhaps the colonel would demand a kit inspection and make me salute.

Chapter 12

I'd decided to treat my visit to Colonel Carisbrooke Dubbins as a surprise attack.

I didn't want him digging into a defensive position to man the barricades.

You get more truth out of interviewees when they haven't had time to prepare their lies.

What bothered me more, as I navigated the MGB through Sussex country lanes towards Heathfield, was whether Dubbins would remember much about the Auxiliary Units. I doubted whether he'd have known more than a few dozen of the scallywags by name. Which meant the odds he knew any of my suspects were low. Even if he had, would he remember anything useful about them twenty-one years after the end of the war?

Heathfield turned out to be a small country town with a mix of old thatched cottages and newer housing estates. The high street was lined with small shops. There was an old-fashioned butcher's with rabbits hanging in the window. There was a baker's with huge cob loaves piled on one another. And there was a quaint little ladies' dress shop called *À la mode*.

Dubbins lived in a large red-brick house on the outskirts of town. It had tall chimneys, wisteria growing around the front door, and a rustic conservatory. A gravel drive ended in a forecourt in front of the building.

I pulled the MGB neatly alongside an old Bentley with maroon coachwork and tan leather seats. The colonel evidently liked his comfort when it came to motoring.

I rang the bell half expecting a butler to open the door. Or, perhaps, as Dubbins had been in the army, a batman who stamped to attention and called me "sah".

Instead, the door was flung open by an elderly gent. He had piercing green eyes, full, almost sensual, lips and a prominent nose. A pair of pince-nez was balanced half way down the schnoz. He had a full head of grey hair parted down the middle.

He was wearing a blue shirt with a button-down collar, a tie with a regimental insignia I didn't recognise, and flannel trousers. Over the lot, he wore a blue-and-white striped chef's apron.

He leaned closer to inspect me and said: "Collar's on wrong way round. You're not the vicar chappie."

I said: "I'm not the vicar chappie. So collar's on right way round."

He nodded. "If you say so. Anything else?" He moved to close the door.

I said: "Can you spare a moment to talk about the scallywags?"

"What did you say? Scallywags? You're too young to be a scallywag."

"I've been speaking to several. They remember you kindly," I lied.

"Bloody fools. I made their life hell. Only a numbskull should think well of me."

"I'd like to ask you some questions."

"What for? Not some kind of writer chappie, are you? I've had them sniffing around before, like a bunch of truffle hounds."

Dubbins adjusted his pince-nez and peered up the driveway.

"Expecting someone, are you?" I said.

"Vicar chappie. Reverend Montgomery something-or-other. Can never remember the fellow's name. But I live alone, fancy a bit of company over the nosebag. Invited him for lunch before. He never turns up."

I put on a hungry look and said: "As it happens, I haven't lunched."

Dubbins squinted at me through his pince-nez.

"Eaten in the officers' mess before, have you?"

"Rarely out of it."

"*Hmmm*. Well, I suppose you better come in."

He marched down the corridor which led from the front door to the back of the house. He waved to me to follow.

"And close the bloody door after you," he shouted over his shoulder.

I hurried down the corridor and entered a large kitchen. An ancient cast-iron range occupied the whole of the far side of the room. There were windows to the left of it, that looked out over a small kitchen garden. A large Welsh dresser stood against the right wall. It held dozens of willow pattern plates, cups and saucers. There were three huge tureens, as bulbous as Buddha's belly, and two large serving platters.

In the centre of the room, a rough wooden table held half a cob loaf on a bread board, a tub of butter, and some cheese. Half a dozen upright wooden chairs were grouped around the table.

Dubbins was over by the range stirring a huge pot. It was more a cauldron, the sort of thing you'd see the witches dancing round in *Macbeth*.

Dubbins turned to me and said: "Sit down. Help yourself to bread."

I said: "Do you always do your own cooking?"

"Special forces, we look after ourselves. Live off the land. For thirty years, I haven't eaten a chicken I haven't killed myself."

Dubbins picked up a ladle and a bowl.

He said: "I take it you'd like some stew."

"I'd love some. Chicken stew, is it?"

"Frog."

"Frog what?"

"It's frog stew. Good nourishing food."

Dubbins plunged the ladle into the cauldron and stirred the contents.

He said: "I take it you'd like a leg. How about an eye?"

"As well as a leg?" I asked.

"They're delicious. There are three frogs in here, so you can have a couple of nostrils, too."

"I've given up nostrils for Lent."

"It's months until Lent."

"I'm doing it early to avoid the rush."

"Suit yourself. I've given you a couple of legs and some giblets."

He thumped the bowl down in front of me. There were some bits of green stuff sticking out of a yellowish slime. I tried the slime. *Hmmm!* It was actually quite… slimy… but also salty and a bit like eating jellied eels.

Dubbins ladled his own portion into a bowl, brought it over to the table, and sat opposite me.

I said: "I expect you've heard that one of your scallywags was murdered."

"Read about it in the *Chronicle*. Wish these newspaper chappies could just stick to the facts. Whole thing was done up with a load of speculation. Can't remember the writer's name now. Crimpton, was it? Perhaps Crumpton."

He tucked into his frog stew with gusto. I took another spoonful and chewed carefully.

I said: "I don't suppose it matters. What's important is that his killer is caught."

"Roger, that. Never thought one of my scallywags would die in his own home when I recruited him. Nazis were knocking on the door, you know. We had to do something. We hid the scallywags in woods and forests. Landowners let us build bunkers where Mr Hitler's stormtroopers would be unlikely to look. But if they did, we built an escape tunnel into each bunker. While the Nazis were knocking at the front door, our chaps would sneak out the back way. Ready to fight another day. We told the scallywags to disrupt Nazi supply lines. Kill high-ranking German officers. Make sure collaborators paid the price. It was going to be dangerous work. I didn't think any of them would last more than twelve days in the field. But they did – because the Germans never came."

I scraped my spoon round the bowl. While Dubbins had been talking, I seemed to have finished my stew.

I said: "No scallywags died on your watch, then?"

Dubbins shook his head so hard his pince-nez fell off. He left it dangling on its cord over his chef's apron.

"I didn't say that. One died through an accident."

"Would that be John King?"

Dubbins gave me a sharp look. "I thought that was still classified. Perhaps I should have you shot. On second thoughts, I'll give you another helping of stew."

Dubbins stood up, crossed to the cauldron, and ladled out another portion. He brought it back to the table.

I tucked in. I was getting good at this. Perhaps I should enrol in the Special Air Service. I'd heard they lived on beetles.

"King's partner Patrick Harrison blew up one of the bunkers," Dubbins said. "There was a hell of a stink at the time. The desk wallahs in London wanted to know what the hell was going on. It turned out Harrison fancied his hand with explosives. He was one of those fellows who's a bit above himself. You sometimes get them in other ranks. Think they should be an officer. Anyway, perhaps Harrison was trying to prove his worth. Thought he'd make a few booby-traps to put the breeze up Mr Hitler and his pals when they came calling. Well, we'd stacked those bunkers with enough explosives to flatten a pyramid. Harrison must have got it wrong. Trouble was, he was away from the bunker when the device went off. King was inside. There wasn't even a body left to identify. We just found his metal identification tag."

"What happened to Harrison?" I asked.

"Never heard of again. Fellow must have had a streak of yellow running through him. He cleared off."

"Deserted?"

"Well, we'd taught the bugger how to lie low and evade the enemy. And now we'd become the enemy – as we wanted to grill him on how it'd happened. Never did – and never got to the bottom of it."

I ploughed on with my second helping of stew. I wondered what we'd have for pudding. Didn't like to ask.

Instead, I said: "What did the scallywags do when the Nazis didn't come?"

"Lied low, mostly."

"Mostly?"

"Well, highly-trained men with nothing to do. It became a problem until we disbanded in 'forty-four. We'd had a bit of trouble early on, and I decided to come down hard. Wouldn't stand for any private enterprise. No capers."

"What kind of capers?" I asked.

"There was talk doing the rounds that a rogue group of scallywags had hijacked an armoured carrier transporting gold."

"Was there any truth in the talk?"

Dubbins stood up and strode to a cupboard. Opened it and took out a carafe of dark crimson liquid and two glasses. Strode back and put them on the table.

"Vintage port," he said. "Might as well conduct ourselves as though we're in the officers' mess."

He poured himself a generous glass and passed the carafe to me. After the frog stew, I decided I deserved it. I filled my glass and took a sip. It was smooth, not too sweet, and had a fleshy aftertaste. Or perhaps that was just the frog repeating on me.

"You were going to explain what might have started the hijack talk," I said.

Dubbins looked baffled. "Was I? Oh, I suppose I was."

He drained his glass and refilled it.

"It was back in May 1940. Brother Bosch had just walked into Belgium without even wiping his feet on the mat. Things looked bad everywhere. Not least the Channel Islands – Jersey, Guernsey and those God-forsaken backwaters. But pukka places for rich coves to stash their ill-gotten gains, or so I've heard.

Count your cash while the tax man looks the other way. On the mainland, we'd prepared a hot welcome if the Bosch stepped ashore, not least from my scallywags. But they had no defences in the Channel Islands."

"And the islands were only a few miles from the French coast," I helpfully added. "The Germans could practically swim there without even puncturing their water wings."

"Quite so. I remember Lord Bognor, the minister responsible for the defence of the islands, was very concerned about it. Expected the Hun to drop in uninvited. Anyway, Bognor and the island bigwigs decided the valuable stuff – especially their gold reserves – had to be sent back to Blighty for the duration. Of course, they'd want it back afterwards. People like that always do. The question was how to do it. The Royal Navy was otherwise engaged. Besides, the idea of a destroyer steaming into St Peter Port in the dead of night and loading up a cargo, would have only attracted attention. It could've become a target for submarine attack as it crossed the Channel back to Britain with the booty on board. So the talk has it the loot was loaded onto a fishing smack."

"Good thinking," I said.

"Almost," Dubbins said. "But the island wallahs wouldn't stash away so much loot without being dead crafty. Sly devils. Wouldn't trust 'em an inch. Anyway, they commissioned a second fishing smack as a decoy. The idea was that one would sail to Shoreham and the other to Newhaven. No-one, not even the captains, would know which held the crates of gold and which held the decoy crates."

"Did both vessels make port safely?"

"So the word has it. And there were identical armoured vehicles and escorts waiting at both ports. They loaded up their cargoes and headed for London."

"But not home and dry?" I said.

Dubbins drained his glass and poured himself more port.

"Far from it. Rogue scallywags held up one of the armoured carriers on its way to London. They took the crates and hid them. Or so the talk has it."

"The crates with the gold?"

"Nobody knows," Dubbins said. "At least, I don't. Don't think anyone does. Of course, we sent out a patrol to hunt the blighters who'd let us down. There was a gunfight and two of them died. Serves the buggers right. If I'd had my way they'd have been strung up by their testicles. But you couldn't do that sort of thing then. What with shortages and rationing, you'd have had to apply for the rope in triplicate."

"And nobody has seen the gold since?" I asked.

"It might've got through. It might be buried somewhere. In wartime, no-one was going to blurt out the truth. And lips haven't loosened in peacetime either."

I drained my port. Thought about pouring another, but remembered I had to drive back to Brighton.

Besides, the frog stew had started to churn in my stomach. Felt like the damned creature had come back to life. Anyway, I'd learnt as much as I would from Dubbins.

I stood up.

"Not going, are you?" Dubbins said.

He reached for the port and poured another glass.

"No need to see me out," I said. "Thanks for the lunch. Next time, I'll bring sandwiches."

Dubbins took a healthy pull at his port. Nodded goodbye.

"Good man," he mumbled.

I wasn't sure whether he was talking about me or himself.

It was late by the time I arrived back in the *Chronicle's* newsroom.

I looked around for Cedric but couldn't see him.

Sally Martin, who edited the woman's page, told me he hadn't been around for most of the afternoon. She'd had to take her own feature on "ten things to do with new season plums" up to the subs herself.

I told her: "If Cedric doesn't show his face soon, I'll be able to add an eleventh thing to that plum article."

Sally chuckled and wandered off to the tearoom.

I sat in my captain's chair and jotted down a few notes from the Dubbins meeting. I wondered what was fact and what was myth about Dubbins' story of the stolen gold. And could any of the scallywags I'd met have been involved? Dubbins had said he thought the rogues were shot.

I was musing on this when Cedric hurried across the newsroom.

He had a grin that bulged his cheeks and lit up his eyes.

He rummaged a piece of paper out of his pocket and handed it to me.

He said: "There's the address of a Mrs Rita Flowers. She's the mother of Pansy Flowers."

I said: "Well done, Cedric. Was it easy to find?"

Cedric shook his head. "No, not at all, Mr Crampton. There were three Flowers listed in the telephone directory for Brighton. I rang all the numbers but none of them knew of a Pansy. I tried in the morgue, but Miss Houndstooth couldn't find a cutting with that name. I was getting worried. I didn't know what to do next. Didn't want to let you down. Then I had a brainwave."

"Are you going to tell me what it was?"

"I remembered that you'd told me it was Pansy's sixth birthday. So I went round to the town hall's registrar department and asked to see the birth certificates for six years ago. Well, I didn't realise there'd be more than two thousand. But you'd told me Pansy's birthday is just coming up. So I narrowed the search to October. There were a couple of hundred for the month and it didn't take long to leaf through them."

"And, of course, you found the mother's and father's address on Pansy's birth certificate."

"You've got it. It shows Pansy's birthday is tomorrow."

"Did it occur to you that six years later the Flowers might not live at the same address?"

Cedric tapped the side of his nose. "No flies on me, Mr Crampton."

"I'm pleased to hear it."

"I went round to their street and knocked on a door three houses down. Asked to see Mrs Flowers, all casual like. The old body who answered said I'd got the wrong house – well, I knew that – and pointed me to the right one. Rita Flowers lives there with Pansy. No Mr Flowers."

I grinned. "That's great work, Cedric. We'll make a reporter of you yet. I fished in my pocket and pulled out a ten-shilling note. Have a drink on me, tonight," I said.

"Well, that's good of you, Mr Crampton. With ten bob in my pocket, I reckon it'll be my lucky night at the palais."

Cedric nearly skipped across the newsroom and pushed through the swing doors.

I sat there and wondered whether it would be my lucky night when I visited Mrs Flowers and Pansy.

Chapter 13

Rita Flowers lived in an end-of-terrace house in one of those streets round the back of Preston Park.

It was just after eight o'clock and dark by the time I parked the MGB. I sat in the car for a moment and wondered whether I should knock on the door. It wasn't going to be easy to ask Rita why a man I'd met for the first time in a pub was giving her daughter a teddy for her birthday.

The house had a bay window on the ground floor. The curtains were drawn but light filtered through a gap. So Rita was at home. I only hoped she was home alone.

I pushed that thought from my mind and climbed out of the car. I walked up a short path to the front door and rang the bell.

The chimes ding-donged inside the house.

The door opened on a chain and a woman's face peered through the gap.

The face was pale and thin. There were worry lines around her mouth and wrinkles in her brow. Her hazel eyes surveyed me suspiciously.

I switched on a smile and asked: "Rita Flowers?"

Rita said: "What do you want?"

I said: "I'd like to speak to you about Fred Youngman."

"What about Fred?"

"He may be in some trouble, but I'm hoping you can clear it up."

"Are you the police?"

I flashed Rita my most disarming smile and said: "Worse than that. The *Evening Chronicle*."

I pulled a card out of my pocket and handed it through the gap.

Rita took the card and looked at it longer than she needed to read my name.

She looked back at me and, this time, there was a hint of defiance in her eyes.

She said: "What would a newspaperman want with Fred? Or me?"

"Could we talk about that inside?"

"Not if it's going to mean trouble."

"We may be able to clear up a misunderstanding." I tried the disarming smile again. It hadn't worked the first time.

I said: "I'll wipe my feet when I come in and I'm fully house-trained."

Rita shrugged. The gap closed, the chain rattled, and the door swung open.

I stepped into the hall.

Rita led me down a passage into a cosy sitting room. There were a couple of easy chairs on either side of a fireplace. One bar of an electric fire glowed red. There was a worn Wilton carpet on the floor and floral wallpaper – climbing roses. There was a table by the bay window. I could see Fred Youngman's teddy bear on it and a pile of cards. But pride of place was reserved for a silver picture frame. It held a photograph of a young man with a broad grin on his handsome face. He was wearing a soldier's uniform.

Rita saw me looking at the picture.

"My husband Charlie – my late husband."

"I'm sorry."

Rita plumped up the cushion in one of the chairs and said: "You'd better sit down."

She slumped into the chair opposite me. She was wearing a grey housecoat and had fluffy blue slippers. She crossed her arms in a no-nonsense way.

She said: "What trouble is Fred in?"

"None, I hope. But I need the answer to some questions to be sure."

I told Rita about Steve Telford's killing.

"I read about it in the paper," Rita said. "But Fred would never be involved in anything like that."

"How can you be sure?"

"Because I've known Fred since I married my Charlie eight years ago. He and Charlie worked together in the war. And Fred has kept in touch after my Charlie passed away. He's looked out for Pansy. He was round earlier and left a teddy bear for her birthday tomorrow."

"So your Charlie was also a scallywag?" I asked.

Rita's eyes opened wider in surprise.

"You know about the scallywags?" she asked.

"It's why I'm here. Steve Telford was a scallywag as well."

"Yeah! And he was a scallywag on his own account, too."

"I know about that also."

"You know a lot. Perhaps too much for your own good."

I thought about that for a moment.

I said: "Did you know Charlie was a scallywag when you married him?"

Rita shook her head. "No. He told me on our wedding night. He said he'd done dangerous work in the past. He said he'd worked with good men – Fred as well as Harry Deakin and Alec Perkins - and they'd remained friends for life. He told me that if I was ever in trouble and he wasn't around to help me, I could trust any of them with my life."

"And have you?"

"Not with my life. But they're all coming to Pansy's birthday party."

Rita stared hard at the red bar in the electric fire.

"Are you too hot?" she asked.

"No."

"Would you like a cup of tea?"

"The cup that cheers. I never thought you'd ask."

The ghost of a smile touched Rita's lips. She stood up and bustled towards the kitchen.

I waited until I could hear her rattling cups and saucers. I stood up and moved over to the table by the bay window. I picked up the cards. They were Pansy's birthday cards – ready for her big day tomorrow. Three of them featured pictures of horses. Others had characters from Disney cartoons. One had a little girl paddling in the sea.

I picked up one of the cards and read inside: "Have a lovely birthday, Pansy, and get well soon with love from Uncle Reg and Auntie Freda."

I put it back exactly as I'd found it and looked at another. "For a brave little girl, have a happy birthday, Mona at the sweet shop. (Enjoy the dolly mixtures!)"

I looked in a third. "Happy birthday, Pansy. Chin up, better times are coming. The scallywags are on your case. Fred Youngman."

Why were the scallywags on Pansy's case? And what was Pansy's case?

I thought about that as I crept round the room. I kept an ear out for activity in the kitchen. The whistle on a kettle screamed. I probably had two minutes before the tea was brewed and poured.

Just behind the door, a small table was stacked with newspapers. There was a *Daily Mirror* folded out to page 12. There was a *Daily Express* a couple of months old also folded open at an inside page. I rummaged, taking care not to rustle the papers. There was a *Daily Sketch*, an *Evening Argus* (boo!), a *Birmingham Post* and a *Manchester Evening News*. They were all folded open at news pages.

I scanned them quickly. Each held a mix of hard news stories. If you believed it was the only news available, you'd have thought the world was going to hell in a handcart. Wages were down. Prices were up. The pound was falling. Crime was rising. I couldn't see any common theme that linked the pages.

I could hear the rattle of teacups on saucers as Rita walked up the passage from the kitchen.

I shot back into my chair and feigned an air of bored insouciance.

Rita came in and put the tray on a sideboard on the far side of the room.

She handed me my tea and took her own to her chair.

I took a sip and said: "When you mentioned you'd not yet had to trust the scallywags with your life, do you know anyone else who has?"

Rita stirred her tea and stared at the tiny whirlpool she'd created in her cup.

She said: "I'm sorry we're out of biscuits."

"I'm not hungry – except for information. Are the scallywags helping Pansy?"

"What's it to you if they are?"

"Because it may help with my broader investigation. It may throw a light on the Telford murder."

"What the scallywags are doing for Pansy has nothing to do with that."

"So they are helping."

"They might be."

"I'll take that as a yes."

Rita raised her cup and took a long gulp of her tea. She looked at me with sullen eyes.

I said: "I don't want to pry unnecessarily into the life of a child, but is Pansy ill? Is that what the scallywags are helping with?"

Rita stood up and carried her cup and saucer over to the sideboard. She put it down, returned to her chair, and sat down.

She said: "Pansy has cancer."

I looked at Rita as she leaned back in her chair. Her eyes radiated with Pansy's pain.

I said: "I'm very sorry – that's terrible."

"It's a very rare form of cancer called Hodgkin's lymphoma.

I didn't believe it when they told me. I couldn't even pronounce it. The docs told me it's usually young people in their twenties who get it, but you can pick it up at any age."

"Can it be treated?"

"It's not easy. A low success rate. But there's this treatment in America. It's called a bone marrow transplant. Apparently, it's new but has an amazing success rate. But it costs ten thousand pounds – paid in dollars, of course."

"Are you going to take Pansy to America?"

Rita gave a mirthless laugh. "Sure. I'm going to hire Sir Bernard and Lady Docker's private plane and fly her there."

"You're short of cash?"

"No, I only live here to make a change from the villa in the south of France."

I said: "How can the scallywags help?"

"You leave the scallywags out of it. They're good men."

"Harry, Alec and Fred are certainly brave men, but I'd say they're also poor men."

"They've been good to me. Are good to me – and Pansy."

"Are the scallywags raising the money so Pansy can go to America for treatment?"

Rita sat up straighter.

"I've invited you in, I've given you tea, and I've answered your questions. And now I want you to go."

I said: "The *Chronicle* could publicise Pansy's plight and help raise funds. Readers can be generous for someone in need."

Rita fixed me with a stern eye. "I don't want a word about Pansy in the *Evening Chronicle*. If you had a six-year-old daughter would you want her paraded in the newspapers as a charity case?"

"Even so, newspapers can be mighty powerful when they put their weight behind a good cause."

"Pansy is not a cause, Mr Crampton. She's a little girl. A frightened little girl and one who may not become a big girl unless she gets the treatment she needs. I and the scallywags will see that she does. And if I read a word about Pansy in your or any other newspaper, I shall complain immediately to the Press Council. The door is this way."

I stood up and followed Rita down the passage-way.

She opened the front door and I stepped through it.

"Good night," she said.

The words on my back felt like an ice storm from the Arctic.

"And, so, I was given the grand order of the boot," I told Shirley.

Shirl grinned. "Not like you to get the bum's rush."

It was half an hour later and we were in a Golden Egg restaurant in West Street. The place had a kaleidoscopic wall of different red and yellow lights. They put you strangely on edge. I suppose the point was to take your mind off the food. Their signature dish was a fried egg and a pile of chips served in a greasy metal platter. If we'd been prisoners-of-war it would probably have breached the Geneva Convention.

I picked up one of the tepid chips and dipped it in my egg yolk. The chip looked like it was covered with yellow pus, like I'd just dipped it in an open wound. I threw it back on my plate.

Shirley said: "Has the shut-out put you off your tucker?"

"Anything would put me off this. We must remember never to come in here again."

Shirl said: "That Rita sounds like a strong woman. She'll need to be with a young daughter struck down with a terrible disease like Hodgkin's."

"She seemed confident she'd raise the money, but I couldn't see how. She lives in a modest place near Preston Park and there were no signs of wealth."

"Perhaps these scallywag guys will rootle up the moolah," Shirley said.

"A flint wall builder, a fisherman, and a grave digger. All honest trades, but unlikely to make them millionaires."

"It's not like you to come away with no idea of what's going on. Are you sure there were no clues in the room?"

"I only had a couple of minutes while Rita made the tea. I spent most of that looking at a pile of old newspapers."

"So, there's your clue. Nobody keeps old newspapers without a reason."

"But what reason?"

"Was there anything in common about the papers?"

"No. Some were nationals, some provincial papers."

I pushed the tin tray with egg and chips away from me.

"But, wait a minute, there was a common factor. All the papers had been folded open to a page," I said.

"There you are then. Work out what was on those pages, and you've solved the mystery."

I closed my eyes and tried to picture the pages.

I said: "The *Daily Mirror* was the first paper I looked at. The lead story on the folded page was about a plane crash in Nebraska. There was a down-page story on the launch of the Beatles' *Revolver* album and a column about a robbery somewhere in London."

"That's a start," Shirley said.

"Then I had a look at the *Daily Express*. I think that was just four or five weeks old. The lead story was about Harold Wilson opening the Commonwealth Prime Minister's conference. There was a sidebar about the South African prime minister Hendrik Verwoerd being stabbed to death. And there was a basement piece…"

"Basement piece?"

"Story across the bottom of the page," I explained. "It was a court report about some robbers being found guilty and sentenced."

"What for?"

"I did read that in the second par, but I can't remember. I really can't recall what was on the pages of the *Birmingham Post* and the *Manchester Evening News*. But the *Daily Sketch* had a backgrounder feature on what it called a "crime epidemic" – wage snatches.

I sat back in my seat and stared at the kaleidoscopic wall.

"I remember now," I said. "The *Express* report was about the sentencing of a crew that had carried out a wage snatch."

I closed my eyes and tried to visualise the *Daily Mirror's* page.

"Yes, there was a photo next to the robbery story in the *Mirror*. It showed a rammed car. Must have been carrying the wages."

Shirley said: "I don't get it. What are these wage snatches?"

"Lots of companies pay their staff in cash in brown envelopes on Friday. So, typically, on Thursday someone goes to the bank to collect the money. In a large firm, it could be thousands of pounds. It's not unusual for a junior clerk in the wages department to be sent to collect the cash in a briefcase. He'll drive in his own car and follow the same route. The robbers know it's easy pickings. They'll follow the clerk for a couple of weeks and pick a spot where they can pounce and grab the cash. The police warn companies to choose more secure methods. They tell wages clerks to vary their routes. But most of them take the attitude: it can't happen to me."

"It's too much of a coincidence that three out of five newspapers should all have stories about the same crime," Shirley said.

I nodded. "And I'm willing to bet that if I could see those other papers again, they'd also carry wage snatch stories."

"But surely those scallywag guys wouldn't stoop to robbery to get the cash for Pansy's treatment?"

"Why not? Just consider how they were trained. To intercept heavily-armed German convoys and destroy them. A couple of harmless clerks in black jackets and pin-striped trousers in an old car would be child's play."

"Well, I guess if the money goes to a good cause…" Shirley began.

"A good cause goes bad when it's financed by stolen money,"

I said.

"All very well for you to say. You're not six years old and dying of cancer."

"Suppose the robbery goes wrong?"

"You've just said it would be child's play."

"There's always the unexpected. Suppose one of the wages clerks was injured, even killed? It's been known."

Shirley said: "But Pansy will definitely die if she doesn't get the treatment."

"Yes," I said. "But perhaps there's another way."

I looked at our congealed eggs.

I said: "Why don't we take the taste out of our mouths and go on for a drink?"

Shirl said: "Yeah! My mouth feels like the rough side of a wallaby's whatsits."

Perhaps a stiff drink will help us to think of a way out of this problem.

But after three stiff drinks we still hadn't thought of an alternative to a wage snatch as a way to finance Pansy's treatment.

I arrived back at my lodgings in Regency Square feeling depressed. I hoped the Widow was long abed.

I inserted my key silently in the lock and crept into the hall. I took especial care not to knock against the hall table with the glass ornaments which tinkled. Or to brush against the reproduction of Holman Hunt's *Light of the World*, which hung on the wall.

The first tread on the stairs creaked only slightly when I stood on it. I was as good as home and dry in my room.

And then the Widow burst out of her parlour.

"I've been listening out for you, Mr Crampton," she said.

"Better than Alistair Cooke on the Home Service," I said.

"I've got a problem."

"Only the one?"

"I haven't been able to go to bed because he's there."

"Where?"

"Bold as brass on Hector's side."

Hector was the Widow's late husband.

"Who are we talking about?" I asked.

"The creepy-crawly."

"You don't mean that Mr Webster from the chemists?"

The Widow shopped there once a week for her Sanatogen Tonic Wine ("Fortifies the Over Forties"). Webster had wrongly interpreted this as a signal that she was up for a bit of rumpy-pumpy.

The Widow stamped her foot and crossed her arms.

"I do not mean Mr Webster. There is a spider in my bed and I require you to remove it. Now, if you would be so kind."

I looked at my shoes. I couldn't tell the Widow what was on my mind.

I nodded and headed towards her bedroom without saying anything. There was no spider on the counterpane. I pulled it back. No spider on the sheets. This was looking good. None on the pillow. I decided not to look under it.

I walked back to the hall a happier man than when I had left it.

"I have removed the creep-crawly," I said. "You will not be hearing from him again."

"And about time, too."

The Widow stomped down the passage.

I let out a deep breath. There was one secret I couldn't reveal to the Widow.

I may have faced down armed gunmen, but the one thing that terrifies me is a spider.

Chapter 14

I was awoken at seven the following morning by the Widow hammering on my bedroom door.

She hollered through the door: "You're wanted, Mr Crampton?"

"By the police?"

"No."

"By whom?" I asked.

(Crampton, master of English grammar, even when half asleep.)

"It's that smelly news editor of yours."

"Is he here?"

"No, he's just telephoned. He wants you in the office right away."

"Did he say why?"

"Only that it was the worst thing that has ever happened. Shall I fry you an egg before you go?"

"No, thank you."

The Widow's eggs ended up like something you could nail on the sole of a leaking shoe.

I scrambled out of bed and headed for the bathroom. Figgis had a genius for turning comedy into tragedy, but he'd never called me at seven in the morning before.

This couldn't have come at a worse time. I'd been awake half the night puzzling over the scallywags. I didn't want to believe they were really planning a wages snatch. But the evidence pointed that way. And, when I thought about it a bit more, I realised that if one of them was Telford's killer, holding up an inoffensive wages clerk would be like lifting a lollipop from a five-year-old.

By the time I'd made it downstairs, the Widow was outside the kitchen door waving a black thing around. It looked like a bit of driftwood she'd picked up on the beach.

"Would you like this before you go?" she said.

"What is it?"

"It's toast."

"Not today, Mrs Gribble. You have it with a glass of Sanatogen."

Her face cracked into a rictus grin.

I charged out of the front door before she invited me to join her.

I barged through the swing doors of the newsroom ten minutes later.

And came up sharp with a shock.

At this time, the newsroom should be alive with the clackety-clack of ancient typewriters as the hacks hammered out their stories for the first edition.

Instead, everyone had left their desks. They were huddled in little groups around the room. They had tense faces. A dozen whispered conversations were taking place.

Frank Figgis crashed through the swing doors as I surveyed the scene, not sure what to do next.

He hurried up to me. The wrinkles on his forehead made deeper furrows than usual. His face was drawn with tension.

He said: "This way."

We went into his office and he closed the door behind us. We sat down.

Figgis fumbled for his Woodbines among the drift of papers that covered his desk.

I said: "What the hell is going on?"

Figgis shook a fag out of the packet and lit up. He drew on the gasper so hard I thought he was going to swallow the damned thing.

He blew out a stream of smoke and relaxed a little.

He said: "The paper's been taken over."

That had my attention.

I said: "Since when? Newspaper acquisitions take weeks to negotiate. When the *Daily Mail* took over the *News Chronicle* in 1960, Rothermere had been talking to the Cadburys for months. If someone was angling for the *Chronicle* we'd have heard about it. Besides Lord Bognor has only just died and the paper is owned by Viscount Rackham."

"Not anymore," Figgis said. "He lost it last night."

"What do you mean, he lost it? You can't lose ownership of a newspaper, like it was a bus ticket that slipped through your fingers."

"He lost it in a game of cards. Poker apparently. At some gaming club in London."

A shiver ran through my body. Like a deadly serum, chilled in a glacier, had been injected into my veins.

I said: "Don't tell me, it was the Clansfield Club."

Figgis' eyes narrowed. "How do you know that?"

I told Figgis about my visit to the club. How I'd followed up a lead in the Telford murder case. How I'd learnt that Telford had worked as a part-time doorman at the club.

I left out the bit about the rumble with Hector Clansfield and how Shirley and I had made our getaway.

Figgis' frown deepened as I spoke.

He picked up a single folded sheet of paper from his desk and handed it to me.

"There was a messenger waiting for me when I arrived this morning. That's what he gave me."

I unfolded it. It was a sheet of Clansfield Club notepaper.

It read: "*I, Viscount Rackham, now seventh Marquess of Bognor, do hereby declare that I intend to pass the ownership of the Brighton* Evening Chronicle, *its trademarks and copyrights, as well as all its premises, goods, chattels and papers including the private papers of the late sixth Marquess of Bognor, to the holder of this promissory note, written, signed and handed to the winner of a game of poker concluded at the Clansfield Club, London. On presentation of the promissory note within seven days of the date of this document, I shall sign over ownership of all the assets described in this document to the holder of the promissory note.*

Signed, Aylmer Garth Mungo Rackham, Marquess of Bognor."

I dropped the paper back on Figgis' desk.

I said: "Is this legal?"

Figgis shook his head in despair. "That, apparently, is a copy of the original. After I'd read it, my first call was to the paper's lawyer. When he'd stopped crying, he said it probably was legal, subject to Rackham signing over the ownership of the paper and its assets within seven days to the promissory note holder."

"It couldn't be worse," I said. "So who is this promissory note holder? Who is the new owner of the *Chronicle*?"

"One Quentin Pell," Figgis said in a monotone voice.

"It just got worse," I said. "Have you heard of this Pell guy?"

"I've just found out this morning he owns some Australian newspapers."

"From what I've heard, comics compared with ours. He fills them with pictures of semi-naked women."

"I can't see His Holiness being happy about that."

"His Holiness won't be around to complain. Pell will sack him – and us – the day he takes control."

"You can't be sure of that. And how do you know about this naked woman business, anyway?"

I told him about Shirley's experience at the photo-shoot.

I said: "Pell is only interested in a paper that carries saucy pictures and scandal. Do you want to work on a paper like that? It's like turning a newspaper into a peep show. It'd be more dignified to scrawl mucky stories on a lavatory wall."

Figgis shrugged. "But what can we do? It's out of our hands. We'll just have to grin and bear it."

I said: "It'll be okay for you. You'll probably pick up a pension. You'll be able to spend some real quality time at home with Mrs

Figgis."

Figgis' eyes flashed with alarm at that prospect. He reached for another Woodbine. Lit it from the stub of the old one.

"On second thoughts, you're right. We should see what we can do to stop this."

He fell silent. Puffed a couple of times on his fag. Let the smoke float down his nose, like his brain had caught fire.

He said: "But what can we do about it? I don't see that there is anything."

"What about His Holiness? Presumably he knows."

"I took the note into his office as soon as I'd read it."

"And…?"

"He read it and handed it back to me. Said who owns the paper wasn't anything to do with us. Our job is to bring it out."

"What did he do then?"

"He went back to mounting stamps in his album. A George the Sixth set from British Honduras, I think."

"So it's up to us to save the *Chronicle* for civilisation," I said.

"I'd be quite happy to save it for my job. But what can we do?"

"We need more information. I'll see if I can find out what happened at the Clansfield Club last night. As business reporter, Susan Wheatcroft should be able to find out more about Pell's finances and his newspapers in Australia. I suggest we meet up at midday to review what we've discovered and plan our tactics."

"What should I do?" Figgis asked.

I pointed towards the newsroom. "There are thirty reporters out there who think the world's about to fall on their heads. You should go and tell them it isn't."

"How am I supposed to do that – when I personally face the prospect of retirement days at home with Mrs Figgis?"

"Summon up the Churchill spirit," I said. "We shall fight Pell in the newsroom, we shall fight him in the print room, we shall fight him on the newsstands, we shall never surrender."

I stood up and headed for the door. I glanced back. Figgis had hunched his shoulders, puffed out his cheeks, and curled his lower lip.

Perhaps I shouldn't have mentioned Churchill after all.

Susan Wheatcroft, Frank Figgis and I met for a late lunch in Prinny's Pleasure.

We huddled round the table at the back of the bar. We stared at a plate of stale sandwiches landlord Jeff Purkiss had just put in front of us. None of us felt like eating.

Figgis raised his glass of stout and took a long pull at it.

He said: "How did my pep talk to the staff go down this morning?"

Ten minutes after I'd suggested he rallied the troops like Churchill, he'd slunk into the newsroom and made a short speech.

I said: "I don't think you should have ended on that Churchill quotation about success consisting of going from failure to failure without loss of enthusiasm."

Susan giggled and her double chins wobbled. She had a gulp of her pint of bitter.

She said: "While Frank was doing his Winston impression, I was on the phone to Algy, an old mate who works on the *Sydney Morning Herald*. I got his phone number after I'd done him a big favour when he visited Britain a few months ago. Quite enjoyed doing the favour myself."

I grinned: "Just get to the point Susan."

"Anyway, turns out that Pell first came up on Algy's radar way back in the late nineteen-forties. Pell had bought a run-down gold mine in Western Australia. Hadn't been worked since the gold rush of the eighteen-nineties. Word was that it was exhausted, but it was less than thirty miles from the mine where the Golden Eagle gold nugget – the largest ever found – was discovered. Algy said Pell was unknown in gold mining circles and no-one knew where he'd got his stake money to buy the mine. There was a rumour he'd won it playing poker. Anyway, at first, the mine worked out in a small way. But he needed more capital, so he brought in a partner – a guy called Slim Richards. Anyway, Richards poured his life savings into the mine, but it turned out there was no more gold. It all turned nasty. Richards claimed Pell had misled him about the prospects. There was talk of a court case. But it never happened. Richards died – victim of an accident in the mine. Part of a tunnel roof caved in."

"Convenient for Pell," Figgis said.

"Sure. But the failure of the mine left him with a life-long obsession with gold, Algy told me."

"So why hasn't he tried his luck again?" I asked.

"Turns out a journalist from the Perth *Daily News* started sniffing around. Pell didn't like it although nothing was ever pinned on him. But it seems it made him realise how owning a newspaper could be a way of winning friends and influencing people. He dropped out of sight for a couple of years. And then he popped up in the early nineteen-fifties by launching a small weekly in Sydney. Nothing more than a scandal sheet with girls, according to Algy. Again, nobody knew where he'd raised the funds. In Oz, sex and scandal proved to be a winning formula. But the word from my guy is that Pell's companies rely heavily on debt for finance. They've expanded too quickly – and now face cash-flow problems. Seen it too often, as a business reporter."

"Our problem is how we stop him taking over the *Chronicle*, for nothing," I said.

"But how?" Figgis said. He finished his stout and lit up a Woodbine.

I said: "After you'd finished your impression of Churchill, I slipped out of the office."

"I thought we'd agreed you'd find out what happened at the

Clansfield Club."

"I needed to make that call in private. Not with thirty other journos earwigging me."

I explained how three nights ago I'd met Archie Stamford at the Clansfield. How we'd watched four men playing poker. How Archie had pointed out that one of them was cheating. I told them how Archie was about to tell me more when he had to leave in a hurry. Frightened off by a bouncer.

"Archie said he'd call me, but he hasn't so I called him this morning."

"And?" Figgis said.

"No reply. I'd hoped he might have been in the club when Rackham lost his bet. He could've explained what happened."

"Any idea why he's not called you?" Susan said.

"Perhaps he's been warned off by the management. Just before he left, I think he was about to tell me the name of the man who was cheating."

"It's Quentin Pell," Figgis said.

"Stands to reason," Susan added. "Cheating at poker is the way Pell raises the start-up funds for his business ventures."

I nodded, slightly miffed they'd both stolen my punch-line. But pleased they were keeping up.

"If we can prove Pell cheated, he didn't win the paper," Figgis said.

"But how can we prove that?" Susan asked.

"We'd never prove what happened in the game," I said. "After all, Rackham accepted the result at the time."

"And he signed that promissory note," Figgis said. "So what can we do?"

He slumped back in his seat. His face was grey and etched with deep worry lines. He looked old.

"I don't know," I said. "I need to think about it some more. There may be an angle we've overlooked."

"I can't see what it is," Susan said.

But I couldn't stop thinking about Pell's obsession and Colonel Dubbins' tale of the stolen gold.

I didn't return to the office with Figgis and Susan.

There didn't seem any point. I'd already written my update on the Telford story for the day – and there were no other developments.

Instead, I headed for the seafront. It was a fine October day. The sun was low in the sky, but the air was warm. I walked towards Black Rock with the sea on my right. A fresh breeze whipped up white horses on the waves which broke on the beach. Seagulls screeched as they wheeled above the sea.

I was trying to think of a plan that would thwart Pell's take-over of the *Chronicle*.

But every plan I thought of was either riddled with flaws or too fantastical to succeed.

Besides, it wasn't my job to cover the tracks of a foolish lord who squandered his inheritance.

Except that if I didn't, I'd be a loser. And so would all my colleagues.

I couldn't get Pansy Flowers out of my mind either. She would lose more than me. Her life. I couldn't believe that the scallywags would really go through with a dangerous crime to fund her treatment in America.

And then there was the question of who'd killed Steve Telford. I didn't think the cops would get very far with that. But I had my suspicions about each of the three scallywags I'd met.

When I reached Black Rock, I turned around and walked back into the town. I sat on a bench not far from West Pier as the sun sank in the west and the light faded from the horizon. The illuminations on the pier sparked alight.

I felt tired…

Ever so tired.

I closed my eyes.

My head lolled forward.

A hand rested softly on my shoulder.

I opened my eyes and looked up.

Shirley stood in front of me smiling.

"How did you know I was here?" I asked.

She sat next to me.

"I called you at the *Chronicle* and they said you'd quit for the day. There seemed to be some trouble there, but no-one would say what it is. Does it involve you?"

I told Shirley everything.

"Jeez! This Rackham guy lost the *Chronicle* on the turn of a card? He's a double Dumbo."

"Triple if you ask me."

"There must be something you can do about it."

"I've walked to Black Rock and back and cudgelled my brains for an answer every foot of the way. It's not just that I want to save the *Chronicle*, I can't forget Pansy. Not now I'm sure I know what a cockeyed plan the scallywags have. And I desperately want to get a line on Steve Telford's murder."

"So just the three problems," Shirley said. "And each of them a brainteaser in itself."

"Yes. Three different problems. And hardly any time to think up a plan to solve even one of them."

Shirley edged around me, leaned forward, and kissed me. She drew back and for a few seconds we just stared into each other's eyes.

She said: "But you have a plan to solve all three of them at the same time."

"How can you tell?"

"Because I found you sitting here. If you hadn't solved it, you'd still be pacing the seafront."

I grinned. "Am I that obvious?"

Shirley kissed me again. "Only to me. So what's the big idea, Einstein?"

"It's risky. Very risky."

"Never bothered you in the past."

"But usually it's just you and me. This time it involves other people, too."

Shirley looped her arm through mine. Snuggled closer.

"Tell me," she said.

"Well, it all starts with a ship bringing a cargo of gold to Britain…"

Chapter 15

Shirley's eyes goggled like a pair of dinner plates.

She said: "This sounds like the leeriest scam you've ever tried. I don't like it. You could end up out of a job. Or in jail. Or dead."

I said: "What's the alternative? There isn't one. Besides, if Pell takes over the *Chronicle*, I'll be out of a job anyway."

We were sitting on the bench looking out to sea. The outline of a cargo vessel sailing down the Channel cut the line of the horizon.

I said: "We have to find a way to trap Quentin Pell, so he's forced to hand back the promissory note. Then he won't be able to take control of the *Chronicle*."

"It's blackmail. He'll call the cops. Your nemesis Alec Tomkins would just love an excuse to slap the bracelets on you."

"In his dreams," I said.

"Okay. Just run through this scam again – and I'll pick out the holes."

"Susan Wheatcroft did some great research on Pell. She found he had an early passion for gold mining. Expected to make himself a millionaire. Ended up with a dusty old mine in Western Australia with barely enough gold to stop a miser's tooth. She reckons the failure has gnawed away at him over the years. He's a guy that can't take failure. So my plan is to play on his obsession. Fool him into thinking that there's a big cache of gold in Sussex just waiting to be found."

"But nobody produced any evidence of gold."

"That doesn't matter. An obsessive isn't driven by facts. He's powered by what he wants to believe, even if it's a myth. For him, myths are real. Besides, I'm going to lay a trail which will fire his obsession until it glows like a furnace. I'll create a credible story to make him believe there's gold in 'them thar hills'."

"You wouldn't fool me, buster."

I grinned. "I know that. But there've been rumours for years about a consignment of gold that was sent from the Channel Islands at the outbreak of war. It's supposed to have been hidden by a pair of rogue scallywags. Carisbrooke Dubbins told me about it – and he didn't entirely discount the story himself. If I can get the three scallywags I've interviewed to help, it will encourage Pell to believe the story."

"But you thought one of them croaked Telford."

"That's possible. Even likely. But I can't tell which one. I've interviewed each of them once and I can't press them more without something to go on. If I can work closely with them, I might pick up a clue."

"Like one of them is going to put their hand up to a murder," Shirley said.

"I don't expect that, but if I see them at close quarters, I might be able to tell who's the most likely culprit."

"I can't see why any one of them would want to put their arses on the line with this crazy scheme."

"These are guys who put their arses on the line in the most noble cause of all. Freedom."

"Granted. They were ready to stuff the Nazis. But that doesn't mean they'll go after an Oz with a gold habit."

"But my scheme isn't as crazy as their idea of a wages snatch to fund Pansy's treatment. They could all end in jail. Rita included. Where would Pansy be then? I'll give them an alternative."

"Yeah! Humiliation if it all goes wrong. At least if they were in jail after a wage snatch, the other cons would respect them. If they wind up in the can when your plan flushes down the dunny, they'll be a laughing stock."

"My plan won't come near the ablutions," I said. "Besides, when I've put it in place, it will seem so real Pell will feel he can almost touch the gold."

"And if he goes for it?"

"We're waiting for the moment when he finds the treasure chest empty. And we warn him we'll go public with a story about the newspaper tycoon who got greedy. The other papers will splash it all over their front pages. He'll be humiliated. Unless he hands back the promissory note. Then the *Chronicle* will be safe."

Shirley said. "But what about Pansy?"

"I'll offer Rackham the promissory note for ten thousand pounds to pay for Pansy's treatment."

"I thought Rackham was one of those aristos who was short of the folding stuff."

"He's got a house packed with paintings and antiques. He could sell an old master or a Georgian commode or something to raise the cash."

Shirl shrugged. "He'll never do it. Nor will the scallywags."

"Let's go and find out," I said.

An hour later Shirley and I were standing on the doorstep outside Rita Flowers' house.

The lights were on in the front room but the curtains were drawn. We could hear music playing. It sounded like the Beach Boys. *Barbara Ann*. Not one of my favourites. The kind of song drunk football fans sing in the back of the coach on their way back from a match they lost.

Shirl said: "Of all the scams you've pulled, this has to be the craziest. It's not too late to change your mind."

I said: "Life is a risk."

"Yeah! With you, the risk comes with knobs on."

"You don't have to come in with me."

"Someone's got to watch your bum."

I grinned. "If that's all you're interested in, perhaps we could go somewhere private."

"Are you sure those scallywag guys are going to be here?"

"Rita told me they were coming for Pansy's birthday. We

need them all in the same place at the same time – and this is our only chance."

Shirley reached around me and pressed the doorbell.

I hardly had time to protest before Rita opened the door.

She was dressed for a party in a blue dress with white polka-dots. She had a paper party hat on her head. Her face was fixed in a beaming smile.

It changed to a scowl as soon as she saw us.

"What do you want?" she demanded.

I held up a book we'd bought in W H Smith's on the way.

"We've brought Pansy a birthday present," I said.

"A picture book of *Alice in Wonderland,*" Shirley added.

Rita gave us a look which my old granny would have described as "old fashioned".

This one was so old fashioned it was practically mediaeval.

"Thanks for the book. I'll give it to Pansy. Now goodnight."

Rita moved to close the door.

Like a brush salesman, I stuck my foot in by the jamb.

I said: "We hoped to *snatch* a moment of your time."

I laid heavy emphasis on the word snatch.

This time Rita gave me an old-fashioned look that was prehistoric.

"What do you mean by that?" she snapped.

"We could explain inside."

"And give Pansy her gift," Shirley said.

Rita treated Shirley to a look from the Jurassic period and said: "Who are you?"

"Shirley Goldsmith, over from Oz."

Rita said: "You better come in – but one hint of trouble and you're out. And I've got guests who can make sure you leave."

Rita turned on her heel and marched up the hall.

We followed behind. Not forgetting, of course, to close the door after us.

Rita led us into the sitting room where I'd confronted her the day before.

This time we weren't alone. The three scallywags were here. And they were ready to party.

Harry Deakin was down on all fours making out like a horse. Fred Youngman was lifting Pansy onto his back. Alec Perkins clapped his hands and shouted: "Giddy-up."

They froze when Shirley and I walked into the room. All except Pansy. She shouted in delight: "A new man for my party. And a pretty lady."

She dug her heels into Harry's ribs like she wanted him to jump Becher's Brook.

I said: "I'm not sure about the horse, but I'd certainly put money on the jockey."

Pansy bounced up and down on Harry's back. She was a small girl with a face like a china doll. I suspected it was usually pale, but Rita would have allowed her a touch of make-up for her party. She was wearing a red dress with a taffeta over-skirt and a princess's tiara.

Alec Perkins glowered at me and said: "What are you doing here?"

I said: "I can never resist a party."

Shirley said: "We've got a present for Pansy."

Pansy squealed: "A present!"

She jumped off Harry's back and ran across the room. Shirley knelt down and showed her the *Alice in Wonderland* book.

Pansy took it and flipped the pages. She pointed at a picture of Alice.

"I like her," she said. "And this White Rabbit."

"If your Mummy doesn't mind, I can read you some of it later," Shirley said.

Pansy turned her expectant face towards Rita. "Can she, Mummy? Please."

Rita looked like she'd swallowed a wasp. "If you like, poppet."

Pansy threw her arms around Shirley's neck and kissed her

on the cheek.

"You speak funny," she said. "Do you come from a long way away, like Hove?"

"I come from Australia, on the other side of the world."

"Our teacher, Miss Latham, told us about Australia. They have kangaroos that hop around there. Have you ever seen a kangaroo?"

Shirley nodded. "There are lots of other strange animals, too, that I could tell you about. Like wallabies and the duck-billed platypus, and cuddly koala bears."

"I've got a cuddly teddy bear. Uncle Fred Youngman brought it for me."

Shirley said: "That's nice. In Australia we've also got wiggly snakes and crawly spiders."

Shirley turned her hand into a spider and made it creep across the carpet towards Pansy. She squealed in delight.

"Not all the spiders are nice, though," Shirley said. "There's a nasty one, very poisonous, called the funnel-web, but we won't let him in here."

Shirley's hand went from being a spider back to a being a hand.

I said to the scallywags: "I don't want to spoil the fun, but I've got a proposition to put to you."

"What kind of proposition?" Alec Perkins demanded.

"The kind that will keep you all out of jail – and could provide the money for you-know-who's treatment."

I glanced at Pansy. But she wasn't interested in me. She was busy looking at her Alice book with Shirley.

"This is Pansy's day," Rita said.

"Yes, it is," I said. "And we all want her to have many more of them. That's why we're here."

"Let's hear him out, Rita," Harry said.

She glanced at Alec and Fred. They both nodded. But neither of them looked like men who wanted to shake me by the hand.

By the throat, possibly.

I said: "Why doesn't Shirley take Pansy up to her bedroom to read her the Alice story, while we talk?"

Shirley picked up the clue. "Would you like me to read you the bit about the Mad Hatter and why he wanted to put the dormouse in the teapot?"

Pansy giggled: "Yes, yes. Can I, Mummy?"

Rita glanced at me with suspicious eyes, but she nodded at Shirley.

Shirley took Pansy by the hand. We could hear Pansy's whoops of delight as Shirley carried her up the stairs.

The three scallywags stood up and moved towards me.

"Now we'd like to know why you're here," Harry said. "And it better be good or we'll put you into the street. And it might not be this one."

I grinned. "I can't resist a warm welcome. Mind if I sit down?"

I didn't wait for an invitation and took the seat by the table.

The rest of them stared at me like I'd just taken an axe to a Chippendale. But they sat down in chairs around the room and glared at me.

I said: "I know about the wages snatch."

"What do you mean?" Alec said.

"There is no wages snatch," Harry said.

"You should watch what you say," Fred added.

They started to exercise their shoulders, move their arms, limber up for a rumble.

"Don't start any trouble," Rita said. "Not here. Not on Pansy's birthday."

From upstairs, we heard Pansy laugh.

We all looked upwards. Then back at one another.

The scallywags knew I was on to them. But they didn't know what to do about it.

They'd been trained to sneak through a forest and blow up German tanks. In covert operations, it was all about staying one step ahead of the enemy.

But now I was the enemy. And they were one step behind.

I decided to make it easy for them.

I said: "What you want to do is laudable. If I were in your position and had known Charlie Flowers as a fellow scallywag, I'd want to do something to help Pansy. But a stunt like a wages snatch won't help her."

"Surprise attack. Sudden overwhelming force to achieve an objective. It's what we were trained for," Fred said.

"Yes, to take down Nazi troops, not some poor old wages clerk. What happens if you injure him in the raid? Or worse?" I asked.

"It was always going to be minimum violence," Harry said. "We were all agreed on that. We'd have no beef with no wages clerk. If he handed over the cash like a good boy, he could go on his way rejoicing."

"Sure, feeling like a failure. That he'd let everyone down," I said.

"How did you know?" Fred asked. "We've told no-one outside this room. Unless we've got a traitor in our midst."

"That's enough of that talk, Fred Youngman," Rita snapped.

I smiled at Fred. He glowered back.

"I look at things," I said. "I put two and two together. Very occasionally, they make four."

"What does that mean?" Fred asked.

I told them how I'd spotted all the newspapers with the wage snatch articles.

Rita's hand flew to her mouth and she sobbed. "I never realised, boys. I'm so sorry."

"You've got nothing to be sorry about," Alec said. "Not when a snooper who pretends to be a journalist comes to call."

He wagged his finger at me. "You write a word of this in your rag and we'll sue you so hard you won't even end up with the clothes you're standing up in."

"That'll cause a bit of stir in the newsroom," I said.

There was more laughter from upstairs. This time both Shirley and Pansy.

We all looked towards the stairs.

I said: "A timely reminder of why we're here. There's another way to raise the money. And it doesn't involve breaking the law. At least, not so much. And, perhaps, not at all. You won't spend the rest of your lives looking over your shoulders wondering whether the man behind is a cop. You won't jump every time there's a knock at the door thinking they've come to arrest you."

"Why should you want to help us?" Rita said.

"Because I've got a problem to solve, too."

I told them about how Rackham had lost the *Chronicle* in a game of poker with Quentin Pell. I said I wanted to recover the promissory note Rackham had given Pell.

"Why should we want to help you?"

"Because if we can recover the note, I can sell it back to Rackham for ten thousand pounds." I looked Rita in the eyes. "That's the money you need for Pansy's treatment. And it comes all legal and above board."

"Only if your plan works," Rita said. But I could tell from her eyes that she was thinking hard.

"What is your plan?" Fred asked.

"Yeah. Why do you need a bunch of retired scallywags?" Alec said.

"You all know the story about the scallywags who held up the gold truck," I said.

"Yeah. We know about that," Fred said.

"Nothing was ever proved," Harry said.

"We don't even know if there is gold out there," Alec said.

"But if someone believes there is…" I said.

I spent the next fifteen minutes describing my plan. The scallywags watched me through narrowed eyes. They didn't know what to make of me. Whether to take my plan seriously.

I wound up. "So that's what we'll do. It will look like I'm researching a story about the hidden gold. I'll drop hints that I've interviewed former scallywags who have new information. I'm betting that Pell won't be able to resist finding out more himself. And that's when we move in for the sting."

"How will that work?" Harry asked.

"Let's come to that when we've got Pell on the hook," I said.

"It's a risk," Alec said.

"But not as much as a wage snatch," Fred said.

"I don't know," Harry said. "Let's leave the decision to Rita."

We all turned towards her.

She stood up and headed for the door.

"It's time for the birthday girl to go to bed," she said. "Haven't you got some planning to do?"

Chapter 16

Shirley speared a chip with her fork, popped it into her mouth, and chewed.

It was half an hour after we'd left the birthday party. We were in Bardsley's fish and chip shop. We were enjoying a cod and chip supper with mushy peas.

Mr Bardsley had asked us whether we'd like our fish battered.

I'd said: "No, just slapped around a bit."

He'd rolled his eyes. He'd heard that one a thousand times. He'd dipped the fish in batter and lowered it into the spitting fat like he was laying a much-loved pet to rest.

Shirl said: "You know, I think Pansy knows she's going to die."

I stopped scooping up some mushy peas and looked hard at Shirley.

"What makes you say that? Rita said Pansy doesn't understand how serious her condition is."

"She's a bright little Sheila. She knows something's not right. She can feel it in her body. She said as much to me when we were lying on her bed reading the story."

"That she was dying?"

"No, not like that. She was lying propped up in a kind of one-sided way on her pillow. I asked her if she'd be more comfy if I plumped up the pillow. But she said she found it easier to lie that way. And then she looked at me and said: 'At least it won't be for ever.'"

"She must have meant she'd get well."

"You didn't see her eyes when she said it. That girl knows what the fates have in store for her."

I ate some of the mushy peas. "Downstairs, we heard her laughing," I said.

"She's full of fun. That's what makes me feel so bad about it all."

I put down my knife and fork and reached across the table for Shirley's hand. She gripped mine and squeezed hard.

"If we can pull this off, Pansy will get her treatment and she'll live a long life. Even a blameless one. Just like mine."

Shirley let go my hand, picked up her fork, and pronged another chip.

"That 'if' is about as big as the endless skies of the Outback. You've never tried anything like this. Besides, even if you manage to make people believe there's gold out there, it's not true is it?"

"How do we know? Carisbrooke Dubbins seemed to think there was something in the story. Besides, newspapers carry speculative stories based on rumours or myths all the time. What about all those stories about sightings of the Loch Ness Monster?"

Shirley shook some vinegar onto her battered cod.

She said: "I'm worried. This whole scam is a gamble, but a child's life is at risk. What happens if this Quentin Pell guy doesn't take the bait?"

I leant across the table. "Everything I've heard about him tells me that he will. In my work, I've met a few chancers in my time, and this guy has it written all over him. In capital letters. Look at his scam with the gold mine. He screwed a partner out of his stake - for all we know by cheating him at poker. I'll bet he knew the mine was a dud all the time."

"Sure, I'll give you that."

"He'll be gagging to find out more about this gold when I break the story."

"So what if all he does is pat you on the back for a good story and walk on by?"

"I can't see him doing that. He'll want a slice of the action. So I'll need to work out a way to hint I know the location of the gold. That way he'll be tempted to get there first. We can be ready and waiting with a camera to catch him in the act of trying to steal a fortune. Except it'll all be moonshine."

"Even if you catch this guy with his dacks down he'll just laugh at you."

"I don't think so. Because he's a chancer, he's always been on the outside. Never got the respect of the legit players in the newspaper world. I figure that's what he craves now. The respect of his peers. He knows the kind of coverage he'd get from this would ruin any chance of that. I think he'll play ball."

Shirley forked up the last of her fish. "I hope you're right. If this goes bad, we could all lose out. Pansy worst of all."

"Don't worry," I said. "I'm going to make it all seem like someone else's idea."

I strode into the press briefing at Brighton police station the following morning ready to deploy a sneaky plan.

I'd spent part of the night thinking it out. The problem was this: if I suggested there was wartime gold buried somewhere in Sussex, everyone would become excited for a few hours. And then, when they realised the gold story was only a rumour, forget about it.

But if the gold was linked to a hard news story, other reporters would have to take it seriously. The question I needed to solve was how to do that. If I stood up at the police press briefing, most of the other journos would just think it was old Crampton with another of his hare-brained notions. Besides, if I was going to fool Pell, the gold idea would seem more genuine if it had come from someone else. It would look like I was following up another journalist's lead. The bonus would be that other papers would be on the story, so we'd have to move fast. That would put pressure on Pell to make up his mind about whether he wanted to make a play for the gold.

Keeping up, so far?

I knew you would.

So how could I gull a fellow journo into making the idea public without him realising he'd been used?

Earlier, I'd sneaked into Figgis' office and taken a sheet of the memo paper from the pad on his desk. The paper was headed: Frank Figgis, News Editor, *Evening Chronicle*.

I'd hurried back to my desk and typed this message on it: *"Colin, about that hidden gold angle on the Telford murder you mentioned to me last night. I've decided we want to play this one close to our chest. If Steve Telford really was part of a renegade team that hijacked wartime gold somewhere in Sussex, we'll have an explosive exclusive. Under no circumstances mention this to anyone else. That means you should not raise it at the police press briefing until I give you express permission to do so."*

I'd signed the memo with the squiggle that usually passed for Figgis' signature.

When I entered the press briefing, the memo was tucked inside the front cover of my notebook.

I saw the victim who was to be my dupe straight away.

Jim Houghton was wearing a crumpled grey suit with an egg stain on the right lapel. His tie hung loose from his collar. He looked as though he'd just been given a haircut with a lawnmower. A faint agricultural smell wafted up from his shoes. He'd stepped in something on his way to the cop shop.

He'd seen me as soon as I'd sauntered through the door. His lips were twisted into the grin of a man who knows he's got a snarky remark – and can't wait to make it.

He limped up to me and said: "Your story in last night's *Chronicle* read like a piece of ancient history. Now if you want to know how to handle real breaking news you should have read my story in the *Argus*."

"I think I saw it, Jim."

Houghton's eyebrows jumped. "You did?"

"Yes. It was wrapped around my girlfriend's cod and chips."

Houghton scowled. "Cocky bastard. You'll get your

comeuppance one day."

I pulled my notebook out of my jacket pocket.

I said: "I'm ready to take notes of this briefing. How about you?"

I flipped through the notebook's pages. Pretended not to see the memo as it fluttered to the ground.

"I'm taking a seat at the front today, Jim."

I marched off before he could say any more.

I didn't see him stoop to pick up the paper. Or see him turn and head for a corner where he could open and read it unobserved.

I didn't need to watch him. I knew exactly what he would do. Exactly what I would do.

He didn't come over to me, look abashed, and say: "I think you dropped this."

Instead, he eventually took a seat at the back.

I looked round. He was sitting at the end of a row next to Angela Eagleton, a young reporter from the *Brighton & Hove Herald*. He was telling Angela how she could be a great reporter if only she was more like him. She was turning her face away from his shoes and trying not to breathe.

There were a dozen reporters in the room, a fair turnout for day six of a provincial murder. Especially one where the cops hadn't made much progress. But "baffled cops" stories always went down well with readers. They reinforced cherished prejudices.

A couple of minutes later, a door opened and Detective Chief Superintendent Alec Tomkins made his grand entrance. His eyes scanned the reporters seated on the half-empty rows as though expecting a round of applause. He sat down behind a table at the head of the room.

He said: "Our investigation into the murder of Steve Telford is making good progress. We have the results of Mr Telford's post-mortem back from the pathologist. It appears the deceased was killed by an insect bite."

"What kind of insect?" I asked without being invited to.

Tomkins glared at me and said: "The lab boffins haven't been able to determine that yet. They say it seems similar to the venom emitted by poisonous spiders in several parts of the world. They need further tests to be more specific."

"How could Tomkins be killed by a bite from a spider from overseas?" I asked.

"We're conducting further enquiries," Tomkins said.

"Perhaps you should call in Spider Man to help with the case."

That won a round of laughter from the press pack.

But Tomkins flushed. "There are many things about this investigation you don't know."

"And many you don't either, if you can't say precisely how Steve Telford died," I said.

Tomkins' voice rumbled like he'd got a bad case of indigestion. I think he said: "No comment."

A stringer for one of the national papers asked: "Do you have a suspect?"

"We are reviewing a number of possibilities," Tomkins said.

A silence fell over the room.

I felt my heart beat a bit faster.

I'd expected Jim to ask a question.

The silence ran on for another ten seconds.

Reporters stared at the blank pages in their notebooks.

I let out a sigh. My ruse had failed.

Then I heard a chair behind me scrape back.

I risked a glance over my shoulder. Jim Houghton was on his feet.

He said: "Chief Superintendent, can you confirm that the Telford killing is linked to a store of hidden wartime gold somewhere in Sussex?"

He sat down again. A buzz of conversation started up. This was new.

Angela said: "Nobody has mentioned wartime gold before. Do you know about that, Mr Tomkins?"

Tomkins looked flustered. He rummaged among the papers on the table in front of him.

Looked around for help. None was coming any time soon.

I chipped in: "Would that be the gold that was rumoured to have been hijacked by a rogue army unit?"

"What rogue army unit?" Tomkins asked.

"I was hoping you could tell us," I said.

By now, the room was in uproar. Everyone was shouting questions. People were on their feet demanding answers.

Tomkins stood up. Held up his hands. "Please, please, one question at a time. We have no information about gold at this time. I will look into the matter."

"When will you be able to comment?" Jim asked.

"I... I don't know. This meeting is adjourned."

Tomkins grabbed his papers and fled the room.

And then there was a stampede for the door as reporters rushed to be first to the phones.

I noticed with satisfaction that Jim had already left.

This was one occasion when I was happy if the *Argus* scooped the *Chronicle*.

But it turned out my triumph at the cop shop was short-lived.

When I returned to the *Chronicle's* newsroom I was in for a shock.

I pushed through the swing doors and came up hard. Instead of the controlled chaos as thirty journalists scrambled towards the deadline, the place was silent. It was like someone had just died. Like being back at school when the whole class had to stay in for detention.

Phil Bailey's fingers pecked at the keys on his typewriter. Susan Wheatcroft wound some newswire paper tape round a pencil. Sally Martin flipped the pages of an old *Vogue* magazine.

They shot dagger glances at my old captain's chair.

A man was sitting in it.

He was so thin he could have stood next to the skeleton in the ghost train on the pier and you'd have been hard pushed to tell them apart. He had a skull of a face. Bony cheeks, a chin like a dagger, eye sockets like inkwells. His lips were thin and moist, and his nose drooped a little. His head was bald and his skin was mottled.

He was wearing a cheap blue suit and brown shoes.

He'd opened the top drawer of my desk and was rifling through the contents.

I stomped towards him.

I said: "Have you found what you're looking for?"

He looked at me through condescending eyes and said: "I don't know what I'm looking for,"

"Then you can close my drawer, get out of my chair, and let me get on with my work."

He said: "You must be Crampton."

I said: "You must be Mr Nosey."

He grinned and revealed a row of sharp, pointy teeth, like he'd been chewing concrete.

He said: "Cold body."

"No, I'm quite warm actually."

"No, that's me, Coldbody. Nigel Coldbody."

"Well, Mr Coldbody, perhaps you'd hot-foot it out of my chair."

Coldbody stood up and surveyed the room like he planned to pulverise it with a ray gun.

He said: "I'm Quentin Pell's eyes and ears."

"I can quite understand why he wanted to get rid of them."

"I'm here to look after his interests until he takes over the paper legally. I'm a practising solicitor."

"In that case, come back when you've learnt to do it properly."

Coldbody curled a lip. Not that he had much to curl.

He said: "I'd heard you could be a difficult customer."

"Too right. And today I'm not buying. So jog off. And in future keep away from my desk."

"Things will be changing around here, Crampton. Just wait until Mr Pell gets his feet under the desk."

"It won't be this one. I'll chop it to pieces before Pell can get within a hundred yards."

Coldbody shot me a malevolent look. He slithered across the newsroom and pushed through the swing doors.

A thin cheer broke out from the other journos.

The temperature seemed to rise about ten degrees.

Telephones started to ring. Typewriters went clackety-clack.

It was like the newsroom had emerged from a nuclear winter.

I sat back and thought about Coldbody. I hadn't expected Pell to move so fast. I'd thought he'd wait until he'd exercised his rights with the promissory note. Until he'd signed the contract to own the paper.

Coldbody's appearance wasn't good news. I'd planned to set up the hidden gold scam and feed Pell the clues from a distance. With Coldbody on the prowl, it would be more difficult to pull off the con.

But perhaps I was looking at this the wrong way. If Coldbody was around, maybe I could use him as a conduit to feed misinformation to Pell. If Coldbody vouched for the stuff, Pell was far more likely to take it at face value.

I could tell Coldbody thought he was shrewd.

But he looked like a sucker to me.

I learnt my first lesson on how to pull a scam at school.

It was during a maths lesson on the law of cosines. Something about angles and the length of the sides of a triangle. It's never come in handy.

Anyway, my mate Ron Trescothick had taken a bet from Badger Bentley. Ron said he could hit the back of old Proudfoot's head – he was the maths teacher – with an ink pellet fired from his desk in the back row of the classroom. Ron was a craftsman when he made an ink pellet. He had a way of folding a piece of tissue paper so it absorbed the maximum amount of ink while retaining all its aerodynamic qualities. Anyway, Ron made one of his finest. He fired it from the end of a foot-long ruler, bent back at an impossible angle.

The pellet hit Proudfoot right on target while he was chalking an equation on the blackboard. The ink splatter across the back of his head looked like a gunshot wound. Of course, there was an immediate search for incriminating evidence. And it was found. Three of Ron's finest pellets. The ones only he could make. His fingerprints all over them. Metaphorically speaking.

And the pellets were in my desk.

I will draw a veil over the repercussions. Suffice it to say, the matter was not satisfactorily concluded until Ron had handed over to me the money he'd won from Badger.

But the lesson was well learned.

When you're pulling a scam, divert attention.

Lurk in the shadows. Let some mug stand in the spotlight.

I'd already suckered Jim Houghton into breaking the story. Now I needed to set some rumours running which would give the story legs.

And I knew just the people to do it.

I sauntered into the morgue with a smug look on my face, like a man who knows something everyone else doesn't.

Mabel, Elsie and Freda were gathered around their table.

If Henrietta Houndstooth was the Queen of the Goss, these three were her princesses. They were three comfortable looking women who clipped the newspapers for cuttings. They were known affectionately around the paper as the Clipping Cousins.

Mabel held a copy of the first edition of the *Evening Argus*. Elsie and Freda were focused on the front page. The headline read: GOLD MYSTERY IN MURDER CASE.

I wandered over to the three and said: "Anything of interest in the rival paper today?"

Mabel turned to me. "You won't like this, Colin."

"There's an exclusive story in the *Argus*," Elsie said.

"You've been scooped," Freda added.

They all looked at me like scooped was a kind of operation and they expected to see me with a bandage wrapped around my head.

I said: "Jim Houghton won't be leading on this story for long, but I need your help."

Mabel flashed a lascivious grin. "I could seduce that Jim Houghton and find out what he knows. There are some men who find surgical stockings a turn-on."

"You wouldn't enjoy seducing Jim. He wears a moth-eaten grey suit."

"I'd soon have that off his back."

"And there are rumours he hasn't changed his underwear since Clement Attlee was prime minister."

"*Ugh!* I shudder to think what I'd find under them."

"Not a lot, the rumours go. Apparently, even Jim can't find it much of the time."

The three giggled.

I said: "I think there might be something in this gold story."

"You think it's true?" Elsie asked.

"I think it could be. The trouble is finding someone somewhere who knows more than the rumour."

"How can you do that?" Freda said.

"That's where I need your help. I need you to spread the word that the story about the gold is true. If someone who knows the truth hears the rumour, they may come forward."

"If anyone knows the truth, they'll read the story in the papers," Freda said.

"Not enough," I said. "Not everyone reads newspapers and

some that do don't believe what they read. They're more likely to believe what someone tells them. That's why I want you to spread the rumour as far and as fast as you can. You can use the telephones here. But don't let on that you're calling from the *Chronicle*. Make it seem like you're doing it privately. Tell everyone to keep it secret – there's no better way to get them to spread it fast."

"Like undercover spies," Elsie said.

"A bit like that," I said.

"What will Henrietta say?" Mabel asked.

"She won't mind. She's helping me with something else to do with the story. And you can start now."

I left them staring at one another, their faces alive with mischief.

I headed for the door.

Within twenty-four hours all of Sussex would be spreading rumours about hidden gold.

Chapter 17

When you write for a newspaper, you soon discover that readers believe what they want.

You spend hours on mind-numbing research. You write a story loaded with irrefutable facts. You lay out a case with damning logic. But if someone doesn't want to believe it, they won't.

I've been railing against people who prefer rumour over reality for years.

Now I planned to use the rumour-mongers to my advantage.

There are suckers out there who believe myths for which there isn't any evidence at all. They believe little green men once landed in a space ship from Mars. They believe Marilyn Monroe is still alive and disguised as a tram driver in San Francisco. They believe a tribe of yetis live at the top of Mount Everest and eat any climber who reaches the peak.

From what I'd learnt about Quentin Pell, his newspapers catered for just such readers. The stories in his papers were laid out in words of one syllable. And for those for whom one syllable was too much of a challenge, there were tits and bums to ogle on page three.

But if Pell lived in a newspaper world drenched in myths and rumours, perhaps he was a sucker for them himself. He'd certainly deny it. But consider this. If a teetotaller walks into a crowded bar on a Saturday night, he'll come out stinking of beer. And he won't smell his own stench.

Why people choose to believe things that aren't true is a question for the philosophers. Or perhaps for the psychoanalysts. But it was going to make my scam easier. Because I was convinced that Quentin Pell would want to believe that gold was hidden somewhere in the green Sussex countryside.

He'd failed to find gold in his own mine. I had Pell down as a man who didn't tolerate failure. That included his own. So the chance to dig up some gold - anywhere - would silence a nag in his brain that hadn't stopped since he quit his Ozzie mine empty-handed.

From what I'd heard so far, Pell was sly and dishonest. He lied and he cheated.

But he wasn't stupid. He'd want to believe the story about the gold. But he'd also want evidence that it really was there.

And through his gofer Coldbody, I was going to provide that evidence for him.

I was in a hot little cubby-hole off the *Chronicle's* main print room. It passed as the office of Mike Spalding, head printer on the paper.

In the print room, the rotary presses roared as they turned out the latest edition – at twenty thousand copies an hour. The floor vibrated and sent little shivers through my feet. An acrid smell – part ink, part paper dust - choked the air.

Mike shut his cubby-hole's door and pushed through a narrow gap between a filing cabinet and his desk. He eased himself into an old canvas chair.

Mike had been with the *Chronicle* almost as long as Frank Figgis. He had a broad open face and crow's feet around his eyes. He had a mop of unruly fair hair which he combed straight back from his forehead. He was wearing a blue printer's jacket and brown corduroy trousers.

He grinned and said: "Not often we see you down here, Colin. Guess if what we've heard is true, we won't be seeing many of the familiar faces in the future."

I said: "I plan to do something about that, but I need your help."

"Anything to save the *Chronicle,*" Mike said.

"I need some press cuttings."

"You should see Henrietta about that."

"Not about these cuttings. Because they never existed."

Mike leaned forward and his forehead creased into a frown.

"Not sure I quite follow you," he said.

"Let me put it this way. I need to persuade someone that something that didn't happen actually did. What better than to let them see press cuttings which describe – or at least hint – at it?"

Mike's grin developed into the rumble of a throaty chuckle.

"I see. In other words, you're pulling the wool over their eyes, as my old mum used to say."

I reached inside my jacket pocket and pulled out a thick wodge of copy paper. I'd spent an hour at my desk in the newsroom busy at my Remington.

I passed the papers across to Mike.

"These are some stories I've written. In each case, I've put a date at the top. That's the date I've decided they appeared in the paper. You'll see the earliest dates from 1940, but the later ones come from just after the war."

Mike rummaged through the papers. He chuckled as he scanned the pages.

"As fine a piece of fiction as I've read," he said. "You should take over where that Edgar Wallace left off."

"I'll consider it one day. But can you set them in type and print them off as though they'd really appeared in the paper?"

Mike scratched at his chin.

"Won't be easy," he said. "For a start, we now print the paper in Times Roman typeface, but until the early nineteen-fifties, we used Century Old Style. The Linotype machines are loaded with Times, but we've still got a hand-picked font of Century at the back of the compositors' hall."

"As long as your guys can set the type without any typos. Not like that one last week."

The paper had published a review of a concert by the Rolling Stones at the Dome. The review caused more trouble than the concert.

The day after, the *Chronicle* printed an apology on page eighteen. *"In our review of the Rolling Stones' concert, we stated that Keith Richards was on guitar, Mick Jagger on vocals and Charlie Watts on drugs. We should like to make it clear that Mr Watts was on drums and apologise to him for the inconvenience caused, including the midnight raid of his hotel room by the police. We should also like to apologise to the six women who were with him at the time. We are sorry the police interrupted their prayer meeting as a result of our innocent error."*

I said: "Anyway, if you've got the Century Old, there's no problem."

"Not exactly. Because even if we set your purple prose in Century Old Style, we've still got a paper problem."

"I don't see that. You've got rolls of newsprint out there, Miles of it."

Mike tapped the pile of articles I'd handed him.

"The newsprint we're printing today's edition on is no good for these stories. Most of them are dated when there was newsprint rationing during and immediately after the war. Not only were we limited in the amount of paper we could use, it was much thinner than today's newsprint. I don't know how familiar your target is with newsprint. An experienced newspaperman would spot the discrepancy between the quality of the paper and the date of the cuttings straight away."

I thought about that. I'd hoped to scam Coldbody and even Pell with these cuttings. But they worked with newspapers. There was a real chance they'd spot the newsprint wasn't contemporary with the date of the content. If they had suspicions, my whole scam would unravel.

I shrugged my shoulders. "So that's the end of my plan," I said.

Mike scratched his chin again.

"Not necessarily," he said. "The galley sheets we use for

proofing each article are a bit thinner than the rolls of newsprint. They don't have to be so thick because they don't bear the strain of running at speed through the rotary presses without breaking. I could spray a few sheets of galley paper very lightly with water to soften the fibres in the paper. Then I could roll the papers sandwiched between blotters through the proofing machine. That would squeeze out the extra water as well as some of the original moisture held within the fibres. The paper would become thinner and slightly crinkly – a bit like wartime newsprint."

"And then you could proof the articles on galley paper and I could clip them out so they became cuttings."

Mike nodded. "Sure. But don't forget to fold them so they look like they've been kept in a dusty file for years. You could even brush a little dust along the folds to give an impression of age."

"Had you ever thought about becoming a forger?" I asked.

This time, Mike roared with laughter. "Sure. Printing is the chief craft of the forger. We should go into business together. We'd make a fortune."

I stood up and edged towards the door.

"If this doesn't come off, we may have to," I said.

I had another thought while I was nipping upstairs to the newsroom after my visit to Mike Spalding.

If I was going to make Pell believe there was gold buried in Sussex, I'd need a map.

A treasure map.

If the gold had been stolen by renegade scallywags, they'd have buried it in one of their hidden bunkers. But I didn't think there'd be a map of the bunkers. Certainly not one the public could see. There might be one hidden in a dusty filing cabinet in the Ministry of Defence. But I'd have as much chance of conning the men from the ministry out of that as being promoted to four-star general.

Back in the newsroom, Cedric was perched on Susan Wheatcroft's desk. He was telling a filthy joke. At least, I assumed it was filthy from the way Susan cackled.

I sauntered up just as he delivered the punch line. "And the actress said to the bishop, 'I didn't realise it went that far up.'"

I grinned and said to Cedric. "What went so far up?"

Cedric's cheeks coloured. "Well, the bishop was showing the actress the cathedral's spire. And it was very high. So she said…"

I cut the lad off. "I know, Cedric. I was telling that one myself when I was your age."

Susan grinned. "Leave him alone, you bully."

"I'm here to ask Cedric a favour."

"You've got a funny way of going about it," Susan said.

I said: "Cedric, I'd like you go to W H Smith and buy an Ordnance Survey map. It'll be the one labelled OL11, which covers Brighton and a big arc of the countryside around the town."

"Right you are, Mr Crampton. You off for a hike in the country, then?"

I winked at Susan. "Something like that," I said.

Cedric hurried off and I crossed the office to my desk.

I sat down in my old captain's chair and thought about what I was doing. The idea that I could con Quentin Pell out of the promissory note was the biggest risk I'd ever taken. It was a ten to one chance. No, a hundred to one. Perhaps a thousand to one. Why should a scam artist, who'd conned more people than I could count, fall for it?

Con-men are always suspicious. So my con would have to be totally convincing. Yet I wasn't sure what more I could do.

I lifted the telephone and called Shirley.

I said: "Meet me for lunch?"

"Where?"

"The café at the end of West Pier."

"Strange choice for you."

"At the moment, I feel all at sea."

In the café, we had a table by the window that overlooked the sea.

We could see the line of the bay. It curved into the distance beyond the white cliffs of the Seven Sisters.

We both chose bowls of tomato soup. It was thin and watery. It came with a dark brown roll which crouched on the plate like a malevolent toad.

Shirley said: "We'd get a better lunch by raiding the dustbins round the back of the Grand hotel."

I nodded. "Sorry. This matched my mood. I feel I've taken on more than I can handle."

"That's not like you. Not like a guy who's faced down killers before."

"This time is different. It's not just that everything I've ever wanted is at stake. It's that so many other people may suffer if I get this wrong."

I told Shirley about the way I hoped to con Pell with the fake press cuttings.

"And if I could identify Steve Telford's killer that would be a bonus. At the moment, I'm not sure I can pull off any of it."

"You say you're planning to set Pell up with a treasure map."

"Yes."

Shirley stirred her soup while she thought. "What you need is some real buried treasure."

"Where am I going to get gold bars from? The Bank of England keeps hundreds of them in its vaults - and they're not for hire."

"You don't need gold bars. Any gold would do. We don't know what was on that ship bringing the gold from Guernsey. It could have been those gold coins they used as money in the old days. What do you call them?"

"Sovereigns. Henry the Seventh first minted them in the fifteenth century. It was after the Wars of the Roses and he wanted a way to unite the houses of York and Lancaster. So the back of the sovereign had a double rose – the white of York and the red of Lancaster. They reissued them after the Battle of Waterloo in the nineteenth century."

"Cut the history lesson, professor."

I grinned. "Sorry. My best subject at school."

"Forget gold bars. I bet if this Pell bozo thinks there's a big stack of buried sovereigns, he won't be able to resist. Trouble is we need a few of them to provide the evidence. I guess they cost a packet."

"Notionally, they're worth one pound. But today, you'll pay twenty or thirty pounds for each."

"So we're stuffed," Shirley said.

"Not necessarily. I know someone who might be persuaded to lend us a few. But we'll need a good cover story."

Gerald Kummer scratched the stubble on his chin and let out a deep sigh.

The air hissed through the gap in his front two teeth. It made a sound somewhere between a boiling kettle and a football referee's whistle.

"Let me get this right," he said. "You want me to lend you a bag of gold sovereigns."

We were in a small shop in The Lanes, the antique traders' quarter of Brighton. The place was called Numismatica. It was a favoured haunt for coin collectors. Personally, I've never been able to see why people do it. I mean, what's the point of collecting coins you're never going to spend?

Kummer scratched his chin again. He was a short stubby man who looked like he'd stopped growing when he was about twelve. But what he lacked in height, he made up for in girth. He reminded me of the roly-poly pictures of Tweedledum and

Tweedledee in a book of *Through the Looking Glass*. He was wearing a check shirt buttoned at the neck. He had a pair of grey trousers which looked as though they'd been made out of a circus tent.

I said: "Gerald, you know I've always been fair and open with you."

Kummer's neck twitched in what passed for a nod.

"You know I kept your name out of the story when you were implicated in the Rottingdean Cash Caper."

Kummer's eyes flashed in alarm. "You know I was innocent in that. How was I to know all those bags of shillings had been nicked from a security lorry?"

"Do people often offer you the chance to buy seventy pounds worth of shillings at a thirty per cent discount?"

"I thought they might have been a bit over-enthusiastic in putting the money by for their gas meter. I'd like to help, Mr Crampton. You know I would. But my hands are tied."

"They could be tied with handcuffs."

Kummer threw up his hands. "Now that's not a nice thing to say."

"Perhaps not. But would it help if Shirley explained why we need the sovereigns?"

I'd noticed Kummer's gaze had strayed to Shirley several times while we'd been talking. He'd looked at her harlequin checked blouse. He'd gawped at her red velvet miniskirt. He drooled over her white calf-length boots. Then his lizard-like eyes had ogled her again – imagining her not wearing any of them. I'd spotted the dribble of spittle that appeared at the side of his mouth.

Shirley moved towards Kummer and flashed her brightest smile.

"You look like the kind of man I like to do business with," she said in a low husky voice.

Kummer gulped. Twice.

Shirley said: "You see, it's like this. I'm a model. A photographic model. And I appear in magazines. Now this photographer wants to hire me for a very special photoshoot. The theme is the Midas touch. You've heard of King Midas. He's that Greek guy. Everything he touched turned to gold. Sounded great until he wanted to eat a sandwich."

Kummer unbuttoned his top shirt button, Ran his finger nervously around the collar.

Shirley moved in closer.

"Well, here's the point. In this photo scene, I'm Midas' concubine. And I'm dressed in a beautiful gown, just like those Greek concubines wore."

"Yeah! I'd heard they looked good," Kummer croaked. His throat was as dry as a bishop's wit.

Shirley let Kummer catch a whiff of her perfume.

She said: "The thing is, this authentic Greek concubine's gown comes over my left shoulder and is cut away to my waist. You know what that means, don't you?"

"No," Kummer said in a hoarse whisper.

"It means my right breast is exposed – which is fine for a Greek concubine, but not for a model from Adelaide. Wouldn't you agree, Gerald?"

"No, er… I mean yes. I think."

"So the photographer has suggested I should hold a bag of sovereigns over my right breast."

"It'll need to be a big bag," Kummer spluttered.

"Well, yes, Gerald. You say the nicest things to a girl."

Kummer's mouth had dropped open. His tongue lolled out of one side.

He said: "What if I give you a bag with pennies inside? Nobody would know the difference."

"I would know the difference, Gerald. How do you think I would feel knowing that I held a bag that told a lie? I wouldn't be able to get into character. And that means the pictures wouldn't be any good. And I wouldn't want to give you a signed picture that didn't show me at my best."

Kummer swallowed hard.

He said: "I don't suppose I could have a picture without you holding the bag."

Shirley winked at Kummer. "*Oooh!* If you're suggesting what I think you are, you're a very naughty man. I like naughty men – especially when they have bags of sovereigns."

Kummer dragged his reptilian gaze away from Shirley and moved towards a large Chubb safe at the back of his office. He reached inside his trouser pocket and pulled out a large key on a piece of string. He opened the safe. Looked back at Shirley.

"If I lend you a bag with twenty sovereigns, I want them back in two days."

"Of course, you darling man," cooed Shirley.

He turned his back on us so we couldn't see inside the safe. He fumbled about inside for a couple of minutes. He turned. He was holding a small red leather pouch, pulled tight at the top with a drawstring.

He came back towards Shirley and handed her the pouch.

"Will this be big enough to cover your, er… embarrassment?"

"It will manage perfectly, you sweet little man," Shirley said.

She leant forward and gave Kummer the lightest of pecks on the cheek.

He beamed like he'd just received a proposal of marriage from Raquel Welch.

He looked up at Shirley. His reptilian gaze had turned into puppy dog eyes. As long as you assumed the puppy was a rottweiler.

He said: "Perhaps you could do me a favour."

"What is it?" Shirley asked.

"Will you have dinner with me?"

"I'd love to have some tucker with you."

"Be careful," I whispered in Shirley's ear.

"How about October the seventeenth?" Kummer asked.

"That's next week," I whispered. Louder this time.

"Perfect," Shirley said. "October the seventeenth. The year after next. My diary's rather full at the moment."

She leaned towards Kummer, undid the top button of her blouse, and dropped the pouch with the sovereigns into her cleavage.

"Don't you think that's a nice safe place to keep them," she said.

She turned and swept out of the shop.

I shrugged at Kummer.

"Put it down to experience," I said. "I usually do."

Chapter 18

When I joined Shirley outside the shop she was giggling like a schoolgirl.

She'd opened the pouch and was counting the sovereigns.

"Twenty, all present and correct," she said.

"Thanks to you. But you've left poor Gerald a quivering blob of priapic jelly."

"He'll get over it."

I said: "I'll take care of the sovereigns, O Greek concubine."

That started Shirley giggling again. But she handed over the pouch.

We jostled through the crowds in The Lanes and strolled towards the seafront.

Shirley said: "We've got the gold, but that's not the most difficult part of your scam. You've got to convince Pell that it's part of a much larger horde."

"If I can convince Coldbody, that should be enough. He'll pass the word to Pell."

"You've forgotten the most important thing, mastermind. You've got to let Coldbody see the gold without him grabbing it."

"I've been wondering about that. I think there might be a way, but I'm going to need help from the three scallywags."

Shirley reached out for my hand and squeezed it.

"And one of them could be a killer," she said.

"I only hope I can spot the one before he realises he's been fingered."

"So what's your next move?"

"I'll get in touch with Rita Flowers. She's in contact with the scallywags. I'll get her to arrange a meeting at her house this evening. By then, I should have a plan. I hope."

I left Shirley outside the Royal Albion hotel. She wandered off to do some shopping and I headed back to the *Chronicle*.

When I walked into the newsroom, it felt like I'd just stepped into a deep freezer.

There was a chill in the air which had nothing to do with the autumn weather.

I counted only six reporters in the room out of a roll-call of thirty. It wasn't hard to work out what had happened. Most of them had scarpered to avoid Coldbody. It's not difficult. You just leave a note in the newsroom's diary that you're "meeting a contact". That phrase can mean anything from a quick drink in the pub to a day at the races.

I walked over to my desk just as Cedric came in from the tearoom.

His eyes looked worried. His lips were pressed tightly together and his jaw was tense. He hustled over to me.

He said: "I'm really sorry, Mr Crampton."

"What's the problem, Cedric?"

"You know you asked me to buy an Ordnance Survey map. Well, that Coldbody caught me coming back into the newsroom with it. He wanted to know why I had it. He pinned me up against the telephone cubicles and said my job depended on telling him the truth. I had to tell him you wanted it. I'm sorry. I'm really sorry. Now he's got the map."

I put a soothing hand on Cedric's shoulder.

"Calm down. No need to apologise. I'll speak to Coldbody. And don't worry. Your job is safe."

I hoped I was right about that. More and more depended on my scam working.

I said: "Do you know where Coldbody is?"

"I last saw him upstairs."

I stormed across the newsroom and charged through the swing doors.

I found Coldbody in the corridor outside the subeditors'

room. He had a bundle of papers under his arm. I could see the map among them. He was standing on tiptoe so he could peer over the frosted glass into the room.

I snuck up behind him and said: "One good shove and you'd go through that window and land on the floor."

He spun round. His eyes blazed with fury and his lips were set in a snarl.

He said: "What are you doing here?"

I said: "I work here. What's your excuse?"

"I'm studying working practices."

"Does that include bullying the copyboy?"

"I asked him what he was doing."

"What he does is no concern of yours."

"It soon will be."

"Which, put another way, means not now. So you can give me my Ordnance Survey map."

Coldbody snarled at me in a low-key sort of way. He rummaged among his papers and handed over the map.

"What do you want that for?" he asked.

"I'm planning a journey."

"Where to?"

"Over the rainbow."

"Which rainbow?"

"The Judy Garland rainbow. I'm hunting for the Wizard of Oz."

Coldbody scoffed. "You won't find the Wizard or the tin man."

"I agree about the tin man. He had no heart. And he's standing right in front of me."

I turned my back on him and stalked down the corridor.

Five minutes later I was in Mike Spalding's cubby-hole.

Outside in the print room the rotary presses thundered as they rolled out the midday edition of the paper.

Mike sat behind his battered old desk with a sunbeam smile on his face. I took his visitor's chair.

Mike laid out three press cuttings on his desk.

He said: "Did these myself. Proved a tad trickier than I'd thought. For a start, each cutting has to be printed on both sides. The active side carries the story that's been clipped, the passive side whatever was on the overleaf page of the paper. For the passive side, I've taken real stories from the years you've specified. Henrietta helped me by looking them up in the morgue."

I picked up the first cutting. It was a single column piece, barely two inches in length. A news-in-brief. It was dated 1940. A small headline read: MYSTERY GUNFIRE IN WOODS. The copy went on to explain a cowhand had heard unexplained gunfire. He hadn't explored further because of War Ministry restrictions on the land. The Ministry had "no comment".

The clipping would support the story that rogue scallywags who'd stolen the gold were later killed in a gunfight.

A larger clipping, with a 1950 date, ran across three columns. It was headed: MINISTER DENIES GOLD RUMOURS. The story said that Douglas Jay MP, financial secretary to the Treasury, had told the House of Commons there was no truth in rumours that a large cache of gold had been hidden in the Sussex countryside. He said that he'd confirmed with authorities in the Channel Islands that they had not sent any gold to mainland Britain at the outset of war.

Of course, Jay had told the Commons no such thing. But Pell was a man who ran newspapers based on rumours. I didn't think he'd check with the primary source of such a statement – Hansard's Parliamentary Reports.

A third report headed DETECTOR MAN WAS SEARCHING FOR GOLD was dated to 1962. It explained that one John Acland had been fined ten pounds by magistrates for aggravated trespass. Acland had been using a metal detector on land owned by the Ministry of Defence. Acland claimed he'd heard rumours of buried gold. But the magistrate, Sir Josiah Humphrey JP, had said the government had categorically denied on numerous occasions that a stash of gold was buried in Sussex. Any further gold searches would be met with a prison sentence, Acland was warned.

I put the cuttings back on Mike's desk.

"This is wonderful work. They'd bamboozle me – and I know the paper well."

"Let's hope they fool Coldbody. I had him snooping down here earlier today. I told him that if he didn't clear out of my print hall there'd be one part of his body that wasn't cold. Then a couple of gorillas from publishing – the guys who load the newspapers on the vans – showed up and he skedaddled fast."

I stood up to leave. "Thanks Mike. And please keep these special cuttings to yourself."

His eyes went blank. "What cuttings?" he said.

Back in the newsroom, there was no sign of Coldbody.

No doubt he was in the tearoom making sure people didn't put too much sugar in their coffee.

I picked up my telephone and called Rita Flowers.

When she came on the line, her voice sounded teary.

I said: "Are you all right?"

"When you live with a girl like Pansy, there is no such thing as right. But she's a brave little trooper. And she loved your girlfriend reading to her last night."

"We need another meeting tonight. I'm sure Shirley would love to read some more *Alice in Wonderland* for Pansy."

I asked Rita to contact the scallywags and make sure they were all at the meeting, too.

"Yes, I'll contact Harry, Alec and Fred," she said.

"And tell them to cancel any work they have for tomorrow. I have a plan and we're going to make it work."

"Are you sure? Will it raise the money for Pansy's treatment?"

"Can't fail," I said.

"I wish I could believe that," she said.

The line went dead.

Frank Figgis stepped out of his office and looked around the newsroom. He spotted me and crossed to my desk.

He said: "Have you seen him lately?"

"If you mean Coldbody, I caught him peering over the frosted glass at the subeditors like a common Peeping Tom."

"Didn't he go blind?"

"Coldbody or Peeping Tom?"

"Peeping Tom."

"Yes. As a punishment for spying on the naked Lady Godiva."

Figgis harrumphed. "Pity we can't arrange an unpleasant end for peeping Coldbody."

I shot Figgis a knowing look.

"What's that look supposed to mean?" he said.

"It's a knowing look."

"Knowing about what?"

"Knowing that I'm not going to tell you what you might like to know, but what you shouldn't know because it won't be good for you."

Figgis shook his head slowly. "Damned if I know what you're talking about."

"Let's just say I may not be around for a couple of days. I have something to do."

"If it comes off, will I want to buy you a drink?"

"A double. At least."

Figgis nodded as though he understood. He turned and sloped back to his office.

I reached into my desk drawer and took out the Ordnance Survey map.

The plan to con Quentin Pell and his Sancho Panza, Coldbody, was taking shape in my mind. But a crucial detail was missing.

If I were to convince them that a stash of gold was buried in Sussex, I'd have to come up with a location. It would need to be somewhere that real scallywags, skilled in the arts of deception and evasion, would choose.

I sat back and thought about it.

Carisbrooke Dubbins had told me that scallywags often hid their bunkers in woods. Deirdre Telford had told me that Viscount Rackham had forbidden her to enter the Dark Wood that stretched for miles around his estate.

I wondered whether the Dark Wood could have been used in the war as a scallywag hiding place. Perhaps there were derelict bunkers still there. Perhaps that was why Rackham didn't want anyone visiting the area.

All that added an extra layer of mystery to the story I was spinning. I decided my fictional gold would be buried in the Dark Wood.

I was musing on this when the newsroom doors burst open and Coldbody walked in.

He launched a ground-to-air guided hate-glare missile at me. Then he sat down at one of the sports reporters' desks. He began to leaf through a pile of papers. But I could tell he was sneaking a peek at me.

I pretended to ignore him and unfolded the Ordnance Survey map. I took a pencil and traced a line from Brighton along roads leading to the Dark Wood, north of Washington. Then I chose a spot in the wood where the map seemed to show a rise in the land, and put a small cross. I folded up the map and made a performance of putting it under a lot of old files in the bottom drawer of my desk.

Next I took the three cuttings Mike had created. I tore a small piece of paper off my blotter. I folded one of the cuttings and put the blotter scrap inside the fold. Then I put all three cuttings in an unsealed envelope. If anyone took the cuttings out of the envelope and unfolded them, the blotter scrap would fall out.

I'd know someone had peeked.

I put the envelope alongside the map in the bottom drawer of my desk. Then I locked the drawer and took the key. That wouldn't stop a determined nosey-parker like Coldbody. It wouldn't stop a child. The desk was so old a quick tug opened the drawers whether they were locked or not.

But it was a show that I wanted to keep the stuff private. Coldbody was the kind of guy who would revel in the idea that he'd got one over on me.

I stood up, crossed the office, and gave Coldbody a cheery wave.

Then I pushed through the swing doors and left him to it.

I was willing to bet he wouldn't last five minutes before he decided to rifle my desk.

Shirley and I arrived at Rita Flowers' house shortly after seven that evening.

Rita and the scallywags were sitting around in the front room. Two bars of the electric fire were on. The room felt like a Turkish bath. The scallywags were drinking beer from pint glasses. It didn't look like it was their first of the evening.

Harry Deakin had a line of beer froth along his upper lip. Alec Perkins had sweat beads on his brow. Fred Youngman's face was beetroot red.

They glanced up as Shirley and I walked through the door. They looked at us like a couple of tax inspectors had just stepped into the room.

I said: "Is there a bit of an atmosphere in here or is the room just too hot?"

Rita scowled at me and said: "I'll turn the fire off." She sounded like I'd just asked her to burn the house down.

Shirley said: "Jeez, this place is as hot as a strumpet's doodah."

Rita said: "We don't get many strumpets around here."

There was a clattering from the stairs and Pansy charged into the room. Her face was wreathed in smiles, but she looked pale. She clutched her *Alice in Wonderland* book and jumped up and down. She held her right arm awkwardly, like she didn't want it attached to the rest of her body.

She didn't look like a six-year-girl who would make it to seven.

She shouted: "Shirley, I want you to read me the bit about the Cheshire Cat. Will you? Will you?"

Shirley bent towards Pansy and scooped her up in her arms. "I'm going to read you that and a lot more," she said. "Let's go up to your bedroom."

"Yes," squealed Pansy.

Shirley winked at me as she left the room.

I said: "I think that's reminded us why we're here."

Harry said: "I thought we were here to save your newspaper."

"That's part of the plan – but Pansy is the other part."

Harry said: "Since you were last here, we've had the coppers on our back. Alec, Fred and me think you've shopped us."

So this was why they had faces like Communist commissars at a Kremlin show trial.

"That's ridiculous. Why should I want the police anywhere near you, when we're all going to be part of the same operation?"

"How did they link us to Steve Telford?" Alec asked.

"They will have done what I'd done days ago. They would have found Telford's daughter Deirdre. She would have told them about you."

"We've all been interviewed under caution by some smart-alec 'tec called Tomkins," Fred said.

"We could tell he thought one of us did it," Alec said.

"I don't think we can go on with this," Rita said. "Not with the cops breathing down our backs."

I said: "They won't be breathing down your backs. I know Tomkins. Half the time, he's hardly breathing at all. If he's done his interviews and got nothing from you, he'll go and bother someone else."

I paused and looked around the room.

"The question is: has he got something on one of you?"

Alec drained his beer glass and thumped it down on a table. "I've already told you I was at sea when Telford was despatched."

He made it sound like Telford had been taken to the post office.

I said: "Alone at sea for five hours. What are you? The Ancient Mariner?"

"What do you know about catching fish?"

"Not a lot. I usually catch criminals."

Alec harrumphed.

I turned to Deakin. "You told me the night Telford was killed, you helped the vicar with a scout meeting. But the vicar told me you weren't there that evening."

Deakin shrugged. "So I got the dates confused. Doesn't make me a killer."

"No, but it leaves you without an alibi for the night of the murder."

"An innocent man doesn't need an alibi."

"As it happens, my alibi is private."

"Ah, I see. I hope she was worth it."

Deakin blushed and the other scallywags chuckled. Rita shot Deakin a dirty look.

Youngman looked at me and said: "Don't you start on me. I've been open with you and I've got nothing more to say."

I said: "That's a pity – especially as you're the scallywag who was in touch with Telford most recently. I was hoping you might be able to help me about those cards that were found at Telford's house the night he died."

"What cards?" Youngman said.

"The Jack of spades, king of diamonds, two of clubs, five of hearts, ace of spades."

"Perhaps he was practising his poker. He always used to like to take a few quid off a sucker."

"Not much of a poker hand, was it. Not for someone whose code name was a playing card."

"No, it wasn't." Fred scratched his head. Thought about something. "Perhaps the cards..."

"What about the cards?"

"Nothing. Ace of spades... Ace high. Not much of a poker hand. Don't know what I was thinking about?"

Rita said: "Are you going to talk all night. I thought we were supposed to discuss a plan."

I nodded. "Yes. I've prepared a detailed plan – even got some gold to give it authenticity."

The scallywags leaned forward in their seats.

"So what is the plan?" Deakin said.

"Well, C-day is eleven hundred hours tomorrow."

"Don't you mean D-day?" Alec said.

"No, C is for con. And this is what we'll do..."

Chapter 19

I arrived at the *Chronicle* the following morning before the paper had woken up for a new day.

I needed to have a quiet word with a couple of people before Coldbody appeared on the scene. One was Muriel who operated the telephone switchboard. I left Muriel grinning like she'd just been offered a night of passion with Kirk Douglas. (She was first through the doors of the Regal every time they screened the *Spartacus* movie.)

The other was fellow reporter Phil Bailey, who always turned up early. He had to review the overnight tapes from the Press Association.

When I told Phil what I wanted him to do, he just nodded and said: "I won't even ask what you're up to now."

I sat down at my desk in the newsroom and shoved the key in my desk drawer's lock. It stuck, a sure sign that Coldbody had forced the lock to look at my map and cuttings. It was easy to yank the old drawer open. Not so easy to close it leaving not a trace behind.

I twiddled the key about and finally forced the drawer open. Sure enough, the little piece of blotting paper I'd folded into one of the cuttings had gone. And the map hadn't been folded up correctly. Coldbody merited only an E-grade for his efforts as a spy.

While I was waiting for Coldbody to appear, I put in a call to Ted Wilson at the cop shop.

I said: "I won't be at the morning briefing, Ted. Anything new to report on the Telford murder?"

"Tomkins will announce he expects to make an arrest soon," Ted said.

Tomkins always said that when he hadn't a clue.

"So no progress," I said.

"Who am I to contradict a member of the fourth estate?"

The line went dead.

Coldbody strode into the newsroom two minutes later. He looked around at the bustle as the reporters ramped up their efforts to get the first edition out.

His gaze landed on me – and didn't move on. He was thinking about something.

I knew exactly what was going through his mind. He was wondering how he could ask me what I was doing with cuttings about a gold heist in my desk without revealing he'd seen them.

He strolled over with a nonchalant air. Like someone who's just stopped by to say hello.

He said: "I don't see any copy paper in your typewriter."

I said: "With those powers of observation, it's no wonder you're allowed out on your own."

"You've got me all wrong. I'm not a hard-nosed business type."

"You're really Albert Schweitzer, but heavily disguised so you can go about your good works unmolested."

Coldbody's neck twitched as though he had a crick.

He said: "Working on anything interesting at the moment?"

"Yes. Trying to get rid of you so I can write a story for the paper."

"You could go far here."

"I thought Pell's plan was to kick out the awkward squad so we were as far away as possible."

"Mr Pell understands newspapers. He'll be looking for a news editor to replace that past-it old prune." He thumbed towards Figgis' office.

"If you mean Frank Massingham Figgis, three-time winner of the Newspaper Publishers' Association news editor-of-the-year award, rather than a dried plum, perhaps you'd do him the courtesy to say so."

"No offence intended," Coldbody mumbled. "Just trying to

be friendly."

"I hadn't noticed."

I took copy paper and rolled it into the carriage of my Remington. My way to tell Coldbody this verbal skirmish was over.

Coldbody sloped off and sat down at a desk on the other side of the newsroom. He started to read some documents.

Phil Bailey looked up from his Press Association tapes. I nodded.

He headed out of the newsroom.

In two minutes, I knew what would happen. I sat back to watch the fun.

The phone on Coldbody's desk rang.

BRRIIING!

A loud insistent noise. Coldbody looked up with open-eyed surprise.

He wasn't expecting a call.

BRRIIING!

Coldbody looked around, like he expected someone to leap up and answer it.

Everybody carried on with their work.

BRRIIING!

Come on, answer the bloody phone, Coldbody. My plan wasn't going to work.

BRIIING!

Coldbody's hand reached out and seized the receiver. He lifted it to his ear. Opened his mouth to speak. But already a voice was talking ten-to-the-dozen so he couldn't get a word in.

Phil was at the switchboard making the call. And I'd schooled him in what to say and how to say it: *"Hi, Colin, this is Reggie Todhunter from the* Guernsey Press and Star. *That tip you gave me on the wartime gold story is coming off. It's checking out at this end. But I had to reach you. Heard that a London national has a tip. We gotta move fast. Hey, Colin, are you there… Colin…"*

Coldbody said something. He paused. Somebody else was speaking.

It was Muriel. *"Sorry, caller, a faulty connection. I'll reconnect you."*

Coldbody's phone went dead. Reluctantly, he replaced the receiver. He looked at the phone, like he'd just learnt the secret of the universe.

My phone rang. I lifted the receiver. Phil's voice said: "I could do this for a living. He didn't get a word in, but I could almost taste his greed."

I said: "He's looking at me. I'll pretend I'm talking to Reggie Todhunter. I'm taking notes in Biro in my notebook. I'm pressing hard so that I leave an impression on the page underneath. I shall tear out the page with notes but leave the page with the impression. It will carry details of the meeting place and time when I'm meeting my co-conspirators. We'll give Coldbody time to hide up and watch us."

"You're a crafty devil," Phil said. "I'm glad we're on the same side."

"Me too. I'll tell you more about this when it's all over."

I made an elaborate act of putting down the phone. I made sure the expression on my face was one of exultant expectation. Sir Donald Wolfit couldn't have done it better.

Then I tore the top page out of my notebook, stood up, and hurried from the newsroom.

I was tempted to come back for a curtain call. But I had a tougher performance ahead.

The first sign that my con might not run according to plan came when I met the scallywags.

We were a man short.

Harry Deakin and Alec Perkins were standing next to Harry's battered old Ford Poplar in the car park of the Frankland Arms in Washington village.

But Fred Youngman was missing.

I said: "Where's Fred?"

Harry shrugged. "No idea. I called his cottage. No answer."

Harry was wearing a long black anorak with a deep hood, like a monk's cowl. He had thick cords and a pair of plimsolls.

I looked at Alec. He shook his head.

Alec was wearing a Harris tweed hacking jacket and plus fours tucked into yellow socks at the knee. He had a pair of brown Oxford brogues on his feet.

I said to him: "Where did you get that clobber at short notice?"

Alec grinned: "My great uncle Percival used to get invited to shooting parties. Of course, that was before he bagged one of the gamekeepers. But he'd kept all the gear. Thought I'd better look a bit county set for my role in this."

"Good thinking."

I was pleased that Harry and Alec had entered into the spirit of the con. Fred's absence was doubly annoying. As a result, I would have to play his part. But the show must go on.

Harry said: "Are you certain this Coldbody will turn up?"

"After the way we've teased him this morning, he won't be able to stay away. Even now he'll be lightly rubbing a pencil over the indentations I left in the sheet under which I'd written the exact location of our little pantomime."

"You're a crafty so-and-so," Alec said.

"I'll take that as a compliment."

I looked out over the countryside. On the other side of a cow pasture, lay the western boundary of the Dark Wood. Three miles away, the eastern boundary was close to the edge of Rackham's estate. That boundary was a few hundred yards from the cottage where Deirdre Telford lived.

When I'd visited Deirdre, I'd noticed a bridleway crossed the estate behind her cottage. The ground from the Dark Wood and the cottage sloped downhill towards a narrow country lane. A hedge of buckthorn, hazel and dog rose cut off the lane from the estate. But a five-barred gate provided an ideal vantage point. I'd marked the spot on the Ordnance Survey map and described it in the indented writing I'd left for Coldbody to decipher.

I'd left so many clues, I'd practically provided him with a Thomas Cook tour guide.

Alec would take his position on the bridleway behind the cottage. Meanwhile, Harry and I would sneak through the Dark Wood and emerge on the path near the cottage. That's where the pantomime I'd planned would play out. If I was right, Coldbody would spy on us from behind the five-barred gate.

I turned back to Harry and Alec. "You know what we've got to do – so let's take up our positions."

I looked at my watch.

"But, first, let's synchronise our watches."

It felt good. I'd always wanted to say that.

An hour later, Harry and I were standing on a track which led out of the Dark Wood and past Deirdre's cottage.

I checked my synchronised watch. Alec should have been hidden on the bridleway behind the cottage.

I was carrying two leather pouches – a small red one and a big brown one. The red one was the pouch with the gold sovereigns Gerald Kummer had loaned Shirley. The brown one was at least four times as big and heavier. It contained a pounds-worth of one penny coins – all 240 of them – I'd borrowed from Jeff at Prinny's Pleasure. They clanked in the pouch in a satisfying monetary way, just as a big pouch of sovereigns would.

I tapped Harry on the shoulder. "Let's go – and let's make it convincing."

We strode along the track and stepped out of the Dark Wood into a watery sunshine.

I snuck a glance towards the five-barred gate by the hedge. I couldn't see anyone. But I could just make out the roof of a car parked about ten yards from the gate. That would be Coldbody's transport. He'd be hiding somewhere. And I was willing to bet he'd have binoculars trained on us.

We walked on. Harry wagged a finger at me. He acted like he wanted the pouches. He pointed at them. Made a grab at one.

I pushed him away. This made him angrier. He stopped in his tracks. Stood in front of me and shook his fists.

I scowled and said: "You're doing great. Keep this up and you'll get a part with the Royal Shakespeare Company." I used plenty of angry gestures.

Harry took a swing at me. I ducked and tried to push him away. But Harry wasn't having any of it. He wanted the pouches. He barged into me and I fell on the ground. I dropped the pouches.

Harry grabbed the brown pouch – the biggest one - and took off up the path towards the Dark Wood. I rolled around on the ground and acted the injured party.

I pulled myself to my feet shaking with simulated anger. I was so angry I purposely didn't notice Harry hadn't taken the red pouch. It was lying on the ground. I took off after Harry in simulated fury. But Harry had now disappeared into the Dark Wood. I reached him a few seconds later. He was hiding behind a sycamore tree. I joined him and we peered around its trunk.

One hundred yards down the path, we could see the red pouch. It shone like a traffic light. We couldn't have made it more obvious. For a minute or more, nothing happened.

Then a figure climbed over the five-barred gate.

It was Coldbody.

He hurried up the path towards the red pouch.

He was halfway up the steep path when an imposing figure emerged on the bridleway from behind Deirdre's cottage. Alec in his gamekeeper fancy dress.

He strolled down the bridleway like he had all the time in the world. Coldbody hurried up the footpath.

"Come on, Alec," I said under my breath. He had to reach the pouch first.

But Coldbody was closer. And then he stumbled in a rabbit hole. Sprawled on the ground. Screamed a four-letter word. It wasn't "gosh".

He was only six feet from the pouch.

He lay on the ground and stretched out his arm towards it.

And then a hairy hand reached down from above him and snaffled it.

Coldbody looked up.

Alec looked down. He was holding the pouch.

Coldbody scrambled to his feet.

The argument started.

We knew this would happen. We wanted it to happen. Alec would play Lord Bognor's imperious gamekeeper. He would make it clear the pouch belonged to the estate.

Alec opened the pouch and let the sovereigns spill into his hand. Coldbody moved closer and stared at them. He practically caught fire with greed for them.

Alec was speaking. He'd be telling Coldbody he'd witnessed the fracas on the path a few moments ago. It was regrettable – a result of rumours about gold hidden in the Dark Wood. But the Dark Wood was off-bounds to anyone.

Alec poured the sovereigns back in the pouch. Put the pouch in a pocket in his hacking jacket. Pointed to the five-barred gate.

Coldbody protested. He waved his arms. He shook his fists. He stamped around like a toddler in a tantrum. But it was no use. Alec was adamant.

Coldbody shook his head like a man who couldn't believe his bad luck. He loped off towards the gate. He looked back over his shoulder. But Alec was standing in the middle of the track, hands on hips, like a gamekeeper who'd just seen off a poacher.

The show was over.

Shirley clicked her chopsticks together, trapped a prawn in

black bean sauce, and swiftly lifted it to her mouth.

I poked around in my chicken with mushrooms and bamboo shoots.

We were in the China Garden restaurant, not far from the seafront. It was early evening and the lamps in Preston Street had just come on.

Shirl said: "What's on your mind?"

I gave up on the bamboo shoots and put down my chopsticks.

"It's been today. I have an awful feeling that everything is going wrong. I fear this time I've taken on too much."

I explained how we'd played the scam to give Coldbody a sight of the gold which we'd supposedly dug up in the Dark Wood.

"Sounds like job done to me," Shirley said.

"Sure, but the plan didn't play out as we'd intended. Fred Youngman didn't turn up so I had to take his part. I was supposed to be invisible, watching what happened from the wood."

"But Coldbody saw how it played out anyway."

"Yes, but he wasn't supposed to know that I was directly involved in discovering the gold. Now I'll have to think up a story to explain why I was there."

Shirley put down her chopsticks and had a sip of her jasmine tea.

She said: "You could say Harry Deakin had told you about the gold. But then he double-crossed you and raced off with the brown pouch full of sovereigns. You chased him, but he got away."

"Doesn't explain why I didn't pick up the red pouch."

"You could say, you didn't realise Harry had dropped it."

"That might work, I suppose. But it's not very convincing."

"No worries. Coldbody has seen real gold. That will trump any doubts he had. He's bound to pass the word to Pell. And you've already said that Pell is obsessed with discovering gold."

"You could be right. Coldbody wasn't at the *Chronicle* when I got back there. Figgis thought he'd gone to London."

"What did you do with the sovereigns?" Shirley asked.

"I asked Cedric to take them back to Kummer with your compliments. I told him to tell Kummer that you'd been keeping them safe in your secret place and they were still warm."

Shirley grinned. "You'll blow the poor guy's blood pressure."

I shrugged, picked up my chopsticks and managed to eat a piece of chicken.

I said: "There's another problem – and it could be a big one."

Shirley put her elbows on the table and leaned forward.

"It's Fred Youngman," I said. "I don't know why he didn't turn up – and he's not been at his job in the cemetery today."

"Not well," Shirley said. "Perhaps too nervous to take part in your cockamamie scheme. Can't say I blame him."

"I wonder whether the real reason is that he was Telford's killer."

"You got evidence for that, cobber?"

"Not directly. But of the three scallywags, he's the one who saw Telford not long before he was killed. Deakin and Perkins both had grudges against Telford, but only Youngman stood to lose his job. Telford had been blackmailing him over a stolen gold photo-frame. I think Youngman didn't turn up this morning because, for some reason, he thought he would give himself away."

"Why should he do that? He'd agreed to take part in your scam when you discussed it with the others."

"Cold feet, perhaps. Anyway, I can't rest until I've confronted Youngman with my suspicions."

"When?"

"Now."

"Jeez! I thought this was supposed to be a quiet dinner. You've hardly touched your chicken."

"You stay and eat it."

"In your dreams, buster. I'm coming with you."

It was dark by the time we drew up outside Youngman's cottage in the hamlet of Wiston.

His place was only two miles from the impressive wrought iron gates to Ethelbert House. Youngman's cottage was surrounded by a broken-down picket fence and a gate hanging off one hinge. The rough track of a lane ran up the far side of the cottage and disappeared behind a high hedge.

The cottage had been built out of Sussex flints. It had two small windows, one on each side of a Dutch door.

We stepped round the gate and made our way up a short brick path. The top half of the Dutch door was slightly ajar. I knocked like the rent man had come to call.

I shouted: "Fred, it's Colin Crampton."

No answer.

I pushed the top half of the door open and released the latch on the lower half.

Shirley and I stepped inside.

I called out again. "Fred, are you in?"

In the room to my right a cat mewled.

I stepped into the room. It was a cosy little parlour. There was a Welsh dresser with willow-pattern plates, a faded floral carpet, and dusty velvet curtains at the window.

There was a big fireplace with a soot-blackened mantlepiece. A pack of cards rested on it. Five of the cards had been propped up along the mantle. Jack of spades, king of diamonds, two of clubs, five of hearts, ace of spades.

In front of the fireplace, there was a small sofa.

And I now knew why Fred had not joined Harry Deakin, Alec Perkins and me when we'd conned Coldbody with the sovereigns.

Fred was slumped on the sofa.

His throat had been sliced open and he was very dead.

Chapter 20

Shirley tried to hustle into the room behind me, but I pushed her out.

She didn't need to see Fred to know what had happened. The gut-wrenching musk of congealed blood hung in the air like a rotting vulture.

Shirl said: "Jeez! What is it with you, Colin? You attract dead bodies like a dunny can brings the flies."

I didn't have time to answer that.

A loud crack as wood splintered came from the back of the house. There was a crash as a door flew back on its hinges. Then the sound of running feet pounding on gravel.

"Stay here," I shouted as I hustled along a short corridor to the back of the house.

I burst into a small kitchen. The door to a backyard swung on its hinges. I raced through.

In the lane beyond a hedge, a car engine fired. Its lights flashed onto full beam. Tyres skidded on loose stones as the motor took off.

I ran back through the cottage.

Shouted at Shirl: "The killer's making his getaway. I'm after him in the MGB. Stay here and call the cops."

"Forget it, whacker."

We shot outside. Bundled into the MGB. Took off along the narrow lane in pursuit of the killer.

Up ahead I could see headlights rise and fall over the hedgerows as the killer's car jounced on its springs.

"I think it's a saloon car," I said as the needle on my MGB's speedo swept past sixty. "We should be able to catch it."

"What then, superman?" Shirl said.

"If we can identify the car number plate, the cops will have a vital lead."

The hedgerows closed in on both sides as the lane narrowed. I swung the wheel sharply to the right and the tyres squealed as we took a tight corner.

"Guess you were wrong about Fred being Telford's killer," Shirl said.

"Not necessarily. Both Fred and Telford were scallywags. If they were linked in some other way, perhaps someone out there has a grievance against both of them."

Shirl grabbed my arm. "Mind that fox!"

Its eyes flashed like nightlights as I stepped on the brake. The tyres shrieked on the road.

The animal jumped a hedge and vanished. "One more for the huntsman," I said.

"You've no heart."

"It's eyes and brain I need when we're chasing a killer."

Shirl strained to look through the windscreen.

"I can't see his lights. We've lost him," she shouted.

"No. There he is."

The road had straightened out. A quarter of a mile ahead tail-lights flashed red as the killer's car braked hard.

"From this distance, it looks like a Humber," I said. "If it is, he'll have enough power to outrun us on the straight."

I floored the accelerator and we closed the gap. But the Humber was still a hundred yards ahead.

"Can you read that number plate?" I asked Shirley.

"Who do you think I am? The woman with X-ray eyes?"

"It was the man."

"Which man? *The Man with X-ray Eyes*. A film with Ray Milland. It came out a couple of years ago."

"Jeez! Does that really matter right now? Besides, at this distance I wouldn't need X-ray eyes. I'd need them hanging off the end of telescopes."

Up ahead, the Humber had vanished. I swung the steering wheel right, then left as we sashayed through an S-bend in the lane.

I said: "Matey is making for the main London to Worthing road. If he can reach it, he'll leave us for dead in a Humber."

"He's already left poor Fred dead," Shirl said.

"Sorry! Poor choice of words."

We flashed past a sign showing a junction three hundred yards ahead.

The road opened out as it approached the junction. We could make out the Humber's tail-lights.

"He's stopped at the junction. What's he waiting for?" Shirley said.

"Other traffic to pass, I expect. This might be our chance to catch him."

But as I closed the gap, the tail-lights moved and the Humber swung left onto the main road.

"At least we'll try to catch him," I shouted over the engine noise.

I accelerated so I could take the junction at speed.

I shot out of the side road and heaved the steering wheel left.

A klaxon roared and I glanced in the rear-view mirror.

A forty-ton truck was bearing down on us. It had been just yards from the junction as I'd swung out.

It loomed over the little MGB. Its headlights reflected in my rear-view mirror and dazzled me.

The klaxon roared again. The truck's engine screamed as the driver slammed down a gear and stamped on the brakes.

But there was no way he could avoid hitting us.

It would be like a steamroller crushing a sardine can.

Shirley yelled: "Colin!"

I swung the wheel left as hard as I could. The MGB jolted like it had hit a wall. But we'd just taken off over a high kerb. The front wheels bounced as they landed on the road's soft grass verge. The engine died.

The klaxon roared again as the truck steamed by.

I looked ahead. Half a mile down the road, the tail-lights of the Humber disappeared into the distance.

"We've lost him," I said.

Detective Chief Superintendent Alec Tomkins raised a mug of steaming cocoa to his lips and had a noisy slurp.

I said: "Don't I get any refreshments?"

We were in interview room one at Brighton Police Station. Shirley was next door in interview room two being interviewed by Ted Wilson. No doubt she'd organised coffee and biscuits for herself.

It was two hours since I'd careened off the road and landed on the grass verge. I'd finally manoeuvred the MGB back on to the road. I'd found a phone box and called the duty reporter in the *Chronicle's* newsroom. I'd asked him to send a back-up reporter and photographer to Youngman's cottage.

Then I'd called the cops.

And now I was trying to explain to Tomkins how I'd come upon Youngman's dead body.

Tomkins put down his mug and said: "Two killings both with different *modus operandi,* as we French speakers say."

I said: "*Modus operandi* is Latin. And with two murders it should be *modi operandi.*"

Tomkins flushed. "Don't you try your clever-dick school book learning with me."

"I just thought you'd want to use the correct *mot juste,* as we French speakers say."

"Any more of that and it'll be *bonne nuit* for you in a cell until tomorrow morning."

"*Mon Dieu!*" I said.

Tomkins let out a deep sigh and finished it off with his trademark snarl.

"Let's start again," he said.

"Why not? I'm Colin Crampton, crime reporter on the *Evening*

Chronicle – and I will have a mug of cocoa."

Tomkins eyes glared. He stood up, stamped over to the door, and heaved it open.

A uniformed plod had been stationed outside in case I decided to make a run for it.

Or perhaps he was expecting Tomkins to lam out of the place.

Tomkins said: "Go and get Crampton a mug of cocoa."

A frown appeared on the plod's forehead. "Does he take sugar?"

"I don't know."

"Would he like a biscuit with it?"

"No."

Tomkins slammed the door and returned to his seat.

I'd been thinking while that little pantomime played out. I'd need to be careful when I answered Tomkins' questions. I'd been first on the scene at both Telford's and Youngman's murders. That would give any cop suspicions. Then there was the scam I'd played on Coldbody. As far as I was concerned, that was a side issue and no concern of the cops. But Youngman should have been in on it. I didn't want the cops fabricating a link between the scam and the killing.

Tomkins said: "Why did you and that Australian girlfriend of yours go to Tomkins' cottage?"

"As you'll know because you interviewed him yesterday, Youngman was one of those brave men in the Auxiliary Units."

"A scallywag."

"Yes. I wanted to ask Youngman if he had any thoughts on why his fellow scallywag Telford was killed."

"Had he?"

"I don't know. He was dead when I arrived."

"And the killer was still on the premises?"

"It seems so. We heard a crash as he escaped by the back door. You already know that we chased him in my car but lost him on the main London road."

"And you didn't touch anything at the murder scene?"

"We left it exactly as we found it," I said. "We didn't have time to touch anything as we raced after the killer."

Tomkins scribbled some notes.

I said: "I've got nothing else to tell you."

Tomkins harrumphed. "If only I could believe that. But you can go. For now."

I stood up and the door opened. The plod stepped in with the cocoa.

I said: "Give it to Mr Tomkins. He's expecting a long night."

Shirley was waiting for me in the police station's reception area when I came out.

We swapped notes about our respective interviews as we walked back to the MGB. It seemed that Shirl had had an easier time with Ted Wilson than I with Tomkins. But that figured. Alone in a room with a gorgeous girl late at night – Ted must have thought his luck had changed.

I said: "Did Ted ask you about the playing cards on Youngman's mantlepiece?"

Shirl shook her head.

"Tomkins didn't raise them with me either. Perhaps they haven't realised the cards are the same as the poker hand we saw at Telford's flat."

"Don't they look at the detail?" Shirley asked.

"They do, but they have their own ideas about what's relevant and what isn't."

"What do you think those cards mean?"

"I don't know. But it has to be more than coincidence that the same cards are found in the same order in both places."

We reached the car, climbed in, and flopped down in the seats.

I was exhausted. And I could tell Shirley felt the same.

I said: "Do you mind if I stay at your place tonight? I can't face the Widow."

Shirl shot me a saucy grin. "And I suppose you're so tired, you just want to hit the sack and fall fast asleep?"

"I may need something to relax me before I sleep."

"Then you've come to the right girl. I've just bought a new tin of Horlicks."

Shirl giggled. I giggled. We were both still giggling when we pulled up outside Shirley's flat.

I didn't think I'd be needing the Horlicks.

I was in a sombre mood when I reached the newsroom the following morning.

I wasn't sure how I'd handle Coldbody when he inevitably questioned me about my part in the great gold con. I only hoped he hadn't realised it was a scam.

The newsroom seemed to be running in slow motion when I pushed through the swing doors. The bustle, the energy, the sheer pizzazz which fizzed through the place as the paper approached deadline had evaporated.

Phil Bailey lounged back in his chair with his feet on the desk. He had his head in last night's *Evening Argus*. Perhaps he planned to jump ship to the rival paper before he was pushed. Sally Martin pulled old copy off her spike, screwed it up, and a tossed it in her waste bin. A couple of sports reporters abandoned copy paper in their typewriters and sloped off to the tearoom. At this rate, the paper would need agency copy to fill columns for the midday edition. Unthinkable.

But there was no sign of Coldbody.

Figgis was on the far side of the room deep in conversation with Susan Wheatcroft. Susan was alternately nodding and shaking her head as Figgis unwound what was obviously a tale of woe. Susan stood up and embraced Figgis. Things must be bad. Susan was a generous girl who'd embrace most men given half the chance. But wrapping her arms around Figgis deserved a medal.

Figgis turned away from Susan and saw me. He pranced across the newsroom.

He said: "Come into my office."

"Bad news?" I asked.

"The worst."

He pushed open his door and slumped down in the chair behind his desk. He reached for his ciggies, shook out a Woodbine, and looked at it.

I said: "You look like a man who's lost the will to live."

He shoved the fag back in the packet. "What's the point?" he said. "The quacks say they kill you."

"A man like you isn't normally put off by unassailable medical evidence. You walk on the wild side."

"But the cancer sticks take time to kill you. I just want to die now."

"Pope hasn't questioned your expenses again?"

"It's worse than that. I've been told I'm fired when Pell takes over."

"It can't be all bad. Early retirement. Slippers, pipe and feet up in front of the telly. Then there'd be days out with Mrs Figgis."

Figgis reached for the Woodbines. "Perhaps I will finish this packet after all. It gets worse."

"What gets worse?"

Figgis struck a Swan Vesta on the side of the desk and lit his coffin nail.

"Pell is making Coldbody news editor. And it turns out the only job he's ever had in journalism was picture editor on one of Pell's girly magazines."

"And I suppose he thinks that will help him keep abreast of the news," I said.

Figgis harrumphed. "Not hard to see what will happen to the *Chronicle's* news coverage when Pell's in charge."

"It will go tits up," I said.

Figgis harrumphed again.

"We have to stop this," I said.

"I don't see what we can do."

I glanced out of the window at the Pavilion Gardens. A couple of Darby and Joan types were strolling along one of the paths towards the refreshment kiosk. It didn't seem like a future for Frank and Esme Figgis.

I said: "It might not happen."

"If you mean Pell's takeover, it already has. He has the promissory note."

"What if there was a way to stop it?"

Figgis stopped puffing on his fag. The smoke cleared and I could see his face. His hard marble eyes bored into me.

"What do you know?" he asked.

"Something it's best you don't know. You've trusted me in the past."

"I suppose so. What have I got to lose?"

I nodded towards the Woodbines on his desk.

Figgis shrugged. "I suppose so." He stubbed out his dog-end and tossed it in his waste bin. Then followed it with the rest of the packet.

I stood up to leave. Figgis followed me to the door. He had a kind of shame-faced look on.

"If I don't see you again, well, we've landed some great stories together," he said. "It's been an… education."

He held out his hand and I shook it.

His eyes were watery – perhaps the cigarette smoke. He turned back to his desk looking hunched and defeated.

I said: "Whatever happens, Frank, it's been the experience of a lifetime to work with you."

I meant what I said. I just wished my voice hadn't cracked when I'd said it.

I opened the door and stepped out.

The first person I saw when I walked back into the newsroom

was Coldbody.

He was over by my desk and rifling through a pile of papers on top of it.

I walked over to him and said: "Whatever you're looking for, you won't find it there, Coldbody."

He turned around with a vulpine grin on his face.

"I know that. I was just passing the time until you turned up."

"Well, pass it somewhere else. Like Timbuctoo."

"You and I ought to get along. Now that we'll be working together."

"Yes, I heard about your proposed promotion. No doubt years in the tits-and-bums business has given you a nose for news."

"Pell's newspapers aren't all tits and bums. We'll need top reporters who can land scoops. Guys like you."

"Sorry, I'd rather be covering parish councils in the Isle of Skye."

Coldbody nodded like a guy who knew he had an ace up his sleeve and had decided the moment had come to play it.

But he hadn't mentioned seeing me yesterday before he'd tried to grab the red gold pouch. He would've assumed I hadn't seen him. I guess he didn't want to admit he was a spy.

He said: "Quentin Pell wants to meet you. In fact, he insists on it."

"Sure, let me know the date of his funeral and I'll be there wearing a party hat."

"You don't want to be too cocky. You won't be the only one to regret it, if you don't meet Pell."

I gave Coldbody a killer look. A few daggers, followed by a machete or two, with a hara-kiri sword thrown in for good measure.

"What do you mean by that?" I asked.

"Just that there's a lot riding on you meeting Pell. Good things could happen. Or bad."

"When does Pell want to meet?"

"Tonight. Eight o'clock. The Clansfield Club in London. Don't be late."

Coldbody turned to leave. Looked back over his shoulder.

"By the way, Quentin enjoys a friendly game of poker. I hope you play."

Chapter 21

Archie Stamford's jaw hung slack, his eyes popped, and his nostrils flared as he leaned over the table.

"You what?" he exclaimed.

"We want to learn how to cheat at poker," I said. "A crash course."

Shirley and I were in the Lyons tea shop in The Strand, less than one hundred yards from Trafalgar Square. As usual, the pigeons in the square were giving Admiral Lord Nelson on his column a hard time.

After Coldbody had left me in the newsroom, I'd felt like a First World War Tommy who'd just seen an unexploded hand grenade lobbed into his trench. Frankly, the idea of meeting Quentin Pell worried me. The suggestion I should play him at poker scared me stiff.

I'd called Stamford and he'd agreed to meet. Then I'd contacted Shirley and explained what had happened. I told her I'd be driving to London for the evening.

She'd said: "Pick me up before you leave, buster. Jeez! Without me to watch your back, you'll lose your shirt on the first hand."

So here we were. Early afternoon in London. Sitting in front of three cups of tepid tea and stale currant buns.

I said: "When you scarpered from the Clansfield Club, Archie, I thought you were going to contact me."

Stamford looked shamefaced. "It's been a difficult time," he said. "I have a feeling Pell is on to me. I had to leave town for a few days to let the situation cool."

"You regard Pell as a threat?" I asked.

"The deadliest," Archie said. "He killed my closest friend. The friend who'd saved my life during the war when we were fighting for King and country in Burma."

"Jeez! That's terrible," Shirley said. "Why isn't Pell in jail?"

"Because when Pell kills someone who stands in his way, he makes sure his fingerprints are nowhere near the crime."

"Yes, I heard his partner died when the gold mine tunnel's roof collapsed," I said. "Was that your friend?"

Archie nodded. "Slim Richards. But it wasn't an accident."

"How did Slim get involved with a rat like Pell?" Shirley asked.

"Slim was the finest man I ever knew," Archie said. "But too trusting. He decided to live in Australia after the war. He'd inherited a little family money – enough for him to be independent in life. Slim was conned out of it by Pell for that mine. Slim saved my life. But I couldn't save his. Since Slim's death, I've made it my mission in life to bring Pell down."

"Perhaps this is the opportunity you've been waiting for," I said.

"Think you can beat him at poker?" Archie asked.

"Why not? I used to play it at school, sometimes at the back of the class in maths lessons. I reckon I could make a fair fist of it. And if I knew how to cheat, I'd have an extra chance."

Stamford leaned back and shook his head in disbelief. "You don't understand. Pell is a master of the cheat. He invented some of them. It'll take more than you to bring him down."

"Sure," Shirley said. "It'll take me, too."

Stamford shrugged. "It's your funeral. And you'll know from your previous visit to the Clansfield, that might not be a metaphor."

"Last time we made the chumps look like bozos," Shirley said.

"This is this time," Stamford said. "And you and Pell will be centre stage. Cheat him at poker? I can't believe it. You'll lose. And even if you win, he'll flatten you. I take it you know the rules of poker. Five card stud poker."

I nodded. "It's what we played at school. Starts with each player getting one card dealt face up and one face down, the hole card."

"Yes, then everyone lays their bets before another card is dealt to each player face up."

"That's called the third street and there's another round of betting," I said.

"Right. And then two more cards are dealt – the fourth and fifth streets – with betting after each round," Archie explained. "And after the fifth street, the last player to bet shows his hole card. If it isn't you, and you know you've lost, you can muck your cards. Otherwise, you show it and scoop the pot. What am I saying? You won't get within touching distance of scooping a Pell pot."

"We will if we cheat," I said. "So how do we do it?"

"First, let's get fresh tea and some of their fruit cake. It's better than these stale buns."

I signalled to a nippy who came over and took our order.

When the nippy had scurried off with our used crocks, Stamford leaned forward.

"What you have to remember is that there's nothing you can teach Pell about dirty play. So your problem becomes doubly difficult. It's not a question of how you cheat – but how you cheat a cheat."

Shirley and I exchanged worried glances.

Archie said: "Pell has different ways to cheat, depending on who he wants to swindle. The night we saw him at work he was using the old collusion technique. I could see the little signs he made – a scratch of the ear, a twitch of an eyebrow – which he used to signal to the two players who were in it with him."

"And they were both gulling the fourth guy?" I asked.

"That's right. He lost a packet. From what you've told me I don't think Pell will use that technique with you."

"Why not?"

"I've studied this scumbag. I know how he works. Sometimes he cheats a mug because he wants to take him down. But sometimes it's because he wants something from the guy. If he can get you in a position where you have to give him what he wants, he's beaten you."

"And you think he'll try that trick with me?"

"That's my reading of the situation. But I could be wrong."

Or not, I thought. Pell would want me to tell him what I knew about the gold. His plan would be to beat me so badly I had no alternative but to reveal every detail.

The nippy returned with a fresh pot of tea and three hearty lumps of fruit cake. We stopped talking while she laid out the cups and saucers. I slipped her a quid and told her to keep the change.

Stamford reached for his cake and took a large bite.

A few crumbs sprayed out as he said: "I think Pell will play you head-to-head. No other players at the table."

I said: "I brought one hundred pounds with me."

"That's loose change to Pell. He'll laugh at stake money that tiny."

"It was all I could screw out of the cash office at the *Chronicle* before we came. And I had to make all kinds of promises to get it."

"We'll come back to that problem," Stamford said. "I think as he's playing one-on-one, he'll use a marked deck."

"You've lost me already, cobber," Shirley said.

"You know that the backs of playing cards have elaborate patterns. Cheats introduce tiny changes to those patterns which identify each card."

"Surely other players would spot them," I said.

"That's not easy if it's done very subtly. Pell is a superstitious type and always plays with a deck of black-backed Bicycle playing cards with the Rider Back design. The centre piece shows a rider on a bike. And the rest of the design consists of lots of whirls, twirls, circles, triangles and other shapes. The key for the card marker is the abstract graphic of a rose's petals down in the bottom left-hand corner of each card. There's a centre circle which represents the flower's stamen. There are eight little teardrop shaped blobs around it that represent the petals. The marker carefully alters the shape of one of those petals to represent a card. For example, in Pell's marked deck, the bottom petal represents a two card. Then he moves clockwise around the petals to cover the three, four, five and so on up to nine cards."

"But what about the ten, aces and picture cards?" I asked.

"That's where the scheme is clever. If the shape of the centre circle is slightly altered together with one of the petals, it's possible to represent those cards. So the centre plus the two petal becomes a ten, the centre plus the three petal a Jack, and so on. If there's no change to the centre circle or a petal, the card is an ace."

"But I don't see how you tell which suit the card's in," Shirley said.

Stamford had another bite of his fruit cake and said: "For that you move a little up and to the left of the rose. There's a whirl in the design of the card which encompasses five small triangles. From right to left, Pell has marked the first four in the order spades, hearts, clubs, diamonds."

"Jeez! We can't mark a pack like that in time for tonight," Shirley said.

"No, and if you did, Pell would notice," Stamford said. "Remember, he's not just an expert poker player, he's an expert cheat, too. But I have got a marked pack of cards."

"You've used it on Pell?" I asked.

Stamford pulled a rueful moue. "Never had the chance, more's the pity. But I'd like to see you take him down with it."

"But you just said he'd spot a marked deck for a ringer right away," Shirley said.

"Not this one. I was watching Pell play at the Clansfield one night, while pretending to mind my own business. There was a misdeal. The dealer, a cocky youngster, flicked a card across the table. It skidded on the others and flew onto the floor. Landed right at my feet. Four of diamonds. Naturally, I'd picked it up even before the player had realised where it'd gone. Turned it over. Spotted the marking design scheme right away. I bought an identical pack of the Bicycle cards and had it doctored by a specialist artist to look like Pell's pack."

"Specialist artist?" queried Shirley.

"He means forger," I said.

"Yes, if you must, a forger," Stamford said. "And a good one. Since then, I've played patience with the cards dozens of times so they have the worn feel of Pell's marked deck. I'd bet you the ace of spades to the Kohinoor diamond, he'd never spot it."

"Wait a minute," I said. "If you've marked your deck the same as Pell's he can still read it."

"I've used the same physical marks on the backs of the cards so that Pell would think he's playing with his own doctored deck. But most of my markings represent different cards to Pell's. Instead of the bottom petal on the rose being a two card, it's a nine. The other numbers move in descending order clockwise. I've changed the order of the picture cards, too. And the suits in the triangles. But thirteen of the cards in my deck have the same markings as Pell's. He can read them as easily as his own. I reckon that will confuse him enough to keep him in a game for a dozen hands if you're playing stud poker. Of course, if you're going to use my deck, you'll need to learn my marking system. I can teach you now."

"Just a minute," Shirley said. "You bozos are missing the big one. How do we get Archie's doctored deck into Pell's hands without him realising?"

"We'll need a distraction."

"Yeah! But you guys are too obvious. I think you better leave that to me."

Shirl stood up.

"Where are you going?" I asked.

"Shopping. When a Sheila wants the big eye on her, she needs to look as fab as a sunrise over Ayers Rock."

The three of us met later in a pub called the Blind Beggar not far from the Clansfield Club.

Shirley was the last to arrive. Heads turned as she walked into the bar. She was wearing a jumpsuit in shimmering black silk. It had a plunging v-neckline and hugged her figure like a second skin. She'd looped the strap of her handbag over her left shoulder.

I said: "You look sensational."

Shirley said: "That's the intention, big boy. You see what happened when I walked into the room? Some guys' eyes popped like they were on springs. Some guys drooled like their tongues had hit the floor. If you want to cause a distraction you gotta distract."

Stamford's eyes goggled like they wanted to leap out of their sockets.

He said: "I had my doubts about whether we could switch the decks of cards. But now I think it might work."

He produced a deck of cards from his pocket. Lifted them to his lips and kissed the top card.

"This is my special marked deck," he said. "Took days of work and cost me a packet. If we use it, I guess we'll never see it again. But if it brings Pell low, it's worth it."

Stamford turned to me: "Are you sure you've learnt the marking code?"

I nodded. "There's logic to it and it's easy to remember."

He said: "I only hope so. The best time to switch the deck will be when Pell has produced his marked cards at the beginning of the game. You should ask to inspect them. Pell won't turn a hair at that. Most experienced poker players expect it. While you're inspecting his deck, Shirley will have to produce the distraction of a lifetime. You slip Pell's cards into your right pocket, and whip out the replacement deck from your left. You get Pell's attention as quickly as possible after that so he doesn't suspect a switch has taken place."

He handed me the cards. I put them in my pocket.

My heart was beating like a steam-hammer. My mouth felt as dry as a dust-bowl. This wasn't going to be easy to pull off. And the consequences of fouling up didn't bear thinking about.

I asked Shirley: "How are you going to distract Pell? You'll need to have the eyes of everyone in the room on you."

Shirl grinned. "You leave that to me. It'll be like Elizabeth Taylor just rode into the room stark naked on a unicycle."

Stamford fidgeted with his tie. Glanced at his watch.

"I think I should go. Best if I arrive at the club before you. Give me fifteen minutes."

"Good luck," I said.

"See ya!" Shirl said.

Stamford gave us a cheery wave and disappeared through the door.

Shirley turned to me. "I'm frightened," she said.

"Me too," I said.

Shirley and I stepped into the entrance lobby of the Clansfield Club a quarter of an hour later.

I felt like a squadron of butterflies were performing aerial acrobatics in my stomach.

Shirl gripped my hand like her life depended on it.

Inside the lobby, Hilary, the doorman, gave us a leery look.

"Didn't expect to see you two back here," he said. "But Mr Pell says you're to be welcomed like old friends. For the time being. Evelyn will take you in."

Evelyn led us through the bar towards the poker room, like a hangman leading his victims to the scaffold.

Inside the room, a small knot of people was standing round

one of the card tables. The knot parted and a man with thinning hair, a full beard, and a nose that was God's gift to cartoonists emerged. He was the man I'd watched playing poker on my first visit to the club.

He was dressed in a royal-blue dinner jacket and bow-tie. He had a scarlet cummerbund around his waist. He wore a dress shirt which gleamed white. You practically needed sunglasses to look at it.

He strode towards us with confident steps.

He walked up to me stuck out his hand and said: "Quentin Pell. I'm your new boss."

I said: "Be careful what you wish for."

"I am always careful, Mr Crampton. It is why I have everything I want."

"You don't have the *Evening Chronicle*."

"Not yet, perhaps. But in a few days…"

"A lot can happen in a few days."

"A lot can happen in one evening – as you are about to discover."

"Is that a threat or a promise?"

"Consider it a prediction."

Shirley stepped forward and Pell's gaze rested upon her.

"Good to meet a fellow Oz so far from home," she said.

"Why, G'day," Pell said, a bit unconvincingly. "Where do you hail from?"

"The proud city of Adelaide."

Pell ogled her up and down like she was a side of beef hanging in a butcher's window.

Shirl caught the look.

She eyed him and said: "So you're a guy who gets off on a good view."

Pell gave an embarrassed cough.

Shirl said: "Next time try the view from the top of the Sydney Harbour bridge."

Pell said hurriedly: "Would you like some champagne?"

Shirl said: "Sure. There's a waiter over there. Please fetch me a glass."

Pell pursed his lips in anger, but gained control. He stomped over to the waiter and returned with two glasses. He handed one to each of us.

We sipped. It was refreshingly cool. Probably the only thing that was in the place.

The knot of hangers-on had dispersed around the room. I noticed that Stamford was among them. He was talking to a woman in a gold lamé dress.

Pell moved closer to me and said: "People find it's more profitable to work with me than against me."

I said: "That sounds like a job offer."

"I like a man who spots an opportunity."

"And I like a man who says what's on his mind. Why am I here, Pell?"

"You're working on a story," he said.

"You don't miss much. I'm always working on a story."

"This is a story that has a special interest to me."

I said: "Is it a story about gold?"

"How do you know that?"

"Because I'm a good journalist. I do my research. And I know everything about you."

For an instant, Pell's eyes clouded with worry. No, it was fear. But then they cleared. Became confident. Even defiant.

He said: "Nobody knows everything about me."

I said: "I know you're a failed gold miner. Not exactly a Forty-niner. But then you were working a mine in Australia. And you didn't have a Clementine."

"I never fail," Pell said. "And you're going to tell me everything I want to know about the gold seized by the scallywags."

Coldbody had evidently fallen for the scam and briefed Pell that the gold story was true.

"Why should I help you to a king's ransom in gold?"

"Because I can help you to save a young girl's life."

That had my attention. I hadn't realised that Coldbody knew about the plan to raise money for Pansy's treatment. That was a secret reserved to a small circle. Could there have been a careless word somewhere?

I said: "Yes, I want to raise ten thousand pounds to save a girl from dying of a rare form of cancer."

Pell grinned: "So here's the deal. We play a round of poker. I'll stake you with five thousand pounds. I'll start the game with the same sum. You win my five thousand and you'll have ten thousand for Pansy."

"And what if I lose?"

"Then you tell me every secret you know about the gold. And I do mean every secret."

I said: "That's not how I see this game."

Pell scowled. He wasn't used to someone who contradicted him. He'd spent his life surrounded by yes-men, not awkward customers with their own demands.

He said: "And how do you see it?"

"If I win the ten thousand pounds, I hand you the money and you return the promissory note you won from Viscount Rackham."

"But then you don't have the money for your charity child."

"Watch your mouth, whacker," Shirley said.

I said: "With the promissory note, I have other plans to raise the money for Pansy."

"And if you lose?"

"Then I'll tell you what I know about the gold."

I looked at Shirl. She shrugged. "You can do it," she said.

With Stamford's marked cards, perhaps I could. But now I was face-to-face with the opportunity, it seemed like a huge risk.

I drained my champagne while Pell thought about it.

"Okay," Pell said. "We'll do it your way. You have a deal. And a game of poker."

Chapter 22

Pell moved towards a card table with the look of a wolf bearing down on a lonely lamb.

He sat down at the table and produced a pack of cards from his pocket. He shuffled them a couple of times. Split the pack and riffled the cards together. He looked like a magician practising a trick. I half expected him to produce the ace of diamonds from his sleeve.

I sat at the table opposite Pell.

The people in the room realised something was about to happen. They crowded around the table eager for the contest.

Hilary and Evelyn shouldered their way to the front of the crowd.

I glanced anxiously at Shirley.

She was still holding her glass of champagne. She hadn't drunk most of it.

I said: "Don't I get to shuffle the cards before we play, Pell?"

He grinned. "Sure. This is a straight game. All fair and square."

Like hell it was.

He handed over the cards and I pretended to fumble a shuffle. A titter of amusement ran around the crowd. They were going to enjoy a novice beaten silly by a poker pro.

I glanced again at Shirley. This was the moment she was supposed to provide a diversion so I could swap decks. But there was no chance I could do that. Pell's eyes bore into me. And there were too many onlookers around the table.

Shirley put her glass of champagne on the card table. She reached into her handbag and pulled out a perfume spray.

She puffed a little behind each ear.

Hilary was standing right behind her. He coughed as the stray perfume misted in his face.

"A girl's gotta be at her bonzer best when she backs her guy," she announced to the crowd.

She stuck out her breasts. An impressive cleavage showed above the plunging v-neckline of the jumpsuit.

She sprayed some perfume towards it. A tiny mist appeared in front of her.

She nudged up closer to Hilary.

"*Owwww!*" she shrieked. She spun round and faced Hilary. "You pinched my bum."

Hilary's face clouded with confusion. He opened his mouth but no words came out.

Shirl stepped back and swung her arm to slap his face.

But her backswing sent her champagne glass flying. The vintage bubbly fizzed over the table and drained into Pell's lap.

He leapt up as a wet patch appeared on his trousers.

I cheered inwardly. Well played, Shirl!

Pell was hopping around like a man who'd just peed in his pants.

Shirl looked at him horrified. She even managed to blush. What a girl!

She produced a handkerchief from her handbag, knelt down, and started to mop furiously at Pell's wet patch.

Everyone's eyes were on Shirley and Pell. He was grinning like a guy who's just lost a race but discovered he's won first prize anyway.

He tried to brush Shirley away. But she wasn't having any of it.

"Hold still, big boy," she said. Rubbed away at the patch.

"My word, you are a big boy," Shirl announced to the crowd.

Pell had a goofy grin on his face. All eyes were on him. For the wrong reason.

Hilary shouted. "I never pinched her bum, boss."

"Shut up, you ape," Pell snapped.

He switched his attention back to me.

"What are you smiling at?" he said.

"Do you want to change your trousers before we play?" I asked.

"No, but we'll need to move to another table. The green baize on this one is soaked."

I gave the deck of cards a random shuffle.

"Hey, hand over those cards," Pell demanded.

I leant across the table and Pell grabbed them from my hand.

He moved away, held them up to his face and studied the back more closely than was needed to determine he had a pack of playing cards in his hand.

"Are you satisfied?" I asked.

"Yeah!"

"Me too."

"Let's play," he said.

"Can't wait," I said.

Pell turned his back and I flashed a quick wink at Shirley.

I sat at the card table with five thousand pounds worth of poker chips in front of me.

I felt richer than I'd ever felt in my life.

And more nervous. Those butterflies were flying circuits and bumps in my stomach.

The room had fallen silent. There was a crush of bodies around the table. Hilary and Evelyn stood on either side of Pell's chair. Shirley was beside mine.

Pell and I had cut cards for dealer. His ten of clubs beat my seven of hearts.

Suited me. I'm no card dealer and even if Pell tried a trick deal – bottom card or second from top in the pack – I'd know what the card was because of Archie's marking system.

Archie had taken an inconspicuous place at the back of the crowd.

I knew that if I was to win Pell's five grand, I'd need to do it quickly. He'd be baffled when he discovered his card marking system wasn't working.

Once or twice he might put it down to misreading the marks. Archie's clever ploy of aligning thirteen cards in his doctored deck with Pell's system would add to confusion. It would keep Pell guessing. But not for ever.

The fact we were playing stud poker acted in my favour. In each five-card hand only one card would be face down. So opportunities to read marked cards were limited. Even so, I couldn't be confident I'd fool Pell for more than half a dozen hands.

Pell shuffled, then riffled, the cards again. He dealt the hole cards.

I peeked at mine. Queen of hearts. But Archie's mark would make Pell think it was the Jack of clubs. I leant forward – all casual like I was making myself more comfortable – and looked at Pell's hole card. King of spades. Useful. It was one of the cards in Archie's pack where the marks coincided with Pell's crooked deck.

Pell dealt the first face-up cards. Nine of diamonds for me. Four of hearts for him.

On the basis of the first two cards, my hand was going nowhere. But neither was Pell's. As his four of hearts was lower than my nine of diamonds, he had to open the betting.

He picked up some chips and tossed them into the centre of the table, like they were bread-crumbs.

"Two hundred pounds," he said.

I matched him.

He dealt the third street cards. Ten of spades for me. Six of spades for him. I was pleased he wasn't taking any notice of the back markings. But why should he? The street cards were all dealt face-up anyway.

My ten of spades outranked his six of spades so I got to bet first. I couldn't see my hand making much, but I tossed in another two hundred pounds. Pell matched it, but didn't raise.

Pell dealt the fourth street. Jack of clubs for me. King of diamonds for him. His king outranked my Jack so he bet first. He looked at my hand. Stared hard again at the hole card. Pell thought I had a pair of Jacks. But he knew he had a pair of kings.

He tossed five hundred pounds into the pot. I shrugged. I had a run of four cards – nine, ten, Jack, queen. If I got lucky with my fifth card, I could have a straight – a run of five cards in any suit. I needed an eight or a king. But Pell already had two of the kings. So there were six cards among the forty-four left in the deck that would give me a straight – a little more than a seven to one shot. What the hell!

I tossed in five hundred to match Pell.

"Brave play," he said. "You must know something I don't."

"What I know that you don't would fill *Encyclopaedia Britannica*," I said.

I sensed tension was rising among the onlookers. They shuffled their feet. Nudged one another knowingly. Whispered comments to each other.

Pell said: "This is where it all counts."

He dealt the fifth street cards. Eight of spades for me. (A silent hooray!) Six of diamonds for Pell.

He grinned. He had two pairs, kings and sixes. He could see that I had four cards of a straight – eight, nine, ten and Jack. But he didn't know I had the queen to make it. He thought I had only a pair of Jacks.

Pell's four face-up cards had a pair of sixes against Jack high in mine, so he started the betting.

He grabbed a handful of chips and slung them into the middle of the table.

"One thousand pounds."

And why not? He was a dead cert to make easy money against a mug. *Moi*.

I made a play of looking like I wasn't sure what to do. I peeked again at my hole card.

Made my hand shake as I counted out one thousand pounds. Tossed them onto the pile in the pot.

Flipped over my hole card.

I said: "A straight."

Pell's eyes popped. His brow furrowed in confusion. His hand had reached for his own hole card. Now it drew back.

"Beats me," he said. He mucked his cards together and added them to the bottom of the deck.

I reached into the centre of the table and scooped the chips towards me.

Shirley gave me a reassuring pat on the shoulder.

I looked up at her. "Beginner's luck."

First hand over - and I was up one thousand nine hundred pounds.

Half an hour later I was sitting at the table with nine thousand pounds worth of chips in front of me.

And I was worried.

With the exception of one hand, Pell had lost consistently. The phony markings on Archie's cards had gulled Pell into making lavish bets.

We'd completed seven hands. I'd expected Pell to realise he'd been played for a sucker after three or four hands at the most. There were only so many times he could write off a wrong call as misreading the marked cards.

He'd just dealt the street. His four face-up cards were a pair of fours, a queen and a seven.

I had a pair of Jacks, a king and a three. My hole card was the king of diamonds. The marks on the back told Pell it was the ten of spades.

I said: "I'll bet one thousand pounds. It's your last chance to stay in the game, Pell."

He grinned. Peeked at his hole card again.

"I might just do that," he said. He pushed his remaining chips into the pot.

He turned over his hole card. "Two pairs, queens high," he said.

I flipped my hole card. "Two pairs, kings high," I said.

Pell stared at the cards like he was looking at some dusty manuscript from the past. He didn't seem to understand what had happened.

"You're looking at a Jack and a king. Two of them," I said.

Pell turned his gaze on me. It wasn't friendly.

He said: "What did you say?"

"Jack King. Twice. Just my little joke. Not often I walk away with ten thousand pounds. But you get the money back when you hand me the promissory note."

Pell looked like a man fighting a demon inside himself. His face contorted with conflicting emotions. Confusion… anger… greed…

Finally, fear.

He turned to Hilary. "Hey, you ape, bring me a scotch. Make it the largest this side of the Hebrides."

Pell switched his attention back to me. I scooped the chips from the pot into my pile.

Pell took a deep breath and made a visible effort to get his emotions under control.

He turned on a smile as bright as limelight. As fake as a con-man's promise.

"Well, newcomer, you played me like a didgeridoo. Guess I have to hand over that promissory note. We'll do it in Hector Clansfield's office."

He stood up and withdrew the note from an inside pocket. It was a single sheet of paper. He waved it about a bit. There was a ripple of applause from the crowd. He reminded me of old newsreels of Neville Chamberlain arriving back from his meeting with Hitler and waving his paper that promised "peace with honour".

That ended badly.

I had a sick feeling Pell's pledge was just as worthless. I was about to find out.

We assembled in Clansfield's office like a party of mourners who'd just attended the funeral of someone they hated.

Clansfield sat behind his continent-sized desk and scowled. Pell strode over to the drinks cabinet and poured himself a scotch. Shirley and I shuffled from foot to foot in front of the sofa. I held a cloth bag with ten thousand pounds of Clansfield Club chips in it.

Hilary and Evelyn, I was disturbed to note, had taken up sentry guard positions on either side of the door.

The fake bonhomie Pell flaunted in the poker room had vanished. The smile had disappeared. He knocked back the scotch and poured himself another one.

Clansfield said with heavy irony: "That's a twenty-year-old Glenlivet single malt you're drinking."

Pell said without irony: "I wouldn't be drinking it if it were monkey's piss."

Clansfield scowled at him.

I held up my bag of chips.

I stepped towards Pell. "I'll also take that promissory note in exchange for these," I said.

Pell fired a death look at me and said: "You can kiss goodbye to the promissory note – and any more lip from you and you can kiss goodbye to your arse, too."

"You're a bad loser," Shirl said. "I thought you'd whinge like a dingo with its donga caught in a trap."

Pell's lip curled into a sneer. "You're gonna find out there are only two losers around here."

"Not us," I said.

Pell downed another scotch.

He said: "I know about your scam. I know how you planned to make a fool of me over the wartime gold. Lure me into a trap – and then humiliate me, wasn't it? I'm speechless a pair of losers like you could ever think you'd outwit me."

That had my attention. For all the wrong reasons. I'd been certain we'd fooled Coldbody. He'd passed along what he knew to Pell. There were no loose ends in the gold scam. How the hell had Pell found out about it?

Shirley and I exchanged worried glances.

I said: "You've got it all wrong."

"No, you've got it all wrong, smart-arse," Pell bellowed. "And now you're gonna pay the price. And you're gonna start by giving me my ten grand back."

I clung on to the cloth bag.

Pell pointed at one of the bouncers.

"You, ape, take that bag off him."

"My name ain't ape."

"What is it, then?"

"Evelyn."

"Jeez! That's a frigging girl's name," Pell said.

"What about Evelyn Waugh?" I asked.

"What about her?" Pell asked.

"His first name was Arthur," I said.

Clansfield's fist hammered down on his desk. The glass bottles in his inkstand rattled.

"For heaven's sake, Evelyn, Arthur, whatever your name is. Get the cloth bag and give it to Pell."

Evelyn walked towards me.

Shirley moved between us.

She faced up to Evelyn. "How'd you like to end the evening with a knee in the nuts?"

Evelyn's brow knitted in confusion. He looked towards Clansfield.

"I only got one set of nuts, boss."

"Then get Hilary to help you. Then you'll have two sets."

"But she's got two knees, boss."

"She can't use them both at the same time, you moron. She'll fall over."

Hilary was already on the move. There was no point in fighting them. We weren't going to win this battle. I handed over the cloth bag.

Evelyn handed it to Pell. He shook it so the chips rattled.

Shirl said: "You're a rat. That money was going to buy the best medical treatment to save a young girl's life."

Pell grinned. "You know you've just given me an idea. I think I'll donate the money to her. When I take control of the *Chronicle*, the paper can run a front-page story about it. Paper's new proprietor saves a young girl's life. You can't pay for publicity like that. I'll be the town's hero."

I felt sick to my stomach. Pell was just the kind of low-life to pull a crude stunt like that.

I said: "I won that money fair and square."

Pell laughed. "Using marked cards. Don't think you can get that past me. In fact, I think we'll run another story in the *Chronicle* – cheating reporter sacked for swindling philanthropist."

I said: "You can't prove I used marked cards."

Pell signalled to Hilary. I hadn't noticed that he'd moved up behind me. He grabbed my arm with one hand and reached into my jacket pocket with the other.

His hand came out of the pocket holding Pell's marked deck. The one I'd swapped for Archie's.

I made a grab for the cards and one slipped out of the deck.

It fluttered to the floor and lay in the middle of Clansfield's fancy Persian rug.

The ace of spades.

Pell gasped. His hand flew involuntarily to his mouth. His eyes shifted from side to side like a guy who's just had a shock.

We all heard the gasp and stared at him.

A silence fell on the room. We shifted our gaze and looked at the card.

Pell was transfixed by it. Like it was the Black Spot – the warning in *Treasure Island* that death stalked the doomed recipient.

I said to him: "Aren't you going to pick it up?"

He opened his mouth. Tried to say something. But no words came out.

What was going on here? It wasn't the first time in the last hour that he'd been shaken by playing cards. There was the Jack and king in the final hand that had troubled him.

I looked at Pell. He was reaching for more scotch. Then I looked again at the ace of spades.

I'd seen the ace of spades before.

Next to Steve Telford's murdered body.

The last of five cards: Jack of spades, king of diamonds, two of clubs, five of hearts, ace of spades.

The same cards in the same order on Fred Youngman's mantlepiece.

A bad poker hand, I'd thought when I first saw it.

But they weren't part of a poker game.

It was like a floodlight, brighter than the sun, had come on in my mind.

They were a message.

In his dying minutes, Telford had named his killer.

With the only thing to hand. His playing cards.

My brain felt like it was plugged into the National Grid.

It throbbed with thoughts about what the cards could mean.

But now I knew why Pell had been shaken by the Jack and king cards in my final poker hand.

And why he now stared at the ace of spades as though it were his death warrant.

The ace of spades had been the code name for one of the

scallywags.

John King. The first two of the five cards were a Jack and a king. But men named John are often called Jack.

And now I knew what the final two cards – the five and the ace – had to mean. The five was the nearest Telford could get to "fifth", the meaning of Quentin, Pell's given name.

Pell was very similar to the French *pelle*. My schoolboy French was just good enough to recall it was one of the words for a spade.

So card for card, Telford's message read: Jack King to Quentin Pell.

In other words, John King now masquerades as Quentin Pell.

But Colonel Carisbrooke Dubbins had told me that John King had died in the bunker explosion – and that fellow scallywag Patrick Harrison had absconded. But it wasn't like that at all.

It was King who'd absconded and Harrison who'd died. And now I knew why.

The night Pell visited the club, Telford was a doorman – and had recognised him. Despite Pell's bushy beard. Despite the dodgy plastic surgery on the nose. Despite the fake Australian front.

Telford had mentioned to Chloe, the lavatory attendant, that he'd seen someone from the past. Chloe had told Shirley that Telford seemed shocked by the meeting.

But Telford made the worst mistake of his life. He tried to blackmail Pell. At first, Pell paid up – he had no choice if he wanted to keep Telford quiet. That explained the two thousand pounds in Telford's flat.

But Pell knew that Telford would be back for more. Blackmailers always are. He had to kill Telford. But he hadn't done it quietly. Stella Armstrong upstairs had told me she'd heard a commotion. So Pell had no time to search and recover the money he'd given Telford. He had to flee fast, before the neighbours investigated.

I turned to Pell. He gawped at the ace of spades.

I said: "Your own code name come back to haunt you. Retribution, Pell. But you're not Quentin Pell, are you? You're John King – a former scallywag - and I know why you murdered Steve Telford."

Chapter 23

Pell pulled himself together, squared up his shoulders, and thrust out his bearded chin.

He said: "You want to be careful making allegations like that. I could drag you through the courts for libel."

I grinned. "At the moment, it's just talk, so it's slander. But your expensive lawyers will tell you that. If you can get them to visit you in your prison cell."

"Besides, it's not slander when the info is ridgy-didge," Shirley chipped in.

Clansfield said: "What's going on here, Quentin?" His gaze had locked on to Pell. He was worried. It was one thing to fleece mug punters. Quite another to kill them.

I could see the cogs turn in his brain. He was calculating how much he'd lose if his posh members resigned to avoid a scandal.

I piled the pressure on Pell. "Not content with killing Telford, last night you called on Youngman and murdered him. Had he recognised you as well? Of course, he must've done – he'd worked out what those playing cards meant. Like Telford, Youngman was a man with his eye on the main chance. What was it this time? Did he want a payoff to keep quiet?"

Pell said: "This is just a heap of dingo doo. You've got no evidence for any of it."

"Haven't I? For a start there's the obvious fact you've had plastic surgery. I guess the surgeon had an off-day when he worked on your nose. Or perhaps he had the plans upside down. But Telford and Youngman still recognised you as King. I'm betting two more scallywags – Harry Deakin and Alec Perkins – will also make a positive I-D."

"So what if I was King? Doesn't mean I'm a killer."

"Back in 1940, a scallywag died in a bunker explosion. Everyone thought it was John King. They identified King's service tag among the wreckage. They imagined that King's partner, Patrick Harrison, had done a bunk because he'd caused the explosion. But you didn't die. It was Harrison who was blown to pieces – by you. After you'd planted your service tag on him. Why did you kill him, Pell?"

Pell started to babble something, but Clansfield's voice boomed above him.

"This has gone far enough, Quentin," he said. "I don't know what the truth of this is, but I want nothing to do with it."

Pell turned on Clansfield with a snarl. "But you're in it up to your neck."

"You know I had nothing to do with any killing."

Clansfield turned to me. "You believe that, don't you? I'm a respected club owner."

"Who runs crooked card games," I said. "That puts you up there on the moral high ground with the Archbishop of Canterbury – I don't think."

Pell said: "I never bargained for this. I'm clearing out, but there's business I have to sort first."

He turned to Hilary and Evelyn. "You apes, go and find some rope."

Hilary shot Evelyn a confused look. "Is he gonna hang himself?" Hilary asked.

"He ain't gonna tie up his Christmas presents," Evelyn said.

Pell pointed at Shirley and me. "I want to tie up these two."

"I don't think we got no rope, boss. Could we use your Sellotape?" Hilary asked Clansfield.

"No, you can't," Clansfield snapped.

He stormed round his desk and faced Pell. "You can't keep prisoners here. What if someone sees them?"

"Lock them in a dark room."

"This will ruin the club."

"The place is finished after this, anyway."

"What the hell am I supposed to do?" Clansfield wailed.

"You just wanna grab as much cash as you can and vamoose," Pell snapped. "Give me twenty-four hours and I'll come back for these two. Take them off your hands. See they can't do us any damage. It'll all be as sweet as a nut, Hector. No comebacks."

He grabbed the bag of poker chips and tossed them to Clansfield. "Here, ten grand for your trouble."

"That's Pansy's cash," I said.

"She can whistle for it," Pell said.

"You got as much class as a 'roo's jacksie," Shirley said.

"That ain't nice," Hilary said.

"Shut up, ape," Clansfield boomed.

He turned on Pell. "This isn't how I expected it to end. But I've got a Plan B. You get back here by this time tomorrow to take care of our friends, and I'll play ball."

"He's gonna want a ball now," Hilary said.

"Football or cricket?" Evelyn said.

"Shut up," shouted Pell.

Pell had moved next to Clansfield's desk.

I edged up alongside him.

I said: "In planning all of this, there's one big problem you haven't considered."

"What is it?"

"This," I said.

I grabbed the bottle of black ink from Clansfield's inkstand and rammed it into Pell's face.

Blood spurted down his nose and the ink splashed around his ears and into his hair.

Hilary laughed.

"It's not funny, you baboon," Clansfield roared.

"What is it with you and monkeys?" Hilary said.

"Fair point," I said.

I grabbed the red ink, swivelled and slammed it into Clansfield's face.

The red splashed over his cheeks and ran down his chin. He

looked like he'd spent too long out in the sun.

Pell had screwed up his eyes and floundered around. He blundered into Clansfield and the pair crashed to the ground.

Clansfield wallowed around on the floor like he was having a swimming lesson on dry land. His eyes were screwed tight to keep the ink out.

He yelled: "Where are you two gorillas?"

"Monkeys again," Hilary complained.

"Actually, I think it's quite masculine to be called a gorilla," Evelyn said.

Hilary nodded towards us. Shirley and I had retreated to the other side of the room. We couldn't get out because Hilary and Evelyn were guarding the door.

Evelyn nodded towards Hilary. "I suppose we better grab them."

Hilary said: "The boss will fire us if we don't."

Evelyn looked uncertainly at me. "You ain't got no more ink?" he asked.

"I'm armed with a rapid-fire Biro," I said.

"There ain't no such thing," Hilary said.

"Wanna find out the hard way?" Shirley teased.

Hilary and Evelyn moved towards us. But it wasn't easy because Pell and Clansfield floundered around on the floor. Pell was dribbling black ink. Clansfield was shaking red ink out of his right ear.

He said: "Haven't you grabbed these jokers yet?"

"It ain't easy, 'cos you're lying in the way," Hilary said.

"I'll get up," Clansfield said.

He raised himself onto one knee. Staggered to his feet.

Pell screamed: "You're standing on my hand, you moron."

Clansfield stumbled. Smashed into his desk and tumbled forwards. He lurched into Hilary and the two crashed to the ground in a melee of thrashing arms and legs.

"Now's our moment," I whispered to Shirl.

"Let's outflank these crazy bastards," Shirl said.

We jumped over Pell. Skirted around Clansfield and Hilary.

But Evelyn still blocked the way.

"Take me," I taunted him.

"Try me," Shirley teased.

Evelyn knew he couldn't take both us. We were six feet apart.

We moved towards him in a pincer movement.

He tried to grab me and trip Shirley, but it didn't work. Shirley stuck out her left leg and he tripped over it. He crashed to the ground next to Clansfield.

I grabbed the door handle. All Shirl and I had to do was fling open the door and rush outside.

I heaved on the door and we launched ourselves towards freedom.

Except that it wasn't.

Beverley and Meredith, the goons from the bicycle chase, blocked the way.

"You know what these clever-dicks always do," Beverley said conversationally to Meredith.

"They overlook the obvious," Meredith said.

I shrugged.

"I think your boss could use some blotting paper," I said.

I turned to Shirley and said: "I've been thinking."

"Pity you didn't do that before we landed in this mess," Shirl said. "What a bozo!"

We were in the wine cellar of the Clansfield Club. Ten feet underground and only one stout door. Locked from the outside. We'd been strong-armed in by Beverley and Meredith. I'd tried an uppercut to Beverley's chin when he accidently let go of my arm. But my fist bounced of his jaw like it was India rubber.

"How long have we been in here?" Shirl asked.

I glanced at my watch. "About two hours," I said. "It's nearly midnight."

There were no sounds from the club upstairs. There'd been some movement, but it had gone quiet. I guessed Clansfield would have wanted to clear the place as soon as possible.

We pulled up a couple of crates and sat down on them.

I said: "The story had been there all the time. I just hadn't put all the pieces together."

"What story?"

"The one about the ship with the gold coming from the Channel Islands to escape the Nazis. None of the gold has ever been found. It's like one of those stories which becomes a myth."

"So it's not true?" Shirley asked.

"Just because no-one's found the gold doesn't mean it didn't happen. Pell's obsession with the gold must be based on something. After all, he was a scallywag during the time all this went down. He knows more than he's letting on. Deakin told me that he was teamed up with Patrick Harrison, the scallywag who was supposed to have gone missing after the bunker exploded. His was the first of three murders we now know Pell has committed."

"Three?"

"Yes. Harrison, Steve Telford and Fred Youngman."

"And Colin Crampton and Shirley Goldsmith if we don't get out of here."

"I think Harrison discovered that Pell – John King then - was one of the scallywags that pulled the gold heist. That's why he had to die."

"But obviously Pell didn't know where the gold was hidden as he'd have recovered it by now."

"I think there are two possibilities there. One is that it has been recovered by one of the other scallywags who took part in the heist. But I don't think that's right. If it was, Pell would know and he wouldn't be going to this trouble to find it. I think more likely is that the other scallywags in the heist were the two who were killed in a gunfight Colonel Dubbins told me about.

That happened just before the bunker explosion where Harrison died. I think they were hunted down and shot. Summary justice at a time of national peril."

"And their knowledge about where the gold is buried died with them?" Shirley asked.

"If it is buried. There's another wrinkle in this story that makes me wonder. Dubbins told me there were two ships – one with the gold and one with a decoy cargo. One docked at Shoreham and one at Newhaven. Both used different routes to take their cargo to London. But no-one knows which was which."

"So could the scallywags have ambushed the decoy truck?" Shirley asked.

"It's possible. Maybe the gold really did make it to London."

"But no-one knows."

"I bet Lord Bognor knew. He was the government minister responsible for defence of the Channel Islands during the war. He would have authorised the movement of the gold."

"He's dead – so he can't tell."

"But the secret may lie in the late Lord Bognor's private papers. Figgis showed me a copy of Pell's promissory note. There's a strange clause in it. If Rackham is forced to sell the *Evening Chronicle,* the sale covers everything in the morgue as well as Bognor's private papers. I think Pell believes he'll find the secret of the gold's location in those papers. Buying the *Chronicle* is just a distraction."

Shirl stood up and stretched her arms and legs. "It's cramped down here and damp," she said.

"If I had a piece of wire, I might be able to twist it into a lockpick and get us out."

Shirl surveyed the racks of fine wines. "No wire in here. Plenty of wine, though. We could have a drink."

"Yes, we can!"

"Have a drink or pick a lock?" Shirley asked.

"Both, with luck."

I stood up and strode over to one of the racks. Selected a fine vintage champagne. Pulled off the gold paper coating over the cork and held the bottle towards Shirley.

"The wire round the cork," I said.

I took care to remove the wire so I could use it in a lockpick. I popped the cork and offered the bottle to Shirley.

"You can have first swig," I said. "I'm opening a second bottle. I need two wires to pick this lock."

I reached for another bottle of the Clansfield's Bollinger and wrestled the wire from around the cork. Then I worked the wire until it was straight. I bent up the last half-inch. I worked the second wire into a wavy line. Then I went to work on the lock.

"How did you get into a shonky caper like lockpicking?" Shirley asked me.

"Click-click taught me. His real name is Denzil Simkins. He's a guy who robs cars mostly. He's an artist with a piece of wire. It was at the time of that case we called *The Tango School Mystery*."

I pushed the wavy wire into the lock and pulled it steadily back. Then I pushed the bent end of the straighter wire in above the wavy and felt for the first pressure point.

"Now this requires a bit of finesse," I said.

"There's something about this gold story I can't figure out," Shirley said.

We were in my MGB speeding around Parliament Square into Millbank and making for the Brighton Road. Big Ben chimed one o'clock as we passed.

I'd made a mental note to send Click-click a few bottles of beer as a thank-you for his lockpicking lessons. He'd taught me well. I'd opened the door of the Clansfield's wine cellar in less than five minutes.

"What part of the story puzzles you?" I said.

"Well, the guys in the Channel Islands sent all their gold to Britain to keep it safe from the Nazis. You'd think after the war, they'd have asked for it back."

"Yes, that adds another layer of mystery. But I think there could be two possible answers. Remember one of the vans taking the gold to London was a decoy."

"It had no gold."

"Correct. Now if the renegade scallywags held up the gold van, they managed to hide the loot before they were killed by the soldiers sent to detain them. So no-one knows where it's hidden. Perhaps it's still there. But perhaps the scallywags intercepted the decoy van – and the gold did reach London."

"So where is it now?"

"Probably in the vaults of the Bank of England, where Britain keeps its gold reserves. I think the government decided to keep it. After all, they could tell the Channel islanders the gold had been hijacked and hidden. There had been a real heist. Everyone knew that for a fact."

"But why should they say that?"

"Britain had huge international debts after the war and it needed all the foreign currency and gold it could get its hands on. There was a new Labour government, with Clement Attlee as prime minister. Labour had always been hostile to the Channel Islands because they were outside the British tax system. Labour thought the Channel Islands were inhabited by tax dodgers who didn't pay their way. And there'd been some collaboration between the Nazis and a few islanders during the war. It would have been easy for the government to say the gold was lost. In reality, there'd be nothing the Channel Islands could do about it."

"And you think that's what happened?" Shirley asked.

"I don't know," I said. "I suspect Pell doesn't think so. He believes the true answer lies in Bognor's papers. Perhaps he knows something we don't. Carisbrooke Dubbins told me that landowners like Lord Bognor let the scallywags build bunkers and tunnels on their land. Perhaps Bognor has maps of those among his papers. Maybe that's why Pell was so keen to buy them."

I flicked the MGB's headlights onto full beam as we left the London suburbs and headed into the countryside.

I said: "I think I know where we'll find Pell."

Chapter 24

"I can sure see why they call this the Dark Wood," Shirley said.

It was little more than an hour since we'd left London. I pulled the MGB into the side of a narrow lane which ran alongside the wood. It was the same spot I'd used when I'd visited Deirdre Telford.

The trees loomed on the left of us like dark sentinels.

In the headlights I could see a weathered sign nailed to a gnarled oak.

Danger. Keep out. Unexploded landmines.

A great way to discourage poachers on the prowl. Or lovers on the hunt for a romantic nook.

But not a journalist chasing a scoop that would win world headlines.

It had started with a murder.

It was ending with… well, I wasn't sure yet. But in the next hour I was confident I'd find out.

I switched off the headlights and killed the engine.

I turned to Shirley. "This could be unpleasant. It may even be dangerous. I think you should stay in the car."

"Yeah! I'll sit here like a good little girl and work on my crochet… I don't think. I'm coming with you, reporter boy."

Shirl opened the door and climbed out. I reached into the car's jump seat and fetched the torch I kept for emergency breakdowns. I joined Shirl by the wall next to the Dark Wood.

The over-hanging branches of the trees blotted out light from a new moon. The branches thrashed in a rising wind. Somewhere deep in the wood, an owl hooted.

We walked a few yards along the lane. It was the point where stones from the wall had fallen. Where I'd climbed in before.

Shirl jumped up on the wall. "Jeez, Colin, this jumpsuit isn't made for a country ramble."

"It looked great in the club. Clansfield couldn't take his eyes off you."

"Dirty old bastard. Yikes! What was that?"

About twenty yards away, a shadow moved swiftly between the trees and disappeared behind a patch of bramble.

"Deer," I said.

"Dear what?"

"Deer, like with antlers."

"Jeez! What next? Buffalo?"

"Take it easy. You're with me."

"And that's supposed to relax me?"

Our feet crunched on dry leaves as we followed a narrow path deep into the wood. The soft smell of pine needles drifted up from the ground.

My torch spread a lonely beam ahead. The light turned spiders' webs into white gossamer. Magical until one wrapped itself around your face. Insect eyes gleamed like pin-prick lanterns. Tree branches creaked and groaned as they swayed in the wind.

Shirley moved closer and looped her arm through mine.

"I guess we're not just taking a night-time stroll," she said.

"You take it right."

"You know where we're going?"

"I have a good idea."

"Like to share it with me?"

"When I studied the Ordnance Survey map for this area, I noticed an unusual feature in the Dark Wood."

"Like unusual good or unusual bad?"

"Like unusual interesting," I said. "There's a deer hay wind here."

"A hay wind?"

"Wind, actually, pronounced like wine. It's a place where deer used to be caught and slaughtered for their venison. It's a bit like a funnel carved out between the trees and undergrowth.

When the deer were hunted, they'd be driven into the broad end of the funnel and forced out of the narrow end into a holding area – usually where a circle of trees had been planted so close together the deer couldn't escape between them. Often the hunters would've built enclosures out of mounds of earth inside the circle. They'd pen the bucks in some and the does in others. These places have been here for centuries – since Saxon times in some cases. That means they're overgrown and look natural. The fact that there are lots of mounds and humps in the ground makes a wind the perfect place to build a hidden bunker with its escape tunnel."

"And you think that's where the scallywags hid out?" Shirley asked.

"I think it's possible. I also think it's likely Pell knows about it. After all, as John King, he was a scallywag. He spent months living a shadowy existence in this countryside before he scarpered."

We trudged on in the dark. We blundered into tree trunks. Tripped over exposed roots. Brushed past nettles. Stepped over pools of brackish water.

We pushed past a tangle of briars into a clearing. When I'd visited Deirdre, I'd followed the path straight through this clearing. But, to the right, it narrowed. I walked over and shone my torch into the darkness.

"I think this is the hay wind," I said.

"I hope we don't end up like the deer," Shirl said.

"This way."

The funnel soon narrowed and we stepped between two pine trees into a circular clearing.

The circle was wide enough for the sky to show through the trees' canopy. A shaft of moonlight lit up the clearing. The place was a maze of broad mounds, three to four feet high. The mounds had flattened tops. They were covered with grass. Saplings and bushes grew on some of them. Between the mounds there were piles of limestone blocks overgrown with moss.

I said: "This is the place. Somewhere here, we'll find an entrance to an old bunker."

We crept through the clearing. It was an eerie experience. The moonlight threw shadows in strange shapes across the ground. Nearby, a fox barked. A small animal scurried through the leaf litter.

Shirley said: "This place gives me the heebie-jeebies."

"We'd better find a way in quickly, then."

I flashed the torch across the clearing.

"Over there," I said. "Those broken branches. I guess Pell has beaten us to it."

"Sure. Speedy Gonzales," Shirl said. "But he wasn't holed up in a wine cellar for a couple of hours."

We felt our way carefully across the clearing. The branches had been broken off a bush which had obscured a hatch in the side of a mound. The hatch was old and rotten, but it would originally have looked like part of a pile of pine logs. Clever disguise.

I lifted the hatch and pointed the torch into the black void beneath.

A ladder led down to an earth floor.

I held the torch under my chin to light up my face and turned to Shirley.

"After me, I think," I said.

I handed Shirley the torch and she pointed it into the void. I put my foot on the top rung of the ladder and started down.

The ladder creaked like it was in pain. But it held my weight and I made it to the floor.

I called softly to Shirley. "Toss me the torch and I'll light the ladder while you climb down."

Clump! The torch landed in my hands.

Seconds later, Shirley was standing beside me.

In front of us was a narrow tunnel lined with rotting wooden panels. The roof was held up by thick oak beams supported by posts.

The place smelt musty, like an old house that hadn't been opened up for years. It was damp and cold.

We stood silently and listened.

Further down the tunnel we could hear a thump, then the sound of wood splintering.

I put my mouth to Shirl's ear and whispered: "Pell has found something."

"Gold?"

"We'll soon find out."

We crept down the tunnel and turned a corner.

The tunnel ended in an opening where there would once have been a door. But no door would fit here now. Two posts served as support for a rotting lintel that sagged under the weight of the earth above it.

The entrance opened into a bunker. So this is where the brave scallywags would have waited for the Nazis to attack.

The bunker was about twenty feet long by ten feet wide. To the left, there was a row of bunks, the mattresses green with moss and mildew.

There was a wooden box on one of them. It had metal catches to close the lid and a handle made from leather.

The right side of the bunker was lined with crates. Tough jobs with battens to reinforce the sides and iron straps to keep them closed.

Pell was bending over one of the crates. He had a heavy crowbar with a forked end. He thrust it under the lid of a crate and heaved down. The wood cracked and the lid slipped sideways to the floor. Pell peered into the crate and cursed.

We stepped into the bunker. Pell was so intent on opening another crate he didn't notice us.

I said: "Not exactly King Solomon's mines is it?"

"And a rat like you would never make Allan Quartermain,"

Shirl added.

Pell glared at us. He brandished the crowbar like it was a club.

I said: "I'll bet you a promissory note to a punch on the snout, there's no gold here."

"How do you know?" Pell said.

"Because it's too obvious. You scallywags were trained in the black arts. If you'd landed a stash of booty, you wouldn't hide it in your own backyard."

Pell nodded as though he'd just understood the meaning of life. He shot a quick look at the box on the bunk.

"That's true," he said. "But I'll find it."

"Unless the cops find you first."

Pell curled his lip. "Find a scallywag? We were invisible. We moved like wraiths. We were like Macavity. We did the business and when people looked, we weren't there. Weeks of training in avoiding capture. I never thought I'd need it now."

"Yes, all that training and here we are – right on your trail."

"That's your mistake," Pell snarled.

"You've got it all wrong, bozo," Shirl chimed in. "You're a killer and we're not letting you leave."

Pell tested the weight of the crowbar in his hands. "You may have noticed that I have the only weapon. And I'm not letting a mouthy tart tell me what I can do. I can use this to crack your pretty little head like a melon."

"You and whose army, buster?" Shirl said.

This was becoming heated. If we were to stop Pell, we needed to cool it.

I said: "I'm curious Pell. How did a man brave enough to join the scallywags go wrong?"

Pell sneered. "Think you can soften me up by taking an interest? You're too obvious, Crampton. But I'll answer your question. Then I'll kill you and your trollop of a Sheila."

"Watch your mouth, scumbag," Shirley said.

Pell ignored her. "First, I didn't join the scallywags. I was conscripted in. No choice about whether I wanted to serve my country or die. I didn't want to do either of them. Why should I? I lived with my Ma and Pa in a three-roomed tied cottage up a cart track on the edge of the Ethelbert estate. We drew our water from an outside pump. And when my Pa asked Lord Bognor to provide us with running water in the house, he got the bum's rush. And then I find myself fighting for King and country. And worse, being paired up in the scallywags with Patrick Harrison."

"What was wrong with Harrison?"

"He was Bognor's bastard son. It was supposed to be a secret, but there were no secrets between scallywags. We spilled our life stories to one another in the bunkers. We didn't expect to live long, so we spoke of our hopes and dreams. That's how I heard that two scallywags were planning to hold up the gold truck. They wanted me to act as look-out. I thought why not? The plan was I'd hide a mile down the road and warn them when the truck was approaching. We'd been issued with short-wave radios as part of our scallywag kit. My two colleagues had a tractor and trailer to haul off the crates and hide them. We'd agreed we'd meet up the next day and decide how to divi up the loot. What we didn't know was that there was a back-up squad in the area. After the hold-up the squad went into action, tracked down the pair. They died in a gunfight – but not before they'd hidden the loot. That night I got pissed. Back in the bunker I blabbed too much to Harrison. When I sobered up, I realised I had to kill him."

I shook my head. "You killed a man in cold blood?"

"But then I had a better idea. I'd kill him and make it look like I was dead. No more king and country for me. I got a passage as a deckhand on a merchant vessel heading to Côte d'Ivoire for a cargo of iron ore."

"The Ivory Coast," I said.

"Yeah! I skipped ship at Abidjan. Seemed far enough away

from the war to let me sit it out in peace."

"So that's where you picked up some French. And decided to name yourself after your codename. Except *pelle* was the closest you could get to spade in French. You made a big mistake there, Pell."

"Sure! I lived through the war when millions didn't. Some mistake! I kept body and soul together by grifting cards with sailors down at the docks. Started with three-card Monte. Moved on to poker later. Became pretty good at double dealing, too. But when the war ended, I decided to make for Australia – far enough away so no-one would remember me – and make some serious money."

"Publishing newspapers for readers who get off on girls showing their tits," Shirl said.

Pell flashed a feral grin at Shirley. "If you want to pose, I'm sure it'll double circulation."

"You won't be publishing anything, Pell."

"What makes you think that?"

"Because the cops know you're a killer. You certainly won't be taking over the *Chronicle*."

"So I move on somewhere. I create a new identity and start again."

"That's why you need the gold, isn't it? You're broke."

I'd just remembered Susan Wheatcroft had told me how Pell's companies had been financed with debt.

"So I need to raise some cash," Pell said. "I've done it before – I played Rackham for a sucker and won the *Chronicle*."

"But you really wanted the late Lord Bognor's private papers because you thought they'd lead you to the gold."

"The scallywags who heisted the gold were miles away when they were shot," Pell said angrily. "They could have hidden the loot in a hundred square miles of countryside. How could I search an area that size without some clues? I hoped Bognor's papers would tell me where to look."

"So that's why the private papers were included in the promissory note," I said. "Well, you're not getting them – or the gold."

"There'll be other suckers," Pell said nonchalantly.

"Who's the sucker, Pell?" I said. "You haven't got the *Chronicle* – and you're going to jail."

"Only if you can keep me in here."

He swung the crowbar in a vicious arc and smashed it down on a crate. The side split and the contents spilt out and fell on the floor.

"Jeez! They're hand grenades," Shirl shrieked. "You better be careful with that rod, buster, or we'll all be meeting in Heaven."

"Pell will be in the other place," I said.

"They're safe until you pull the pin," Pell said.

"Not after sitting in a crate for twenty-five years," I said.

I was terrified. Pell had lost it. There was no telling what damage he could do. We knew he'd killed three people – perhaps more. He wouldn't hesitate to kill us. One blow from that crowbar could finish each of us.

Besides, I was worried what the ammo might do. With Pell doing his bull-in-a-china-shop act, it could blow at any minute. We all had to get out.

Fast.

I said: "Right, Pell. Let's strike a deal."

"Sure. You lie on the floor. And I won't kill you."

"You've got more slime than a wombat in season," Shirl said.

"I've got the crowbar," Pell sneered.

He advanced on us swinging it viciously.

I held up my hands. "Okay, Pell. We see what you've got. What we've got is the opportunity for you to walk out of here without us trying to stop you. Interested?"

"I'm listening."

"You give me the promissory note and we'll let you go."

Pell rested his head to one side while he thought about that.

He walked over to the bunk and picked up the box with the leather handle.

"I'm going anyway."

"Only if you manage to down both of us at the same time. Think you can do it in this confined space. And, remember, we're younger than you."

"And smarter," Shirl added.

Pell was silent for a moment while he considered that one.

"This is what we do. You sit on that bunk. I hand you the promissory note. You guarantee not to come after me for half an hour. By then, I can be on my way to anywhere."

Shirl whispered in my ear. "Don't take the deal. We can stop him."

"We can't," I whispered back. "He'll kill us or injure us and still get away, Better, we're still fit to track him down if the cops don't get him first."

"They won't," Shirl said.

Pell said: "Hey, you two, stop whispering. Do you go for the deal?"

I nodded. "Agreed."

We moved across to one of the bunks and sat down.

Pell pulled a folded paper out of his inside pocket and handed it to me. I unfolded it and read the brief text.

"This is the promissory note," I said.

"Beats me why you want it, it's worthless to me now," Pell said.

He held the crowbar under his arm and flipped the catches off the box with the leather handle.

"You're wrong about me killing Steve Telford," he said. "I left it to one of my little friends. Now I'll leave them to you."

He walked to where the door had been. Stepped through. Tossed the box into the room. It split open and spilled its contents.

But we didn't have time to look at that.

Because Pell slammed the crowbar into the lintel above the opening. The heavy iron cut through the rotten wood and the lintel collapsed. An avalanche of earth and rocks roared into the bunker. The place filled with a cloud of choking dust. Our ears popped as the air pressure changed.

We coughed up dust and rubbed grit from our eyes.

As the air cleared, we saw the way out was blocked by tons of earth.

"Strewth, Colin. We're trapped," Shirley said.

"And that's not our only problem."

I pointed to the floor. Spiders were crawling over it.

Shirley looked at me like she'd seen her own death.

"They're not any spiders," she said. "They're funnel-webs. The deadliest spiders in the world."

I stamped hard a couple of times on the floor.

"That's two that won't hurt us."

"It's only a matter of time."

"Not if we can get out. Colonel Dubbins told me that these bunkers have an escape tunnel. The idea was that if the Nazis were coming through the front door, the scallywags could get away through the back."

"I don't see any door in here."

Shirl did a couple of quick steps and two more funnel-webs ended up as a slime on the earth floor.

"The way out will be hidden. It'll be behind the crates or perhaps the bunks."

I went over to the crates and peered into one Pell had smashed open. There was an unpleasant smell, like bad eggs at the gasworks.

"We need to move fast," I said. "These munitions are sweating."

"Look down," Shirley shrieked.

I spun round. A funnel-web had clambered onto my left shoe. I kicked it off with my right and stamped on it.

I said: "Let's pull out these bunks."

We yanked at one. It swayed and creaked and finally collapsed in pieces.

"What's that?" Shirl said.

She pointed at a metal grille on the wall. It looked like an air vent.

I bent over and looked closer. There was a small latch in one side. I grabbed it and heaved. It creaked but didn't shift. I kicked the wall and dust fell on the floor. I tried the latch again. It squealed as it came free. A section of the wall swung out like a trapdoor.

I grabbed the torch and shone the beam into the opening.

There was a tunnel which ran slightly uphill. I could feel a draught. It must open above ground somewhere. But it was low and we'd have to crawl through it.

I said: "This is our way out. Ladies first."

Shirley scrambled down and disappeared into the tunnel.

I followed.

We crawled along a rough earth floor. It was hard on the hands and knees. My trousers would be good for nothing at the end of it. And as for Shirley's jumpsuit…

"I can't go any further," Shirley said. "There's some kind of wall here."

"It must be the way out. Give it a hard shove."

I watched as Shirl heaved her shoulder at it. I scrambled alongside her. We pushed together. The obstruction collapsed outwards. A blast of fresh night air blew into our faces.

We hustled out of the tunnel and stood in a moonlit woodland clearing. Our chests heaved as we breathed in the fresh air.

And then the ground shook. A rumble like distant thunder echoed through the wood. The tree canopy shuddered around us. A cloud of dust blew out of the tunnel. The munitions in the bunker had blown.

"That was a close call," Shirley said

"At least we're safe now," I said. "That explosion will have finished those damned spiders."

Shirl's eyes goggled with a fear I'd never seen before.

She grabbed the torch from me. Shone it on my sleeve.

A funnel-web was climbing over my shoulder. Towards my neck.

My body went rigid. I swear every muscle had turned to concrete. I was so terrified I had to fight for every breath.

I said: "Get a stick from the ground and knock it off."

Shirl bent down and felt around.

She didn't take her eyes from my shoulder.

I felt the spider's front legs feel around my collar. It tapped its legs on my neck. Like it was testing my skin. Sweat burst through pores all over my body. But I shivered like I was entombed in ice. The spider moved closer. It crawled onto my skin. I felt its every leg move. Like a death dance. I wanted to run. But my feet were welded to the ground. I wanted to hide. To jump in the sea. To fly to the moon. Anything to stop this horror.

Shirl moved ever so slowly with a stick.

She positioned it carefully.

The spider's legs were feeling around the nape of my neck. It crawled slowly over my skin.

Shirl raised the stick to knock it away.

And I felt something sharp puncture my skin. My hand flew instinctively to my neck. I knocked the filthy thing to the ground.

I heard Shirl speak, like her voice was a trumpet. It played a fanfare. And inside my head there was a riot of colours, like Salvador Dali had taken the world and painted it into crazy shapes. Then Shirl's voice faded, like a dying violin. The moonbeams in the clearing became green. And the dark night became blacker.

I felt the organs in my body begin to shut down.

And then I fell, fell, fell... into a chasm with no end.

Chapter 25

My eyes were closed but I could sense there was light beyond my lids.

Perhaps the light came from the halo above St Peter's head. He was waiting to welcome me at the celestial gates.

That was nice of him.

Or perhaps I was wrong. Maybe the light came from the torch carried by Charon, the boatman waiting to ferry me across the River Styx into the underworld. *Hmmm!* Perhaps I might enjoy that more.

In Heaven, I'd have to sit on a cloud and play a harp. Never an instrument I've enjoyed. Besides, everyone would be a Goody Two-shoes. It would be like having Sunday school every day of the week.

In the underworld, there'd be a running bar with gin and tonic, an endless parade of rogues and villains, and perhaps some dancing girls.

The air changed and I smelt smoke. Of course, there was also fire in the underworld. Brimstone, too, although I wasn't sure what that was.

A woman's voice harsh and strident said: "How many times have I told you not to smoke in here?"

I opened my mouth to say I'd never smoked, but no words came out.

So I opened my eyes instead.

I was in a hospital bed. Frank Figgis sat beside it. He took a leisurely drag on his Woodbine and blew a perfect smoke ring.

He turned to a nurse with a starched uniform and a face like a dented bedpan.

He said: "And I've told you, Nurse Ratched, this is a private room and Mr Crampton has given me permission to smoke."

"Mr Crampton has been unconscious since he was brought in

five hours ago. And the name is Ratchick."

She stomped towards the door.

"Rat poison," Figgis said under his breath.

"I heard that," she said

She went out and slammed the door.

I turned towards Figgis and croaked: "I think this is the point where I say in a quavering voice, 'Where am I?'".

Figgis stubbed out his fag.

"You're in a private room at the Royal Sussex County Hospital. And if you want to know how you got here, you can read it in an exclusive report in the midday edition of the *Chronicle*."

"And if I can't wait until then?"

"A brief precis. When that spider bit you, your girl Shirley knew she had to act instantly to save you. Lucky she comes from Australia. They know all about spiders over there. Anyway, apparently the spider's venom takes less than a minute to enter the blood stream from the bite. If it had, you'd have been a goner – and I'd have had a heap of hassle looking for another crime reporter."

"And we couldn't have that."

"It seems a tiny amount of the venom got into your blood which is why you threw a wobbly and collapsed. But Shirley got down and squeezed the skin around the bite to stop most of the venom spreading. She spat saliva into the wound to dilute the venom. Then she pressed hard to squeeze the diluted venom out. Kept doing it until she saw clear red blood running."

I felt towards my neck. There was a large dressing over the bite area.

Figgis said: "Of course, when the blood flowed, it showed the venom had cleared – apart from the stuff that had already knocked you sideways – but she had to stop you bleeding to death. So she grabbed a piece of paper from your pocket and rolled it up so tightly it was like a little bandage. Then she spread some of her lippy on each end to make it stick and pressed it onto the wound. Seemed to slow the blood loss."

No! The paper would have been the promissory note.

I said: "What happened to the paper bandage?"

"It was taken off and replaced with a proper one," Figgis said. "It was soaked with blood, so they'll have burnt it as medical waste."

I felt sick. I'd hoped to use the promissory note to finagle ten thousand pounds out of Rackham to pay for Pansy's treatment. Now I'd have no lever I could use to get the cash. Rita Flowers, Harry Deakin and Alec Perkins would be devastated.

"What I can't understand is how medical help arrived. Shirley and I were alone in the Dark Wood."

"You'll recall there'd been an explosion when the bunker went up. A loud one with earth tremors by all accounts. They heard it in the cottages on the Ethelbert estate. The ones where Rackham's so-called Little Darlings live. Anyway, it turns out they'd been getting the hump over the way his lordship was treating them since he was pushed upstairs into the House of Lords. Apparently, he spends all his time there now. He'd forbidden them to go into the Dark Wood. But they thought someone might have been hurt. So they set off with torches to search for survivors. Shirley saw the lights and shouted for help. They all carried you back to the big house and called an ambulance. And here you are safe and sound – and ready for work."

I looked around me. I had some kind of needle in my arm attached to a tube hanging from a plastic bottle.

"What's that?" I asked.

Figgis shrugged. "I wouldn't think it's gin and tonic."

"And what do you mean 'ready for work'? I'm an invalid."

"Not to worry. I've got everything you need."

Figgis stood up. Wheeled up one of those tables you see over hospital beds.

He said: "As you can see, I've brought over your typewriter

from the office and there's a big stack of copy paper. Sally Martin has interviewed Shirley and got her story. Phil Bailey is researching a backgrounder on the Rackham estate. And Susan Wheatcroft is delving into Pell's shady past and what goes on at that Clansfield club. We've had a bit of luck there. A guy called Archie Stamford called the newsroom this morning. Apparently, you've met him. He's offered to fill in some background on Pell and the club."

I smiled. It was good to hear that Archie had got out of the club after last night's fracas.

But it wasn't all good news. An image of Pell trapping Shirley and me in the bunker flashed in my mind and I shivered.

"You all right?" Figgis asked. "Shall I get Nurse Ratchet to bring another blanket?"

"No, I've just remembered something terrible. I can't believe Pell escaped."

"He didn't. The cops found him dead in his car. One of those spiders he'd smuggled into the country must've got out. They found it crawling around the steering wheel. Pell's hands still gripped the wheel in *rigour mortis,* I'm told. The cops say there was a bag of dead flies on the car's passenger seat. Looks like Pell had been feeding the spiders in the car. That's probably when it got out."

"It's a relief Pell won't be taking over the *Chronicle,*" I said.

"It's great news. And speaking of great news, I want the full inside story from you. We'll splash it on the front page and run it over pages two and three. Cedric is waiting outside. He'll bring the copy to the office as soon as you've finished."

"I feel tired," I said.

"Come on, now, sit up," Figgis said. "I don't pay you to lie down on the job."

I discharged myself from the hospital later that afternoon, after Nurse Ratched threatened to give me a blanket bath.

That morning, I'd sat in bed and typed more than three thousand words telling the whole story. How Pell was really John King, a renegade scallywag presumed killed in an explosion. How he killed fellow scallywag Patrick Harrison. How Pell had changed his identity and pursued the myth of hidden gold. How he'd murdered Steve Telford and Fred Youngman. And how other brave scallywags had tried to raise money to save the life of a six-year-old girl.

Nurse Ratched had just served my lunch – watery mince and lumpy mashed potato – when Cedric brought round the midday special edition. The headline on the front page read: BACK FROM THE DEAD. It summed up the mayhem caused by John King's reappearance as Pell.

Those of us on the *Chronicle* knew it had a second meaning for the paper as well. We'd seen off Pell's attempt to take it over.

But we didn't know whether the new Lord Bognor – as we now had to call Rackham – would continue the same generous editorial policies as his father. I'd saved Rackham a lot of embarrassment by not mentioning his loss of the paper and the promissory note in my front-page story. So when it came to talking about editorial independence, I guessed we'd have some goodwill to trade. And, if not, I knew I'd be able to learn enough of Rackham's dirty secrets from the Little Darlings to keep him under control.

Blackmail is great when you know how to use it in a noble cause.

After I'd quit the hospital, I took a taxi to the railway station. (I didn't know where my MGB was. Probably still parked in the lane by the Dark Wood.) I bought the largest bouquet of flowers the seller outside the station could make up. Then I bought a bottle of the finest champagne from the off-licence in Queen's Road.

Shirley answered the door to her flat wearing blue jeans and a sloppy Joe sweater.

She said: "Jeez! You look like an old man."

"Thanks for the vote of confidence. But without you I'd be lying in a wooden box."

Shirl stepped aside to let me in and closed the door behind me.

I handed her the flowers.

She grinned. "Looks like you've raided the municipal gardens. Hope the park warden didn't catch you."

She put the flowers on a table.

I held up the champagne. "I pulled a heist at the off-licence as well," I said.

Shirl put her arms around me and kissed me softly on my neck. Not where the spider had bit. That still had a dressing. On the other side.

She whispered softly in my ear. "Would you like me to pop your cork?"

I smiled. "You're talking about the champagne. Right?"

"At least you won't need to turn the wire into a lockpick."

"I wouldn't mind being locked in here with you for ever."

"With only one bottle of champagne to drink? We'd die of thirst."

I walked into Shirley's kitchen and fetched a couple of glasses. I opened the champagne and poured our drinks.

I touched my glass against hers.

"Thanks for giving me back my life last night."

"No worries, buster."

We both drank.

I said: "I heard you rolled the promissory note into a temporary bandage to stop me bleeding to death."

The little crinkle of a frown appeared on Shirley's forehead. "Didn't have any other options at the time. I realised afterwards you planned to use it to screw Pansy's treatment money out of Rackham. Without the note, I guess that's the end of the line for the poor kid."

We sat down on the sofa and I put my arm around Shirley. She snuggled up close.

"I was thinking about Pansy on the way here. I have a feeling we haven't heard the last of her story."

Epilogue

27th October 1977

The young woman pushed open the swing doors and took three cautious steps into the *Evening Chronicle* newsroom.

She stood still while the doors shuddered shut behind her. She bit her lower lip nervously.

Her fair hair normally cascaded over her shoulders. But today she'd tied it in a business-like bun. She had clear blue eyes, a pert nose, and a strong chin.

She was wearing a pink sweater under a light grey jacket and a black skirt. All new. All worn for the first time today. Just like her black court shoes.

Her gaze darted around the newsroom but it was empty. She shuffled anxiously from foot to foot. It wasn't yet seven o'clock. She'd been told to be on time. So she'd taken the precaution of setting her alarm for half past five.

And now she was early.

Perhaps she ought to return to the reception downstairs and wait until someone else arrived.

She took another three cautious steps into the room. She sniffed. The place had a curious smell. It wasn't quite like freshly sawn wood. Nor like hot oil. Nor crushed flower petals. Nor the musky aroma of furniture polish. Nor freshly-baked cinnamon buns. There was a bit of all of them in it.

This is how wonder smells, she thought.

She felt her heart beating faster. She put her hand to her cheek. Yes, there was a slight flush. She was excited.

The swing doors banged open behind her. She spun round.

A large woman barged in carrying a cup and saucer in one hand and a plate with three doughnuts in the other.

The young woman jumped out of the way.

"Hi," said the large woman. "I'm Susan Wheatcroft, business correspondent and trouble-shooter around here. You must be the new trainee reporter."

The young woman nodded. "Yes, I'm Pansy Flowers."

"Sorry I wasn't here to greet you. I've just been to the tearoom. Would you like a doughnut?"

Pansy shook her head.

The two stood silently sizing one another up. An awkward moment when both weren't sure who should speak next.

Then Susan said: "So, your first day as a reporter."

"I wondered what this moment would be like. I've wanted to be a reporter since I was a child. And now I am."

"Don't let the stardust get to you, kid. It's just a job – and a tough one."

"No, not just a job. It's a job that saved my life. I was ill when I was a kid – a rare kind of cancer. But there was a story about some murders and the reporter who wrote it mentioned that a young girl needed money for treatment to save her life."

"That was Colin Crampton's story."

"Well, thousands of pounds poured in from readers. And I got the treatment I needed in America. I beat the cancer."

Susan nodded. "Yeah! I remember the piece. It was that story about the scallywags."

"They'd been trying to help me."

Susan frowned as she tried to recall the details. "I can't remember their names."

"Harry Deakin and Alec Perkins."

"I remember now. Whatever happened to them?"

"Harry is still building his flint walls. Says it gives him time to think. But Alec is dead. Brain tumour."

"Horrible way to go."

"He actually drowned at sea. His fishing boat was found abandoned by the coastguards five miles out in the English Channel. There were two empty rum bottles rolling around on the deck. There was a note propped up in the wheelhouse. 'Only one way for a seaman and a scallywag to die.'"

Susan nodded thoughtfully. "Brave man."

Pansy looked around the newsroom. "Do you know which desk will be mine?"

"The junior reporter normally sits at the one on the end of the front row."

"And who sits in that old captain's chair."

"That's Colin's."

"I've been longing to meet Mr Crampton again. I've not seen him since I was a child. Will he be here today?"

"Maybe. He's out on a big story that broke last night. It seems that a huge cache of wartime gold has been discovered in somewhere called the Dark Wood."

Crampton of the Chronicle will be back in a new adventure published in 2020.

Read more Crampton of the Chronicle stories at:

www.colincrampton.com

Author's note and acknowledgements

The idea for this book came to me when I discovered the secret history of the Auxiliary Units. Not many people have heard of them, but they were particularly important in the part of Britain in which I live – the county of Sussex. In Kent, also. I'm told that something like 500 bunkers, like the imaginary one featured in this book, were built across the two counties. The fact the scallywags of the Auxiliary Units never had to face invading Nazis does not detract from their bravery in rising to the challenge.

I wondered what would happen if a group of former scallywags got together years after the war to use the skills they'd learnt in training for another purpose. And, so, the plot started to take shape in my mind. I hope you've enjoyed the book.

I've mentioned before that any Crampton of the Chronicle adventure couldn't appear without help from many people. Barney Skinner has designed the cover and typeset and formatted the book for both the e-book and paperback editions. Barney is also the designer behind the Crampton of the Chronicle website. Members of the Crampton Advanced Readers' Team read the manuscript and made many helpful suggestions and corrections. The members of the team who helped are (in alphabetical order) Nancy Ashby, Andrew Grand, Jenny Jones, Doc Kelly, Andy Mayes, Amanda Perrott and Christopher Roden. Thanks to you all! Needless to say, any errors that remain are mine and mine alone.

Finally, a big thankyou to you, the reader, for reading this book. If you've enjoyed it, please recommend it to your friends! In these days of internet sales, online book reviews are very important for authors. So if you have a few minutes to leave one on Amazon and/or Goodreads, I would be very grateful. Thank you.

Peter Bartram, November 2019

About the author

Peter Bartram brings years of experience as a journalist to his Crampton of the Chronicle crime mystery series. His novels are fast-paced and humorous - the action is matched by the laughs. The books feature a host of colourful characters as befits stories set in Brighton, one of Britain's most trend-setting towns.

Peter began his career as a reporter on a local weekly newspaper before working as an editor in London and finally becoming freelance. He has done most things in journalism from door-stepping for quotes to writing serious editorials. He's pursued stories in locations as diverse as 700-feet down a coal mine and Buckingham Palace. Peter wrote 21 non-fiction books, including five ghost-written, before turning to crime – and penning the Crampton of the Chronicle series. There are now 12 books in the series.

Follow Peter Bartram on Facebook at: www.facebook.com/peterbartramauthor
Follow Peter Bartram on Twitter at: @PeterFBartram

More great books from Peter Bartram…

HEADLINE MURDER

When the owner of a miniature golf course goes missing, ace crime reporter Colin Crampton uncovers the dark secrets of a 22-year-old murder.

STOP PRESS MURDER

The murder of a night watchman and the theft of a saucy film of a nude woman bathing set Colin off on a madcap investigation with a stunning surprise ending.

FRONT PAGE MURDER

Archie Flowerdew is sentenced to hang for killing rival artist Percy Despart. Archie's niece Tammy believes he's innocent and convinces Colin to take up the case. Trouble is, the more Colin investigates, the more it looks like Archie is guilty.

THE TANGO SCHOOL MYSTERY

Colin Crampton and girlfriend Shirley Goldsmith are tucking into their meal when Shirley discovers more blood on her rare steak than she'd expected. The pair are drawn into investigating a sinister conspiracy which seems to centre on a tango school.

THE MOTHER'S DAY MYSTERY

There are just four days to Mother's Day and crime reporter Colin Crampton is under pressure to find a front-page story to fit the theme. Then Colin and his feisty girlfriend Shirley Goldsmith stumble across a body late at night on a lonely country road...

THE COMEDY CLUB MYSTERY

When theatrical agent Daniel Bernstein turns up murdered, any of five comedians competing for a place on a top TV show could be behind the killing. Colin and Shirley take on identical twin gangsters and tangle with an unlikely cast of misfits as they set out to solve the mystery.

THE MORNING, NOON & NIGHT TRILOGY

Three books in one

The adventure starts in ***Murder in the Morning Edition***... when crime reporter Colin Crampton and feisty girlfriend Shirley Goldsmith witness an audacious train robbery

The mystery deepens in ***Murder in the Afternoon Extra***... as the body count climbs and Colin finds himself hunted by a ruthless killer.

The climax explodes in ***Murder in the Night Final***... when Colin and Shirley uncover the stunning secret behind the robbery and the murders.

Read all three books in The Morning, Noon & Night Omnibus Edition or listen to them on the audiobooks available from Audible, Amazon and iTunes.

Printed in Great Britain
by Amazon

56688622R00168